NOT AS FAR
AS VELMA

NOT AS FAR AS VELMA

NICOLAS FREELING

THE MYSTERIOUS PRESS

New York • London • Tokyo

Writers seldom love Publishers.
Publishers always hate Writers.

So to Tom Rosenthal
with love
since this is a book about love

Copyright © 1989 by Nicolas Freeling
All rights reserved.
The Mysterious Press, 129 West 56th Street, New York, N.Y. 10019

Printed in the United States of America
First U.S.A. Printing: June 1989
10 9 8 7 6 5 4 3 2 1

Library of Congress Cataloging in Publication Data

Freeling, Nicolas.
  Not as Far as Velma / Nicolas Freeling.
      p.   cm.
    ISBN 0-89296-380-8
    I. Title.
PR6056.R4N64   1989   88-39333
823′.914—dc 19   CIP

'If I help the poor, I'm a saint. If I ask why they are poor, I'm a Communist.'

Dom Helder Camara

'You could see a long way, but not as far as Velma had gone.'

Raymond Chandler

1

When the doorbell rang he remembered that Gabrielle had gone marketing. He laid the brush down, went along the passage. There is no point in not answering. The interruption has been made.

He had a long look, though, first, through the lens of the spyhole. The concierge isn't particular about the street door. Half the time it's on the latch and anyone can walk in: she's leaning on a broom somewhere, gossiping. A house, in Paris now, needs to be a fortress. You are in no hurry to open the apartment door to strangers.

After the bright light of the studio the landing is dim, yellowish, and the lens distorts. Two men. Indeterminate age, unremarkable clothes, empty faces waiting placidly, knowing they are being observed. One carries a black briefcase. But two men. So not insurance or the gas. Two, in his experience, means . . . But they could still be selling something; an older one training a younger one, maybe. He put the door on the chain, opened it a crack, stood back and said "Yes?"

"Monsieur Marklake?"

"And then?"

"Police." Peacefully; one could remember when they weren't.

They know the routine, holding the plastic card with the red-white-blue diagonal stripe well up, for the cautious householder to study carefully. There are a lot of these cards and they look alike. The old man is suspicious, clicking a light on, pushing his glasses up on his forehead. Police d'Etat. Stapo. It does not increase his confidence, but used to distrust they wait patiently.

At least not secret-stapo. Police Judiciaire. What's it about? Since not, presumably, a bicycle stolen out of the basement.

"So tell me more." A deep, dragging voice.

"It's only a routine enquiry. Concerns you, though; or so we're given to suppose. Simple verification. Papers and things," apologetically. "We'd prefer to come in if you'd let us." People are right to be cautious. Phony, fast-talking cops with glib tales have wormed their way in to old ladies; poor but with pension money in a retired handbag on a closet shelf. Oh, they could switch on a shouting, bullying manner, no strain, but this old boy has eyes which have seen a lot, in his life. They don't know him from Adam, but one learns to judge from little signs. He too has something of a cop look.

He unhooks, stands back, motions them along the passage. Big studio, bright from a whole wall of window: one of those the Ville de Paris keeps for artists. Eating-space, a round table with a Persian runner and on it even in winter a big vase of flowers. Living-space, tatty old sofas with a lot of cushions. Working-space, canvases on stretchers stacked face to the wall, canvas on easel, jars with a lot of brushes. Rail running the whole length of the side wall, with many framed canvases suspended on chains; the old man's showroom. Everywhere an oriental sense of profusion and comfort and even shabby luxury. Pervading everything the pungent smell of paint and high-grade turps; sharp tingle quite unlike cheap cleaning-fluid.

"Sit," says the old man pointing to the dining-table, and goes to clean his brush with care: this will evidently take some time, for the elder is dragging armfuls of bureaucracy out of that big briefcase . . . The police are painstaking over detail of stupefying minuteness. They can also be highly devious. Good; be patient; one will hear.

The officer starts with a town, a town in the north; one of those historic fortresses of Flanders and Picardy that have been battered, besieged, captured and sacked by more armies than I've had hot cups of tea. Know it well, if not for some years: he's an oldish man and has known many towns.

"Been there recently, at all? Not last November? Nor since? Sure, are you, of that?"

A shrug. Sure he is sure. He was right here, working. How to prove it? Who is going to bear witness to that? Mama, perhaps? He has been in and out, since November: here and there. He has seen friends. They are mostly like himself, elderly; forgetful; what interest have they in when they saw him last? A feastday of the Blessed Virgin, maybe? The day they elected a new mayor? But he is unworried. The war is fifty years behind us and this is France. Antisemitic they are and always were, but nobody's getting in an uproar. These police types aren't trying to build anything. Marginal notes, on their bits of paper. Like the man says, verification.

"Know a little hotel there? 'Caravane'? Near the station; street – I've got it here somewhere, Rue de la Grange?"

"No. One I know is old. 'Duc de Bourgogne'. One eats well there – in a sidestreet, quiet."

"Account for this at all then, can you?" His big moment, piece of paper across the table. I'm not offering them anything to drink. Be polite, but why butter them up?

A photostat. Hotel register of oldfashioned sort, spaces for nationality and passport number and stuff. Sometimes they have little cards, and sometimes they don't bother. *Fiche de voyageur*, an antiquated piece of bullshit they've revived, now there are terrorists everywhere.

Name right. Address right. And what does that mean? Nothing that I can see to stop you filling in Humphrey Bogart and the address in Casablanca.

The old man put his glasses up, spread his hands.

"What's this then? My cheques are forged? Pocket full of stolen credit cards? Look." He borrowed a piece of paper, a ballpoint. "There. My signature. My writing. Like there at the bottom, all those pictures." Tap with the ballpoint on the photostat, flowing easy capitals, educated writing but the most you'd say would be someone used to addressing envelopes. "Not me. I could write Charles de Gaulle, David ben Gurion,

3

but it would be my handwriting. Here is someone I don't know."

"So why forge your name? Pretty uncommon, no other. Marklake in the phonebook. Fellow forges a name he writes Martin, Simon. Got the address right too."

"Fellow having me on. Having you on. Why? I don't know."

"So you can't think of anybody, might like to make trouble for you? Grudge maybe, little trick of malice."

"Antisemites, you'll find anywhere; three a penny. Personal, no. I can't prove anything. What does an innocent man have to prove? Where was I in November, I should write in my diary?"

The cop had picked up the ballpoint; tapping his teeth with it, Morse code maybe. The other just sat, didn't utter; there at all only for the record, drive the car.

"Well, I've asked you, noted your answer. Type out a report to that effect, maybe you won't mind dropping round the office to sign it. We've nothing whatever against you, Mr Marklake, no suspicions or presumptions. But it's unaccountable. Maybe someone else won't feel happy, up in the north they might want to ask you something further, who knows but you may hear more of it. Sorry to have put you to the trouble." He thought he distrusted them when polite more than when they pointed with a stick and said 'Get in line there, you'. He grunted, shut the door, and said, "Mama!"

"I heard." Hadn't even got her shopping-bag inside the door before her nose told her . . . A thin woman with large beautiful eyes and a gift for silence, her speech was to the point. "I'll think about it."

He stumped back to the easel but the work didn't go well. A hair is only a hair until it gets in your soup. Of what stuff are our earliest memories? There is in California an old, old Russian lady, who remembers holding on to her mother's skirts. She is aged two. There is a railway station. Her mother is crying, pleading. There is a very big policeman, with a moustache. He is in the grand uniform of the Austro-Hungarian Empire. Where is this? She is unsure. The Empire reached right up into Galicia. Perhaps Przemysl.

4

Many children have memories of the police. A large sweaty oaf, rather frightening? If you were a small boy, perhaps a recollection of being taken unpleasantly by the ear? Then the likelihood is that you are not Jewish. Fear does not taste like this.

"This I don't much like," said Marklake, cleaning his brushes.

"Then pinch it off at the start." Gabrielle was slapping plates on the table, preparatory to Mittagessen. Living in Paris since nineteen thirty-eight there were still German words that got mixed with the French, and his accent can still sound comically thick and Polish.

"They say it's nothing and tomorrow again they're at your door with another story."

"Where does it start? A town in the North – then go there, and tell them to explain themselves, have it out there between you. I'll pack you a bag."

"A waste of time."

"Better you waste your time your money both than sit here every time the doorbell rings you drop something on the floor. Sit, take a glass of wine, take your pill; eat, I tell you."

The advice is good. Also it is a fine town. There are even good pictures there.

Castang on a winter morning. The Public – in this instance the ruffled Mr Marklake – would be indignant to know how little his mind was on his work. This particular piece of work had been forgotten altogether. To be fair, he has thought about it, quite a lot. It was not in police terms important, but it could be interesting. Interesting is not enough: he knew too little and the rest was speculation. Imagining things makes for bad police work and has got him into trouble before now.

He has forgotten all about it because last November he put out a trace to have this old chap Marklake checked up. Paris receives a great many requests of the sort from provincial sources, treats them with no great sense of urgency. Chronically overburdened by the legal and administrative systems of France which are complicated and laborious in the extreme. One PJ officer with influenza in the month of January creates yet another bottleneck and another week is lost. Castang, well accustomed to this, for he has himself worked in Paris and in exactly this dogsbody job, put it out of his mind.

Ask him, and he will reply – sighing – that there are three sorts of police enquiry. 'The flags': the legal phrase *flagrante delicto* means caught-in-the-act. Some notion of urgency and speed, so one does try to get a move on, even if most of them are petty delinquency and nobody much interested. Preliminary: the police is wondering whether a case exists, collects material to send to the Prosecutor, who decides upon legal pursuit. And rogatory commission, meaning there is a case, a judge of instruction is working on it, and has ordered the police to do some work, hopefully to shed light.

Castang's enquiry being only a preliminary has the least priority. Paris has better things to do than run after a verification concerning a woman who has vanished. Women vanish every day, and a lot of them in Paris.

He would explain, to any member of the public who was really interested – like poor Mr Marklake who imagines that the Stapo has its eye fixed upon him (we do have a Gestapo too but it is more interested in Arabs nowadays than Jews) – that it's really quite normal that Paris should take three months getting around to this. He won't mention that he has meanwhile forgotten all about it, and is trying now to recall what it was all about in the first place.

Castang is in his forties; a Principal, the middle rank of Commissaire: a senior police officer but not very senior nor very important. Sent to this obscurish corner of northern France because he'd been a nuisance elsewhere and here can cool his heels awhile learning not to trouble authority. Meaning get along with routine work and be noticed – either by Authority, the Public or the Press – as little as may be.

In this he has done fairly well. He is a good administrator and a competent, experienced officer. In three years he has had one major case, a noisy homicide involving a wealthy local magnate: he handled that well and got a Good Mark in Paris where the promotions are made. He also got involved in a stupid nonsense which wasn't even in his district, resulting in a small official bad note for a lot of shit with political overtones, balanced by a small unofficial good note for tactful handling of said shit. He will be left another year or so in this backwood. Then he might have purged his contempt or dreed his weird or whatever it's called, and might get a better job elsewhere. And being quite a good sort of cop, after learning not to be too goddamn bright and shaken off those bad socialist tendencies, he might even get his seniority step and become a Division-naire. That means chief of a Regional Service of the Police Judiciaire. Big deal. There are some twentyfive of these in France not counting Paris which is special and where Divisional Commissaires are three a penny. In the provinces. Some are good. One or two are gaudy: the plum is Versailles which includes the outer Paris suburbs. What he'll get, if at all, will be small and unpublicised like Limoges, say: not one cop in a hundred could even find it on the map.

This is what, leaving his house, in reality a rented flat, quite pleasant, of a morning, Monsieur Castang thinks of. He has no house. He had had a country cottage and he sold it. For a nice profit. He is well paid, and he economises. Without gambling on the Stock Exchange like a capitalist he still has Capital. He would like to buy or build (that's tricky) a country house. For holidays first and then retirement. Where – south or north?

His active years will just about see out the school, maybe even university years of his children: he has two girls, would have liked a boy but too bad; tough titty. Since the Regional Services are all in university towns that is no big problem. Should the house be near the sea? Vera has become Marine in her interests: himself, show him a boat he gets sick all over it. He stumps along. It is ten minutes' walk from his apartment to the office and he walks it. Bit of exercise if no fresh air; gets you in shape for the day to come; gearing up, huh, for the hard detective stuff. Or something. Like the first cigarette of the day; tell yourself that when cutting down you enjoy them more.

One metre seventyeight or say five feet ten: fifty years ago it would have been called tall. A shaved, lippy face; lot of lines there. The belly is still flat; the left elbow, shot out by a crooked cop with a large bullet, is made of precious metals. He did gymnastics upon a time and is still elastic, and light upon the feet. On the feet are expensive shoes, kept well-polished; is this a luxury, or just a mania? The clothes have an odd English look, like a maths professor showing he's an outdoor man at heart. Tattersall check shirt, tweed hacking jacket, pullover (good but with darned elbows) and extremely elegant trousers, whipcord. His wife had also been a gymnast, until she broke her spine falling off bars: she walks now again but limps. His arm and her back, it must be symbolic but what of? Togetherness perhaps; they are what is called a devoted couple. There is much love there, and frequent furious detestation.

He likes to swim, but the pool is always full of foul-mannered schoolchildren. She likes to swim, wishes she were rich and had a private pool. Since she is the limping one it is he who carries a stick: sometimes as today an umbrella. There are large ominous clouds in the northern sky, black and bulgy: it will either rain or snow depending on how it feels, quite probably both together. He has a loden coat. They are nice but smell so when wet, like dogs.

He looks both French and not-French. There are some doubts about his father, definable as a person-unknown. Said to have come from Aquitaine, a province occupied in former times by English soldiery who behaved badly. This might account for English mannerisms, like sitting with crossed legs, and a habit of irony. His former chief, Commissaire Richard, who had an evil tongue, described him as a type who hangs about racing-stables, giving bad tips: that horsy world, said Richard, is full of English stallions jumping upon French mares. The many pockets of the tweed jackets doubtless stuffed with banned veterinary drugs. His subordinates deplore an uncertain temper and eccentricities, but once you know the funny little ways he isn't bad to work for.

He reaches the office early, so as to set a good example.

Marklake, journeying (the night before) towards the north, thought about the police and decided that it was silly to do so (working oneself up to nightmares about the camp: what the hell; he had survived the camp. How many were left, who could say that? A thousand, still? Fewer, by now. All had been more or less crippled, were kept alive by complicated medicaments. He had himself the extraordinary Polish physique to thank: even in middle age he could arm-wrestle almost anybody. And art.)

So think about art. Passing out of the Ile de France – the only really French part of France, peeling grey paint and gothic cathedrals, the only ones which really do look gothic – into Picardy, where Frenchness starts to mingle with Flemishness, and Spanishness. He knows a good deal of history, since it is art-history, and here are the towns for whose possession the crafty French king wrestled with the Duke of Burgundy who had been less crafty than his forebears. The French got Burgundy, but Spain got the Netherlands. It is an astounding, tragic fairystory.

These towns are all now safely-French up to the Belgian border. They have been so fought over, for so many hundreds of years, are full of so much mixed blood, one may doubt whether they feel safe, or feel French. The traditional sources of their immense wealth, textiles, coal and iron, have vanished. They are poor now. But the people have character. They will think of ways. And they are full of art. Once finished with the police – stand for no nonsense, but do not lose your temper – he would find much to look at, to study, to inspire.

Marklake was elderly but had always been an oldfashioned painter, believing in draughtsmanship, carefully-prepared canvases, meticulous groundwork and the very best of Winsor and Newton arranged in a lean, sober, classical palette: gaudy chemicals he needed like a hole in his head. Thanks, he knew how to get light upon a canvas. Nothing of his would fade or crackle or turn blue. You could see down into his glazes the way you could see down into a rockpool ten feet deep. He painted as though the world would never come to an end. He looked forward with as clear an eye as he looked back. Here in the world to fight with God, and the angel; like Jacob. He had no use for modern painters – let them turn blue! All they are good for. Abstraction is a nonsense, a dead end, for fools, conjurors, illusionists, get-rich-quicks. How many even can draw?

It was raining – of course: the fine, greasy northern rain. This too he loves, and trudges well content to his hotel, a place of monastic quiet, in a cul-de-sac where the roar of traffic does not reach, where he sleeps well, waking at dawn to the gentle, discordant bell of some nunnery. Before he had drunk a cup of coffee the sun was out, watery in the washed stepaside street of peeling grey paint and closed shutters. His feet echoing deliberate upon the slippery cobbles. Upon the boulevard a hard cheerful racket, and young girls in clean aprons, sweeping the pavements in front of butcher and greengrocer.

Police stations are the same the world over; bovine in the north or siesta in the south, supinely uninterested. In France the air of barely-controlled irascibility, aimed at discouraging the public. In recent years some perfunctory effort has been made at tidying them up.

"Nothing to do with us at all. Police Judiciaire."

"Where's that?" quite prepared to be told they didn't know. A long way: if you don't feel guilty now, you will by the time you get there.

A gloomy building of rusticated stone, occupied by the Land Registry. He was concluding he'd got it wrong again when the eye was caught by a faded notice saying 'PJ First Floor'. Flight of stone steps, door saying Enquiries, and inside that a lobby with two wooden benches and a door with a sliding panel saying Knock and Wait. It could just as well have been the Land Registry.

But the panel slid open at once; a fat female peered at him; he explained himself, haltingly.

"Oh yes," with an unctuous courtesy one felt to be more ominous than rudeness. "The door to your left, Mr Marklake." Inside was a surprise, walls of a pleasant creamy colour and even a potted plant on her desk. Of course, if there'd been one outside, this being France, it would have been pinched the same day. She leaned across, smelling of peppermint, and pointed with her pen.

"Down the little passage," archly as though he'd asked for the lavatory, "and the second door on the right, and that's Inspector Louppes and he'll be glad to talk to you." The old man thanked her politely. "At your service," she said with a trill.

The door was open, to a small office with nobody in it, and no furniture save a metal desk, a typewriter-table to the side, two chairs and a metal filing-cabinet, but it still managed to look amazingly untidy. Paper lay about everywhere including the floor, and in motley colours pinned to the wall; movie posters, record sleeves, three or four calendars, portraits of pop singers, some dashing, fairly obscene female nudes. He sat, since there was nothing else to do; took off his fur hat and after a moment his overcoat; the radiator was turned too high. Inspector Louppes' leather jacket hung on the back of his chair: his ashtray showed that he smoked too much. The window was barred. The offices seemed quiet. One could hear a murmur of conversation and the intermittent tap of a typewriter.

Presently there was a weird noise, high-pitched and rhythmical, A-da-da-Doing-a-doing-da, recognisable as imitating Lionel Hampton's vibraphone and breaking into cheerful song as it neared the doorway.

"Mister Sta-cey – Ring dem Bells – who the hell are you?"

"Your good lady," getting up, "said to go on in."

"She'd no business saying anything of the sort. Since you are in, well, sit down. Tell me about it." He threw himself into his own chair. A shortish, thickset young man in his mid-twenties, a bullish neck and a broad heavy head. The eyes were widely spaced, a pale angry blue, protuberant. Mousy straight hair cut in a fringe hid most of the forehead. Untidily shaved, as though he'd come to work in a hurry; fair bristles showed on the lumpy jaw. Wide, thick-lipped mouth and strong, stained teeth. Nasty young man, thought Marklake going through his explanations, but bright and quick. A cocky, confident look, saying "My name is Patrick Louppes; two pees and an ess." He wore a light blue shirt, open-necked, definitely on its second day, under a dark blue pullover and tight faded jeans. The butt of a big magnum revolver showed behind his right hipbone. While the old man spoke, sounding to himself confused, thick, Polish, his expression became vague, opaque; the mouth pursed, the jaw got lumpier and the voice said "O-ho" as though about to unmask fierce biting questions, but all that came out was, "Yes . . . We're glad to see you . . . Rather a funny business, this of yours."

"Except that it isn't mine." Louppes gave the indulgent smile of Yes-yes, that's what they all say; irritatingly. "Someone is usurping my identity. That is serious. It is why I have come all this way. To understand it."

"And what is your explanation?"

"I have none. I have not made myself clear? I am here to find out. I am an old man. I was deported, in the war. My good name is important to me." Louppes looked in silence before taking a cigarette and lighting it, observing the old man, bulky and solid. Wearing a good brown suit, a greenish silk tie somewhat faded. In the buttonhole of the lapel, the thin red cord of a Legion of Honour. He held the hard blank glare with the cigarette between his teeth and the head cocked to keep the smoke out of his face; the knowing, toughy look they have while still young. He got up.

"Please stay where you are." And went out. Big brogue shoes with thick rubber soles, but a light silent step. Marklake thought: I have come from curiosity. Certainly, to put a stop to lengthy administrative persecutions. You complain, say, at an excessive phone bill, and they make your life a misery. No administration will ever admit to being in the wrong. I will be

patient. Whatever they do or say, warned Gabrielle, do not lose your temper.

"The Commissaire would like to see you." He had come back on his silent feet while Marklake was staring out of the window, at the vista of people who have gone to prison because the administration does not admit to making mistakes.

They went along the passage. The chief would have the corner office. Yes, but this too was a surprise; a square biggish room lit by two windows; a nice reeded wallpaper, linen curtains a paler shade of green, sand-coloured carpeting, a rattan stand with half a dozen green plants. The man behind the desk had got up and was holding his hand out.

"Monsieur Marklake? My name is Castang. Sit down, please. I'll let you know, Louppes. Tell Varennes, would you, that I'd like a word. I don't want to be interrupted afterwards. Forgive me just a moment," over his shoulder. He held a short conference in the passage with a big, rawboned young woman with a bell of fair hair, a man with a neat, slim back to me, in informal trousers and pullover but authority in his manner; a voice soft-pitched. But he too is a cop: we must be careful. The ones of most charm can be the most dangerous.

When he came back to sit behind his desk, unhurriedly taking a small cigar from a tin of them, there was nothing remarkable about the face – bony, full of planes and hollows – but a painter would notice that the man was well constructed; a good carriage to the head, and quick, well-shaped hands. The eyes weren't missing much either.

Louppes came in with a cardboard file, dumped it wordlessly on the desk: a moment later the young woman came with another, satisfying her curiosity by a good look at the old man. Castang flicked through the papers, like a man who knew his facts but is marshalling his command of them, remarking, "Good of you to have come, like this." He pushed the files aside and said,

"This is quite a puzzling matter, that probably has some very simple explanation which escapes us. Let's see what we can make of it together."

13

"I ask nothing better," said the old man.

"It seems clear enough that you had nothing to do with it, but you've come all this way. Why?" Marklake explained about the administration's reluctance to admit an error in the phone bill, and he laughed. He had a ready, open laugh, crinkling at the outer corners of the eyes.

"Yes, that's alarmingly frequent."

"I am curious, too."

"Are you? So am I. I could let all this fall into oblivion. There's no sign of any criminal act or intent. It's a loose end, that's all. A woman vanishes. She's middle-aged, of well-conducted life, a small but adequate income, no known family ties; been a widow some years. People who knew her, there aren't many, are astonished and have no suggestions to offer. This hotel register contains blameless names, easily verifiable. Yours was the only oddity, apart from being the last. Let me be candid with you."

A remark often made by people who are nothing of the sort. Puts one on guard. Castang is in fact candid. Since few people expect candour from a cop he uses it like a footballer, feinting inside a defender to pass outside.

"Lady vanishes, there might be sinister reasons. Inheritance, insurance. We aren't quick, here, to imagine ghoulish happenings. We have learned to practise a famous rule of conduct for civil servants: not to show too much zeal. But there are one or two puzzling features about this, nonetheless."

"Like who forged my name on a hotel fiche."

"Yes, if he wanted to mislead, why not choose a name that attracts no attention? You exclude anyone known to you – no after-thoughts about that? Malice, an ill-placed sense of humour?"

"Candidly, no."

"Well, let's go and view the scene. You're a painter. You'll maybe notice things that I haven't and which might provide us with a clue." He got up, shrugged on his jacket, an old one but well cut and expensive once. He was wearing no gun. Tja, a Commissaire; he will be well paid, and he has people to carry

the gun. He paused in the corner by the door, where he had two or three sticks and an umbrella.

"It's not raining much. If I take the umbrella it'll only tempt it to rain more." An English rather than Jewish sense of humour; it was sunny out. "Good, this isn't Corsica. We'll walk, with your permission. It isn't far."

"I like to walk."

"I'll be at the Hotel Caravane, Madame Metz. Very possibly I won't be back this morning."

Outside, large beautiful clouds were gathering. Castang saw them too, earning a good mark from the old man. He made the classic joke which is the same all across this part of northern Europe. If you can see far, it's going to rain. If you can't it's raining already. If it stops raining, means you've left the country. Marklake likes the painter's light of the north.

It puffs him, keeping up: Castang is a brisk walker, a dashing crosser of roads against traffic. There is a stinging, coastal wind that makes the eyes water, reddens Castang's tan which is dark even in midwinter, as though he came of a long line of fisherfolk: Spanish looks that one can see also in the faces hereabouts. He talks too.

"Her name is Adrienne Sergent. Parents refugee, appeared here around the end of the last war, of unknown, probably Central European background. Sergent, who married her, was a quiet decent man. Sold insurance, was a well-known amateur footballer. Also a skilful handyman, bought this house cheap in poor condition, put all his savings into it, fitted it up nicely, left it to her. Died quite young. He knew, I think, he was going to die. Sensible man, he took precautions for the widow." A cop, thought the old man, will not often talk like this.

It was a small street, wide enough only for one-way traffic; quiet since it led only to others like itself, yet only a minute or so from the broad boulevards in front of the railway station: a dull, flat-chested little street of dingy grey houses, none too clean outside and lord knew what they would be like within, but an unventilated essence of cabbage, dust, gas and floor-polish is readily deduced. In most French towns the façade will

15

be a leprous stucco, but in the North of brick. This house was cleaner than the others.

High up, a small neon sign would catch the eye when turned on. It read *Hotel Caravane* in cursive script, ending in a long curving arrow that pointed to the front door, where now a handprinted cardboard notice said HOTEL CLOSED behind the glass. Even now, it struck one as fresher and more attractive than the thousands of little fleabag hotels still to be found in the older quarters of French towns. Dim, stuffy, World-War-One plumbing, they do not lack custom, and are comfortingly cheap. Castang produced keys and let them in. A narrow passage had in it a side door to a small room overlooking the street. Half livingroom, with armchairs facing a television set; half office, with a bureau and a bookcase full of box files. It was clean and tidy, the heating on enough to banish damp. Castang turned up the thermostat, motioned the old man to an armchair and sat on the bureau chair himself. There was an amused grin on his face at Marklake's astonishment.

2

Castang had been here often enough for astonishment to have long given way to pleasure. It amused him to see the little surprise of others, and now it completed a piece of simple police work to see the old man taken aback. He had plainly told the truth, that he had never set foot here.

Everything was frilly, flouncy, but this was no parody of a bordel style but a femininity quite serious and totally successful. The old boy was shaking his head in disbelief.

"That places like this should still exist!" his thick rumbly voice tasting, relishing.

The chairs were crimson plush, with satin cords at the seams and ropework ornament. An oriental carpet of dark blues and greens glowed like stained glass. On the walls were many little bracket lamps with parchment shades. The door and the passage glistened with fresh white gloss. There were tapestries and a firescreen embroidered in petit-point. The potted plants looked healthy and cared for. The Edwardian cosiness which had asphyxiated Castang at first sight now welcomed and delighted him.

"She had a woman," he explained, "the only real fulltime helper; her children are grown-up. She comes in every day to dust. Why not? – there's money in the bank, to pay her, for some months. She knows nothing, understands nothing. She knew Ada well and didn't know her at all. She says 'Madame will be back' with a certainty she can't explain. She may be right, at that. I give it weight, that sort of instinct.

"Furthermore," with enjoyment, "she has a dreamworld husband, a sort of one-legged sailor whose joy is to paint and carpenter and invent ingenious contraptions. They agree: Ada was fair, kind, considerate, a pleasure to work for; very reserved and never familiar. They trust her, so they keep coming. Look!" He threw a door open theatrically. The kitchen beyond winked with oiled teak, polished brass and copper. "Christ, and my house always looks as though bombed the night before. She didn't do meals for guests except perhaps as a favour. Rather a one for special favours. No," to the unspoken question, "there's no hint whatever that she slept with them, quite the contrary as you'll see. She gave them a marvellous breakfast, though. Listen!" and another of his little surprises. Between the doors there was a sliding panel, sailor-contrived in the wall. From the space beyond could be heard the chirping of many tiny birds.

"An aviary!" said Marklake when light dawned.

"Come and look." From the passage a glass door muslin-curtained led to a diningroom running the width of the house. There were two large aviaries. The back wall was glass with sliding doors and behind, the more exquisite for being unex-pected, was a paved courtyard with little trees, bushes and standard roses beautifully kept; a suntrap where wild birds lived. "One can't ever tell what may lie behind the front. A smelly dump or a little paradise. Upstairs is the same. Only seven bedrooms counting her own, and so little space you can't modernise. The municipality wouldn't give her more than lodging-house status, in consequence. The nautical gentleman did his best with bathrooms. There are only two, and tiny. But she treated her people so well the house was always full of regular customers and she made a good living. She kept the front door locked and anyone she didn't fancy the looks of she turned away. Except for the two mentioned, no other help, so that her expenses were not great. She put the best quality mattresses and linen on her beds. She worked hard, and all to one singleminded end; making people comfortable, especially men. And it still wasn't a bordel!

"It's time for a drink. I'm about to astonish you afresh – this is the bar. Tell me what you think." Along the wall between kitchen and diningroom stood a very beautiful old buffet, of some silky tropical wood with brass corners and fittings. The old man chuckled and muttered, passing his hands along the finish.

"A thing like this I've only seen once in my life and that was in a malouinière, one of those houses ship-owners and rich captains built in Brittany: this comes off an East Indiaman and that's very rare. Worth a fortune this is, I am telling you, how does it get here?"

"I was goddamn jealous too. Funny things happened, during the war. Consequence of shelling is looting, right? And loot got sold cheap off barrows." Castang opened the doors gleefully. "I kept the police-judiciaire savages out of here! Grateful customers brought her a bottle now and again would have been my guess. Or a friend in the trade – look at that, I haven't seen Danziger Goldwasser in twenty years."

"Give me a little," said the old man. "In thirty I haven't tasted."

"Too sweet for me," helping himself to Macallan malt. "But if you're feeling Polish there's thirty-year-old gin there. Comfort!" sitting back and patting his stomach. "Lucky for me my wife can't see me now." He switched from farce to serious. "She reigned here of an evening, like a queen. I have witnesses."

"Then I don't understand. How does she come to leave, if you think no foul play?"

"Yes," said Castang, "that's the question. Virtually everybody who was here, these six months, we have identified without trouble. The mysterious stranger who signed your name, him we haven't."

"You are not still thinking that I have anything to do with this!"

"Of course not. But I've thought about you. You aren't in fashion and you don't bother with fashion. In fact you're rather like this house! You have a circle, not very wide but of good customers, who understand and appreciate your work. You don't need a noisy write-up in the press, or some lousy gallery taking a cut." The old boy didn't look too pleased at this description, but admitted that it was so.

"Somebody who signs your name is somebody who knows you. It doesn't sound like the customers of this hotel. Those are two worlds which don't intersect. But there was a point of intersection. You ought to be able to find it for me."

"This is nonsense you are talking; I have been painting pictures for fifty years; they carry my name. Photographs, records, sales, you ask my wife. Work there – the whole police judiciaire you can keep busy running around." Castang was perhaps grinning but hiding it.

"We'll go and have lunch," he said comfortably. "Plenty of time. Enjoy your drink. Perhaps we'll go to your hotel; one eats well there, the head waiter is a character. Do you get flustered by ideas like maybe there's been a pork chop in the same pot?"

"Fromme Jüden," said the old man disgustedly, making him laugh out loud, "this sort of pious Jew thank God I am not."

"Have some more. Look around you. Let the atmosphere soak in. It's all we have of her."

"She was Jewish?" asked the old man suddenly: it had only just occurred to him.

"It's possible. We don't know. Sergent was a man of forty, married a girl of twenty. She lived with her father. Her mother died early, she has said she never knew her mother. The father was a refugee; nobody's quite sure where he came from nor along what route."

"There were a lot of Displaced Persons."

"As you say, and there's small point in speculating. A quiet man and skilful with machines, found work, kept it, talked to no one much – his work spoke for him. Died only some eighteen months ago. Nobody was interested in him; why should they be?"

"Until you."

"And perhaps you. He had a little flat, lived by himself but she used to pop in. She was much attached to him, we are told. Just as well, since there was nobody else. She was loyal, caring, good. That's the word which comes up over and over. She had *bonté*. That's not a word which is used much nowadays. Goodness isn't much valued any more."

"This I understand . . . She disappeared," said Marklake suddenly. "Why don't you let her disappear, forget it? Why go scratching after it? Five million Jews disappeared. Maybe six. One million not accounted for. Now maybe one million and one. She wasn't Jewish, we've plenty more. Communists, gipsies, homosexuals. How many Poles? How many Russian soldiers, women, children, old peasants. Jews make a big fuss and people say, typical those people, always making a noise, why can't they keep quiet? Six million Russians, nobody gives a damn."

"Yes indeed," said Castang. "I can find things closer to home. Just round the corner here – practically across the road, this is the battlefield of the Somme. Thiepval, High Wood, Delville Wood, Vimy Ridge, right?"

"Yes of course. You are telling me that many vanished here, in fragments, under the mud, whatever, never more found, nothing to put under these dreadful little white crosses."

"Exactly. Families still come here, knowing nothing but that somewhere under these fields and trees – illegible. So that's one thing. It is part of my job to look for people. In Paris probably I wouldn't bother."

"Good. This too I understand. So you look. What do you find?"

"I never know what I might find," said Castang. "There was a woman, a year or two ago. She disappeared and it was thought her husband might have killed her, until she reappeared six months later, been under everyone's nose the whole time."

"And then what happened?"

"They both got killed. She killed him, or he killed her; once they were both dead policemen also lose interest. Nobody was left, you see."

"Here too nobody is left."

"Can we be quite sure? All right, it's time for lunch. I hate talking business during lunch."

True to his word Castang does not 'talk business' over lunch. "There are two people I want you to meet," he says with his mouth full of bread and butter. "This evening. You've things to do? Enjoy yourself, rest, walk about. There's an evening train you can get." He asks if Marklake knows the northern countries – Belgium, Holland? Of course; how could any serious painter not? And England? Like all Jewish people the old boy has a 'soft spot' for this country. Castang agrees, but 'in streaks, like bacon'. More questions, mostly naïve, about painting: Marklake does not know that his wife has training in graphics from her native Slovakia, has been experimenting – a battle – with 'real paint': the results are promising but uneven.

"Like when she paints eyes, the face tends to look as though holes had been cut in it, for the eyes to fit into." The old man laughs, amused. A frequent problem, he agrees gravely, and suggests with a touching formal politeness that if she cares to visit him in Paris he could show her a few technical effects.

Meantime they eat well, also true to word. The hotel is pleasingly oldfashioned about good food at an honest price, and plenty of it. The head waiter also is as promised: a man of distinction. Plainly he knows Castang but does not show it; avoids the title 'Commissaire'; gives them a table clear of potential eavesdroppers; serves them himself. Asks simply "Do you like herring?" and when the old man, instantly Polish, says "Very much" nods and goes away. A little local charcuterie with winter salad. The herrings which are fresh and grilled with mustard butter. A red-wine beef stew, with baked chestnuts and brussels sprouts. All of it is good and so is the local still champagne. When it comes to cheese there is an admirable ripe Valençay as well as the robust local jobs.

"And what is that?" asks Castang, pointing.

"That is a camembert."

"Pull the other one."

22

"They have peeled off the crust and substituted bread-crumb."

"Why?"

"In order that there should be in France three hundred and three varieties instead of only three hundred and two," a deft push sending the trolley exactly where he wanted it.

"If only we lived," says Castang rhetorical, "in the simple world of Lord Wimsey."

"Lord *Peter* Wimsey," gravely marching away.

"Could one not," suggested Marklake, "have the handwriting on that register analysed?" Castang drank his coffee and lit one of his little cigars.

"You don't know a lot about police procedure. An expert's study and report can only be authorised by a judge. They are expensive, and chargeable to public funds. We have here no instruction, thus no judge. In the process called flagrant delict I can do much, but we've no delict. We have only the preliminary enquiry. My authority goes no further than the geographical limit of the region. Anything else whatever, I need the Procureur's permission and a mandate from a judge. Our powers are small and strictly limited."

"In the light of some of my experiences with police, that's just as well." Castang smiled.

"Pick me up about five at the office, we'll have a Belgian beer in a low pub, and I'll show you what I can do."

Castang has spoken the exact truth, as in most instances a little over half the real or whole truth.

In this medium-sized town, a focus for part of a large thickly populated region, he commands a smallish group technically known as an 'antenna', semi-autonomous but dependent on the big PJ service in Lille, whose chief, Divisional Commissaire Sabatier, a handsome silver-haired gentleman, likes the peace, comfort and dignity of his position and does not bother Castang overmuch.

Nonetheless the position demands skills and crafts, some of which Castang possesses. Thus he is quite a good administrator of his small world. His in-tray is empty, messages are logged, papers are filed: he does this by working harder than his staff. He is efficient. It wouldn't do though to be too efficient – more so, say, than they are in Lille: that would be officious.

He can use his staff to bend the rules he has described, which are stringent and quite often severely interpreted by the juridical authorities. If the rules were not bent one would get no work done. To old Marklake who has lived over forty years in France it doesn't need much explaining: a little more is due to the stranger to the devious and tortuous bureaucracy of the Republic. Put as briefly as may be, Castang's left hand does a lot of work he doesn't allow his right hand to know about.

This afternoon he is pestering his junior inspector (the lowest grade of officer in French police hierarchies), the young woman called Varennes. She had had the tedious chore of identifying the people in the hotel register.

"How do I identify something just called Koopman–Amsterdam? I looked it up in the phonebook; there's about fourteen pages of the thing."

"Where are your wits? It's a name and an address. It recurs. Sufficiently obvious that he no longer bothers writing it all down, that he's a regular customer."

"I looked for previous volumes. There aren't any. The neighbours" – she means the municipal police – "didn't bother until all this terrorist nonsense."

"Then you had better go to Amsterdam and get a nice big Dutch policeman to help you."

"Go to Amsterdam!" appalled. French schooling teaches you to be extremely articulate in your own language and monosyllabic in all others. It also leaves the pupil with a general notion that everywhere outside France is both very far and menacingly barbarian. Amsterdam is about an hour and a half by train. Kamchatka, roughly. Doubtless ice-bound for ten months of the twelve. "Oh God."

"I want this within fortyeight hours. He's a man. Not a Co-op or a cooper." Probably she's Flemish herself. She has the build and the looks. Her name would be Varen. Her granny might have spoken Flemish at home. Suppressed by the family for fear of sounding peasant. The child is now alarmed at having to speak English in Holland and appearing ridiculous. End of sociology lesson.

"It will do you good," curtly. "Say 'The Leith police dismisseth us' rather quick. Now try it in Dutch . . ."

The Land Registry people downstairs, chilly souls, keep the heating turned too high. It is a thorn in Castang's flesh that he hasn't a thermostat on his radiator. If he asked for one he would be told that the budget did not allow for such luxuries. Wasting heat is cheaper. You must understand the bureaucratic mind.

It wasn't cold, but high up some colder current of air was passing because it had begun to snow, sparse and fine, and outside his window it fell slow and straight, but down in the street the draughts blew it into whirlwind patterns, complicated and unpredictable. Old Marklake came originally from Poland. Adrienne Sergent's father might have been Polish. Did that mean anything?

Castang looks at his watch, shrugs himself back into – in France it's called a pull, in German a Pulli and in America a sweater, and he calls it his woolly, and the hell with it. He remembers English lessons from his friend Geoffrey Dawson. His pretty wife Emma-Emmeline; one must not say Em.

'Can't say pullover; that's like eating pudding with your fork.'

'Send for the fishknives, Norman.' Giggles.

'Only foreigners ever speak proper English.'

'My poor father, who'd been to Cambridge for his sins, used always to talk about his jumper.'

'What about all these officers in the Secret Service, then, who speak German like natives?'

'No no, Castang, they are playing the Great Game.' And we are only policemen.

He took Marklake to the sort of pub which is in Amsterdam called a brown café; much, and self-consciously touted as a tourist attraction. The brown has nothing to do with coffee. Probably it was centuries of cheap tobacco-smoke. Nowadays they preserve the brown with varnish. Any day now there'll be a 'hostess' clicking her tongue with disapproval when you light up in the non-smoking section.

In Belgium there are strict rules governing the sale of alcoholic liquors: these do not include beer. But here we are in France, and northern France, so there is a nice flavour of gin, and corn schnaps as well as cheap cognac, and whisky too if you're feeling snobbish. Saving only Brittany, there are more alcoholics to the square centimetre hereabouts than anywhere. The Belgian beer comes in goblets the size of a baby's head. This is really nice.

And the atmosphere is deliciously thick. Your serious drinker likes his air to have flavour. Not so much of the Marlboro-Country which tastes of nothing at all, as of the contraband from Holland. A roll-your-own, fine-cut dark tobacco known as shaggie, which comes in dark blue packets sporting a picture of a stormy sea and a lighthouse, and the legend in art-nouveau script 'In Hope of Salvation'. The Surgeon-General has the cheek to say this is bad for your health? He can stick his preachments straight up his bum.

In the nicer of these pubs there are tables of wood, scrubbed until the grain looks like the isometric map of the South China Sea. You can't see through the windows. Not just condensation but thick serge curtains with a woolly fringe of bobbles. At the back there is generally a billiard table. You would be wiser not to make bets. Castang likes all this very much. So does old Marklake. In that powerful perfume there is a hint – moss, ferns, roses? – no, Baltic herring. Happily he orders a jug of Côtes-du-Rhône, itself a subtle cocktail of components from Italy, Algeria and Argentina, such as would be absolutely forbidden by Gabrielle at home. He had been displeased by the pictures. Primitives much over-painted. But this is something like. Almost one warms to Ensor, Marquet, Delvaux, Magritte: there is something about these Belgians after all. Yes, this is something like. Gabrielle is back knitting in Paris. He doubles in size. He tells old, consecrated Jewish jokes.

"Man in a Lada, yes, must brake suddenly, old woman on

the road. Screech – bang, behind him a Ferrari crashes into him, into the Ferrari crashes a RollsRoyce, paf-paf, they are all kapot. Man of Rossroyce gets out cross yes. You break my car, that cost me three days' salary. Man of Ferrari angrier, Du Arschloch, I lose there three weeks' income. Man of Lada, he say, Sorry but me, I lose three years my work. The two men they look at him, they can't understand. 'But then why you buy so dear an auto?'" Castang happy!

"Here's our man coming now." A sort of giant had appeared at the door.

He was not a real giant. He did not amble, shamble, or look diffident. He was an ordinary man, unusually well-coordinated, nodding, shaking hands, sitting and calling for a beer. But hardly unobtrusive. One metre ninety, six-foot-five if you'd like it in Fahrenheit, and two hundred pounds without an ounce of fat.

"And this is Nelson Walter. Always known as Nelly. And generally known as the number-eight of the New Zealand Rugby Team; that, my sons, is an AllBlack." How would an elderly Jewish-Parisien painter have the remotest notion what that animal could be? But Castang is from the south-west in origin; a rugby fan from way back.

One might have seen him however fleetingly and accidentally on television. The small screen diminishes.

Nelson will take it easy whatever happens. The roar of sixty thousand throats in Auckland or Toulouse bothers him no more than some girl saying My, you're a big one then, aren't you? A Tiger in Montreal is in Sydney just another farmer in from the outback, and in New Delhi no space for your knees. Try Holiday Inn, they got kingsized beds over there. Content enough not to be American because of the astronaut get-up their footballers wear. In Moscow you'd make the icehockey team and at least that would mean proper housing. All in all, it's preferable to a poke in the eye with a sharp stick. The Pope in Rome is indifferent to there being another Pope in Christchurch.

Here is just right. There is a good school of high-tech

agricultural sciences, so that asked what he does he says Oh, soil chemistry and stuff, y'd find it pretty boring. A good rugby club, without everybody going fanatic. Not like down in Agen or Béziers you know, where they think of nothing else. Were anyone to ask – they do – how he stands the bloody climate, he will smile. You haven't been to Auckland yet, mate.

Old Marklake is entranced, seeing him in full armour. Just so, one day in a Madrid café, some trick of light reflecting off a piece of metal turned a blue-chinned Spanish businessman peacefully eating shrimps into a portrait by Titian. A bandit – a *condottiere*. Have they no plazas in New Zealand, suitable for a fullsize equestrian bronze? I should be Verrocchio! In New Zealand the free flow of physical strength. Apollo rather than Dionysos. He sees lucidity, intelligence. The stillness in movement; tense in the saddle while sitting absolutely loose, lance-butt on the stirrup.

Mr Walter has lowered his first beer in one go and is now nursing his second, easy along. Mildmannered young man of twentysix and the best to come; number-eights take longer to mature. He has quite a modest travelling scholarship. The Federation likes to give its young men some European seasoning. By summer – winter down there – he'll be back in Christchurch, trailing the shining-eyed small boys along the pavement, perhaps remembering the little hotel in provincial France where he learned about love. Sex is okay. Welcome like that first beer. But love is something else and right then sex is not that important any more and don't get in my way.

'You see, there's something very special about Madame Sergent." Never Adrienne, Adri or Ada. Maybe it's that they're still strictly brought up, boys in New Zealand; taught to show respect for married women? She has taught him French, which he speaks with ease and fluency. On the field a famous reader of the game, as he is for balance, for economical deftness of movement. But it had to be learned. It was a lumbering, uncouth boy who got off the train, with French, impatient and incomprehensible, around him, and Christ, the people worse than their effing language. Lumbered with the raincoat and the

28

suitcase and the big tote-bag, knowing fuck-all, just wanting somewhere, put the junk down and take a breath to look about him.

"Sure I'd been in France before. On tour it's all taken care of. Out the plane, there's the bus, off the bus and there's the hotel, good one too, swimmingpool, terrace, terrific food, who wants to know the price? Two to a room, your mates are with you, nothing to think of till next day out with the trainer in y'r sweat suit, you haven't even asked what town this is. Manager is tough, talks discipline, this is your country's prestige, no beer, no girls, you're here to play it and you're here to win it and that's All She Wrote. You're the baby in the pram, belch when the man claps you on the back; the rest, nix, these boys might look big but mentally they're three months old." He had wandered around, desolate: hotels that look cheap, sure don't look clean – France! mean t'say, after Auckland . . . He saw that curving neon arrow saying Caravan and that looked all right.

And what did Ada Sergent think when she glanced through her peephole and saw an AllBlack on her doorstep?

"I reckon she saw a silly big boy and felt sorry for 'm."

"When you saw all the frilly bits, lace and little mats, you didn't feel it smothering?"

"Plenty of homes like that down our way. We aren't very . . ."

"Sophisticated?" suggested Castang. Mistake. Nelson's eye, a bright sapphire blue, rested on him without hostility, and no favour either.

"We can be pretty oldfashioned." Being a kindly man, and seeing that Castang felt ashamed of himself, "I'd have felt it at home," he added. "I've an auntie with a house full of china animals – I used to want to reach my foot out and kick it all over.

"There were these dollies on all the beds. I was maybe twelve, I turned up one of those flouncy Andalusian skirts see whether she's wearing knickers, my auntie caught me and what I caught was a real ringer round the earhole." Castang's laugh, rather too loud, makes people at the bar turn round.

"So Madame Sergent made me feel at home." Nelson paused, uncertain of the next bit; went straight at it. "I don't know how many ways there are of loving people. The word keeps meaning different things. Fellow says he loves New York, he loves Lucy, what's he talking about?"

"Some people say they love God," suggested the old man.

"And I love me," added Castang.

"Your mother. Your sister."

"A movie star."

"It is also possible to love a friend."

"And which sex that friend is."

"And you don't go to bed with your friends, right?"

"And if you do you lose them fast."

"You can also love a child."

"You can go to bed with a sword between you."

"You can go to bed with a whore and still love her."

"I haven't tried the sword bit yet – not sure, come to that, how many swords you'd find in Hawke Bay."

"And this is liable to go on and on. You're telling us, Nelson, you loved her and she loved you and neither of you did anything to spoil it."

"Not bad for a cop."

"She had love in her," said the old man gently.

"And she gave it. And she was straight. I don't know much but I'd say it was pretty rare. A lot of people, they haven't much and grudge that."

"That's like the Commissaire said. People who love themselves, for them other people turn into things. You also love your country."

"It's a small country," said Nelson.

"That is good. People who love big countries want to make them bigger."

"Some people in New Zealand," ruefully, "think it's bigger 'n bloody China."

A figure had joined the group, without noise or obtrusion, taking a chair from another table, turning it to sit with his forearms loosely over the backrest. Despite this he took up little space and although biggish, heavyset, a man of fifty or more, he was compact, his movements neat, knowing how to make himself small. Painters see figures in space, noticing how they occupy it. The casual French handshake across the table showed he knew the other two.

"Monsieur Delaunay," said Castang. "He's a controller on the railways." This explained at once how a big man can make himself small – and something else indefinable about him: that he was accustomed to wearing a uniform. The big banana-fingered hand stretched to shake was loose and firm (a polite taker and returner of tickets), of a texture soft and slightly roughened like suède leather. Hands tell a painter much. Faces also. The face of a good liver, but nowise gross from eating or drinking. In a moment he got it: the over-developed look of the ex-athlete, whose muscles have turned to fat, but a cheerful, solid fat, easily worn and lightly carried. Nelson Walter's big frame, carrying a few surplus ounces, showed that in twentyfive years' time . . . Castang was going on, as though the newcomer had been there all the time.

"How long were you there, Nelly, staying, I mean?"

"Two–three weeks. Take your time, she said, lodgings are tricky, let me see. She wouldn't let me close a deal without coming to look for herself. I came back of course, an evening or two a week, except before a match.

"We aren't that fussy," he explained. "When you're in fair condition, which is by maybe January here in the north, an hour on the training pitch is enough to sweat off a few beers. French players aim to hit their peak for the tournament with England 'n the others so I go along. I'll lay off in April or I'll be stale for the season at home. After a match I go out with the boys. But they know I'm a bit of a loner."

"Everybody there was a bit of a loner. She was that way herself," said Delaunay speaking for the first time, a deep voice, soft and a little hoarse. Around the eyes were wedges of fat but the eyes were pale grey, sharp with intelligence and humour below a broad balding forehead.

"Rugby-player too?" asked Marklake.

"Naw," smiling, "but used to play a bit of football."

"Good with his head," grinned Nelson; plainly it was a well-worn joke between them. "Jump 'n nod it down. That big ol' head has to be good for something. We'd have made a centre threequarter of him maybe, knock people over with it." The old man, who does not know the difference between football and rugby, sees the kinship between the men.

"I'd like to play golf only it costs too much, wish I lived in New Zealand. Only they don't have trains – right, Nelly? – they got horses and buggies. Nelly's a killer, he likes ice-hockey."

"Sure. If I'd been Czech or Canadian; it's how it takes you as a boy." It was a meaningless kidding, but Castang realised that they were showing how it had been, evenings in that quiet club with its four or five members. Disliking the television, putting it on sometimes for a laugh with the sound turned out and supplying their own dialogue. But a lot of silence. Adrienne and her pieces of embroidery, hardly speaking.

They could neither make nor accept simplistic definitions. Both men knew and loved her, be it at fifty or at twentyfive, it changes and it doesn't. Cool; warm – neither; both. Upright: yes. Unless you mean straitlaced: no. You knew her, and you didn't know her at all.

"There wasn't any need," said Delaunay hitting it.

"Looking at a picture is exactly the same," said the old man.

"But you were neither of you there, when she went?" Castang knew this already; it was for Marklake's benefit.

"We had an away match," said Nelson. "Down the Spanish frontier, about as far as you c'n go 'n still stay in France. Didn't get back till next day, I'd missed classes at school, a lot to catch up on. Farmers our way have got on all these years on lime and sheepshit but it isn't good enough any more, we got to invent some new kiwis before the Israelis pinch them all," grinning.

"We get night shifts every so often," said Delaunay. "You get a few hours' sleep in the shelter provided – some are quite good and some are bloody awful! – and you get a day train to take back. Twentyfour hours off but it's not only catching up on sleep. I got a wife. I like to get away from her, and I like too to be with her. One can also love several people at the same time." The old man nodded his agreement.

"It makes sense," said Castang. "She wouldn't have wanted to do any stupid explaining either."

"It would be like her, to go that way," said Delaunay.

"Why?"

"She was – no, secretive I won't call it. Private, yes, but stronger than that – a sort of unobtrusiveness."

"So she disliked drawing attention to herself?"

"Yes and putting anyone out, even in something small like opening a door for her or carrying a tray of glasses – leave me alone, I can manage, she'd say quite vexed."

"What I don't see is her leaving the birds," said Castang.

"It would need to be something powerful," agreeing.

"Like a man?" They looked at each other; disbelievingly. But wanting to disbelieve. They were injured by her desertion.

"But we both agree on this," said Delaunay suddenly. "Nothing squalid happened, and nothing guilty."

"Couldn't be crook if she tried," Nelson said.

"I'd go my oath nobody round here," stoutly.

"Somebody from the past, maybe?"

"It could be. She didn't talk about the past."

"Didn't talk about herself, period."

"Among subjects of conversation, painting ever come up? Or a painter – you know, pictures."

"Painter?" No no, total blank.

"No no!" said the old man, remembering the wool tapestries on the wall.

"This gentleman's a painter." They'd thought him a bit odd; had been too polite to enquire. "He's from Paris. That last day, someone signed his name, in the book." It meant nothing whatever, to either of them. The note introduced was so false, so jarring, that without a word spoken they decided they'd had enough. Nelson Walter got up. Leaning over the table he looked very formidable.

"You find out," he said to Castang, "and let me know."

3

Mr Marklake took the evening train back to Paris, regretting that he was unable to be of help to the police in their enquiries. Asking for an assurance – and getting it – that there would be no more sinister young men ringing his doorbell. By which Castang meant that he'd come himself, although he did not say so: he has a residue of curiosity about this old man.

Finding out rather more; giving the matter more thought: to be sure. One revolves such things in the mind, walking home (the temperature is at freezing-point and this snow is likely to make pavements treacherous tomorrow morning). It's a matter of resources. The police can find out many, perhaps most things if it tries hard enough: a laborious process and without more to go on – such as VV turning up some unexpected grain of gold in Amsterdam – there's not much likelihood of that. Residues of curiosity there might be, and often are, but they have a way of being put out of mind by things – what was the phrase the railwayman used? – more squalid; more guilty.

He is quite right: it's about to happen and it will be both. And not nice; not nice at all.

A winter landscape, but neither pretty nor pleasing. There are no robins on logs: it is raw and misty out, studying the street through his window while half dressed and drinking coffee. That wretched snow has lived up to expectations, melting and then freezing and forming films and lumps of black ice; a nasty surprise for people going out early to the baker's. Dawn, meaning neither night nor day, has been going on already for hours, and the municipality has rounded up everyone it can lay hands on, sweepers, gardeners, a lot of chaps

34

who'd rather have had breakfast brought them in bed, to whizz about scattering a vile mix of salt and grit which makes the streets much nastier if supposedly safer. The radio announces two old ladies who have broken their pelvis on the doorstep, and a fine crop of minor road accidents. A spokesman for the Prime Minister in Paris said late last night that the Lebanon – Bang!

A big bang, rattling and shaking his windows.

"What was that?" said Vera, startled.

"Hard to say how near. Gas, at a guess." It hurries him a little. Wintry mornings provoke more than road accidents – the people who will block up every source of ventilation, who set themselves on fire with unsafe electrical heating, whose gas arrives through perished crumbling joints . . . there are also people who choose this way of committing suicide: misery alas exasperates egoism. Sure enough, the not-very-distant wail of the fire-brigade's sirens and the insistent re-fa re-fa of an ambulance. He hurries dressing; on days like this disasters come in multiples. He is lacing his boots when the phone goes. A voice known to him, that of a fire officer, but made scratchy by hurry, worry and an unexpected dimension of nastiness.

"Castang? Lucky I caught you. Rue Saint-Jacques, 's quick 's you can. This one's for you. Plastic." Oh dear Jesus, that was all we needed.

"Good, I'll be there; you've cordoned the street?"

"I do what I can. Goddamn Sipo's all over the town writing off lampposts." The-Municipal-Police-is-separating-indignant-drivers-who-have-skidded-into-one-another-out-of-their-own-goddamn-stupidity.

"I'll do likewise." Glance at watch, Madame Metz will be in the office even if no one else is, smelly she may be but conscientious she is: dialling. "Castang. Bomb, Rue Saint-Jacques. I'm on my way, everybody you have and stand by to alert Lille."

"Roger," she sings, exactly as though it were Churchill ringing from the dugout under the Admiralty. Metz loves a drama.

The Rue Saint-Jacques is in the old town, not very far and

he doesn't forget to lock all the car doors: nowhere were there more pickpockets than at public executions. He is not a bomb squad and has no specific anti-terrorist training, but he can recognise the vile cobwebby traces of plastic explosive. The firemen, stoneface, are quite ready to turn the hose on to the press of morbid voyeurs. Vicious, he goes for the nearest woman on the nearest doorstep. "Police Judiciaire, I want to use your phone."

"Metz, patch me through to Lille, smartish . . . Castang here, urgent, give me Commissaire Sabatier at his home and no time lost. He isn't? Ve-ry well," rather slow and clear. "Sous-chef not in yet? Get them off their ass, we've a Big Red One right here, send them over, find the boss. I don't care where he fucking well is, he'll want to know. We have a bomb. Paris, your urgent procedure, on the computer right away. Alert all regional services, Belgium, Holland, Luxemburg, Germany. Make it Italy, Spain, we have a weirdo here, it's a convent. Yes, you heard me, a convent of nuns – make what they like out of that. Now repeat my instruction, verbatim, signature and authorisation Castang." Ve-ry slow-ly. "Step on it, dear girl."

Madame Metz was sufficiently thrilled she didn't even trill her words.

"Patron, Paddy Campbell will be with you inside five minutes."

"My house." The woman is standing there among the sparkling shards of her front windows, the expression fixed in a small timid grin of shock. "What are they going to do about . . . The government ought to see to it that . . ." She has understood that he is the Law; he is Authority. The French, poor devils, are so accustomed to being governed. "I was just standing in my back kitchen waiting for the coffee to perk when – "

"Missis. Make a big pot. Drink a lot. As hot as you can. Give some to the firemen. They'll be grateful. They'll clear this up for you. It'll all be put back. As good as new. Make yourself useful." His boots crunch hideously. Give them time! Just a little and they'll all be as busy as bees working on the damage estimates in which a wornout runner becomes a Persian carpet and a china dog a valuable antique, telling each other loudly that if the Insurance won't pay the Government will jolly well have to, that's all, it's their job to protect us, isn't it?

Yes, the shutters, their hinges probably rusted through, had torn straight off. Blown – sucked by a gigantic vacuum-cleaner – blast did very odd things; he was no technical expert and it isn't his job.

There are three ambulances, now. The first was the 'Samu' emergency team of doctor, intern and nurses equipped and skilled for just about anything – except when you're dead already. The second was working methodically along the street, on shock and minor injuries. The third was there for the dead: there were two. The 'convent' is an ordinary residential house of a late nineteenth-century pattern. The front blown at street level and the façade of the stories above had folded down on top of that. Captain Robin, the fire chief and the man with the sense to have phoned him, had gone straight in at the risk of the roof coming down on them. The Samu doctor had gone in there with them. As happens, all too often, courage had not paid off. One dead from blast, the doctor told Castang. Young woman with reddish hair, now greyish-white from dust and plaster.

"You don't want it technical. Massive, put it – the breath blown straight out her body. Instantaneous. The other, crushing and multiple fracture, skeletal framework smashed – literally – by rubble. We reached her but there was nothing to be done. One caught by a beam, it's not too bad, internal injuries but spleen and liver all right, pelvic arch took most of it. Can't get her out until the firemen have it jacked and I can't answer yet for the vertebrae: I'll say only she stands a good chance: it's stabilised. So you've two homicides, busterboy, for your Criminal Investigation Department – yes, I'm coming."

"What's the blood on your overall?"

"Oh, it's not mine, a fireman got cut by some glass. You'll excuse me, laddy." He doesn't mind being called laddy – or even busterboy. She had just put her own vertebrae on the line, and her pelvic arch too.

His senior inspector Paddy Campbell is at his elbow; so-called because his father was an Ulsterman, he acts 'dour' and never calls Castang 'Patron' or even Chief but just says 'You'.

"The others are accounted for – got out the back. A few scrapes and cuts, treatment for shock."

"Lille is on the way, Paddy, or bloody should be. Hold the fort and don't let no goddamn soul but firemen – where's young Louppes?"

Paddy points wordlessly: experienced, he has given the order. The junior inspector, camera up to his eye, is systematically taking pictures. When screened, with the magnifier, they may have something to tell.

"And Fabre?"

"Listing the witnesses." Right, can't be too quick in the elements for the 'neighbourhood enquiry'. Who dragged who, how many times, round the walls of where? It isn't Troy and it sure wasn't Achilles.

"Robin." What Castang wants is any trace or fragment of 'the thing'. Parcel, suitcase, shopping bag or . . . Going off this hour of the morning, an electronic command from a distance is unlikely on the face of it. Bits of what might be a timing mechanism might . . .

"Yes, yes." Captain Robin is a senior officer, experienced. "We've got to get it shored up. No good Lille mucking about in there and risk it tumbling on their nose. Job like that can take days. And then get the whole thing tarpaulined."

"Right." And with that much secured – his job is not little microscopic fragments of mechanism or tissue. The bomb-squad technicians can borrow specialised artificers, army engin-eers if they want them. Castang's job is human beings.

Lasserre, from the Municipal Police, is gloomily making arrangements for the Sanitary Department to clean up the mess, nail slats across windows, filling his notebook with Particulars Taken, and burdened with the company of the Town Councillor for Leisure Facilities, a peculiar choice in the circumstances but the first municipal dignitary available. In a little while there will be the Mayor and the Prefect but Castang hopes that Commissaire Sabatier will be here by then. The press arrives too, cross at being fished out of bed at this unholy hour. There are far too many people; who let them all in? Castang turning bumped into a tall man in a grey suit and said irritably, "Who are you then?" Faint smile, almost diffident.

"I'm the Bishop of this diocese."

"Oh. Sorry, Monseigneur." There was a time when Castang who has anticlerical tendencies would not have said 'My Lord' (like Paddy Campbell), but he has learned better manners.

"I am sorry," said the bishop mildly, "I'm hindering your work. But I live just along the road, you see, and these are my people."

"This is a bad business." A conventional remark to which he expected a conventional answer in mayoral, prefectoral words like odious or lamentable.

"The worse because these women are the best there are."

"I haven't had time yet to find out."

"You are Monsieur Castang, aren't you? PJ?"

"The local responsible, yes."

"I'm wondering whether you'd like to come and see me. On second thoughts you're a very busy man and I should come to see you."

"First way is the best, Monseigneur, if you don't mind."

"At your convenience," politely. We both would have raised our hats. If we'd had hats.

They had got the injured woman out and taken her off to hospital. The firemen went on working, to get out the second dead one. The group of minor-injuries had also been taken off, in a police van, for out-patient check-up.

"Radiology for at least three," said the doctor, "one certain minor fracture," looking at his clipboard, "two suspected and a cranial I'm not very happy with. Concussion all round and all need their ears looked at – that was a big bang, Castang. A couple will be out and about again today, probably. A tough lot. Nurses, admittedly, but even so – two simply said it reminded them of the earthquake, I didn't ask where, and one said she'd had exactly the same experience when a house fell in on top of her under heavy artillery fire. All in the day's work, say. If it's interviews you're after I heard Monseigneur say he'd fix them temporary quarters in the Palace, this afternoon I'd say you could."

Castang was interrupted by a noisy arrival. Commissaire Sabatier in his top-of-the-basket Renault, the turbo model with the V-6 motor, stuffed with gadgetry and computers. To Castang asking one day what all these were for (cars do not interest him), the evil-minded Mr Campbell answered that they were to tell Le Grand Patron what he should be doing next.

He got out of the car with a crisp little jump. Almost a skip, thinks Castang. He is fond of these athletic movements which show how fit he is, and is given to running up stairs three at a time; is forever telling his beastly subordinates to stop smoking, and legend says he has threatened to make them all take part in an Early Morning Run. The joke goes that you must explain things to him slowly and in very simple words. This is all nonsense, but he is better at administration than police work, very hot on paper and reluctant to appear in the field. That he has in common with many divisional commissaires. He runs the big Lille service (Paris apart, with Lyon the biggest in France) smoothly and skilfully, and is almost never in the office. He is a more than competent politician – although highly right-wing managing to stay on the most amicable of terms with the Socialist Mayor of Lille, a formidable personality.

He is a fresh-faced man, always smiling and very well dressed. His wife, an ambitious hostess, is even better dressed. This lavish display of moneyed ease causes people to mutter that he swallows enormous bribes. Nonsense, dear boy; he has Private Means and made a clever marriage. Certainly he reads the stock-exchange reports with a lot more attention than the telex.

There is no great fondness between himself and Castang, but he does have one big plus-point: he leaves people alone (as long as they don't stir up shit).

"Well now, Castang," all virile stride, wafts of toothpaste and aftershave, shirt beautifully pressed and slightly starched.

"Morning, Patron."

"Very bad morning. Ah, there they are." Peugeot station wagon, with a scream of brakes and rubber, bomb squad showing zeal but care taken not to arrive before the boss has. "All right, boys, get to it. Liaison with – what's his name, Castang? – Campbell, yes yes, the Red Hand of Ulster. They'll take over all angles in the technical sense, Castang, you'll remain in charge of the enquiry and report to me; if need be I'll have three or four crim-brig officers put under your orders. That the Mayor? I'd better have a quick word, what? Prefect not here yet? Told me he'd be along. You did well, Castang, I confirmed the orders you gave. Spoke to Paris on the phone coming along." He loved using the ship-to-shore while cruising along the autoroute. "I told Paris you're a competent chap – which of course they know – and that I'd just as soon see the matter left in your hands. Until we know more, at least. That, I told them, or take it away from us altogether, send your flying squad, all glare and glamour, we'll go back to reading up the phony marriage agencies in the *Voix du Nord*. But one thing or the other; don't mess us about. Well well, they've said, see what the preliminary indications give, is it part of something bigger and especially something known? Action Directe, anything like that. Or something isolated, some dotty new group? Well, Castang, what's it look like? Nothing local, I hope; or you'd know. Eh?" In answer to this flow of tittuppery, a military and monosyllabic attitude must be taken.

"You don't want premature judgments. Earliest preliminary opinion this far – non-political choice of target. Nuns, that's weird. If it were gelignite, mine or quarry stuff we might look for some acute, psychopathic grievance. But plastic points to professional if irresponsible splinter, loony islam, Lebanese maybe. No attribution claimed so far. Eleven women, two are dead, one badly injured, the others taken for treatment but I'll have them this afternoon, learn perhaps how the parcel was passed or presented. I've a good man on the neighbourhood for any untoward movement or loiterer, Campbell is with the firemen for anything he can get, we've two-three rolls of film taken, we'll hope for something from press or radio, and the witnesses as soon as I can get them. There may have been a threat or warning which they kept dark. I'd suggest moving it to the office, Patron, we'll do no good here and the boys are on the job."

"Do that. Make my number with the neighbours and the Prefecture, and I'll be with you."

"Nuns," said Monsieur Sabatier, sitting in Castang's chair and accepting coffee, "that's really weird."

The tone was querulous; the nuns had plainly done it on purpose to annoy, and Castang recognised the need to be soothed.

"I'll go after their background. These are nursing nuns, used to some tough spots. One mentioned being under shellfire, that could be Lebanon, something they did upset a rival faction. Another talked about an earthquake."

"Do they have earthquakes in Lebanon?" Vague on this point Castang was unhappily aware that a great many places on the earth's surface also enjoyed artillery bombardments.

"They come under some authority," thinking of the bishop, "and it will be possible to find out where they were and if they incurred hostile feelings."

"No peculiar characters hanging about, Castang? No sudden increase in semitic features and swarthy complexions? Your finger kept well on the pulse, is it, huh?"

"Just our usual quota of Turks."

"Never know with Turks," darkly. "Kurds, Armenians, all sorts of shady doings. Iranians!" struck by a sudden attack of geography, "how are we off for mad ayatollahs?" More ointment needed but what emollient action could one take? Would he feel happier were one to bark out 'Madame Metz! Bring me our file on mad ayatollahs!' The northern provinces of France have the lowest Moslem populations because they don't like to

42

stray too far from homely Mediterranean smells and sounds, like their climates hot, and feel uneasy with these potato-guzzling palefaces of the north. To be sure, we have our Foreign Legion. We have Spanish, Italian and Portuguese battalions (we have also our strong floating contingent of Brit tourists). We have our Chinese and our Vietnamese. Besides our Turks. They all stick together in clannish cohesion in their streets, their little 'quartier'. Paddy Campbell, whose car is a Mercedes, uses the generic 'Unterturkheim' (after the Daimler-Benz address in Stuttgart) to describe them.

Even the palest potato learns to tell at a glance which group it is. The food is an accurate guide. Demonstrated entertainingly the week before to him, walking through municipal garden-plots.

"Italian," said his guide, pointing. "That many tomato plants can be nothing else. Tell a Spanish one because it'll be full of beans."

It would be smugly superficial to say, as people do, that the National Front flourishes only where Arabs are thick on the ground. Not for nothing is their Führer a Breton. Gazing peacefully into Monsieur Sabatier's kind blue eyes, Castang is saying 'racist bastard' to himself while being very reassuring about having all the subhumans correctly computerised. It is true that the 'neighbours' of the uniformed branch have been getting more zealous lately at saying 'Papers' at anyone with a suntan.

"Keep a tight ship," advised Monsieur Sabatier looking at his gold Rolex Oyster (as James Bond remarked, you can always use it as a knuckleduster), "and that way your dusky brothers don't get out of hand. I must run, I've a Chamber of Commerce lunch in Dunkerque." And Castang, who has been longing to be rid of him so as to get on with the work, winds his telephone and his telex and his Madame-Metz up to redhot pitch before going home to his wife, who has many abominable vices but not those of a Syndicat d'Initiative in Dunkerque.

* * *

She is called Annunziata. She denies, and pretty sharply, being any sort of 'Mother Superior'.

"We don't have one. We are a team, a team has a chief, I'm it."

"Primus inter pares?" suggests Castang wishing to be tactful.

"What?" For two pins, it crosses his mind, she'd have said 'I'm no schoolmarm at the snake dances' like Marlowe to the Hollywood Indian. Cutting out the pig latin, it also crosses his mind that she's still in shock. She was not cut or bruised, but "Sorry, I'm finding it difficult to hear you; my ears are still ringing from the blast."

She is a good six foot tall, lean but broad of shoulder and hip, and has a facial resemblance – in character too? – to General de Gaulle. She has some fine features. Her hands are beautiful although larger than his. A wide and well-cut mouth above a long obstinate chin; the sharp little grey eyes above a prominent knobbly nose bring into relief the serene planes of a beautifully modelled forehead. Large well-shaped ears are half-hid by coarse grey hair smartly cut into a springy wave. She is irritable at this reconnaissance and uses – like the General – barrackroom language to knock him over.

"I can see," disgustedly, "that your notion of nuns is medieval. The Sister of Mercy dishing out wanks to wounded chinese sailors is out of date. I'm sorry," seeing him out of countenance, "that was brutal and vulgar as well as quite uncalled-for."

"It's all right. You took a very heavy punch there this morning."

"Sandbagged!" she agreed with a laugh like the sun coming out in a black sky: Castang is going to learn that these women have a conspicuous talent for laughing. She wears a wide skirt gathered into a waistband, with two big pockets. Her nervous strain is manifest in the way she hides her hands in these and fiddles with objects: useful tools, decided Castang, Swiss Army penknives, a compass for finding one's way in the bush . . . On her top she wears a cotton T-shirt washed so fiercely that it has stretched in every direction, some unexpected. She has a man's wristwatch, Longines in plain steel. The moment she realised

44

she was rummaging she made herself stop it. Her facial skin is fine, scarcely wrinkled: she could be any age between forty and sixty.

"Well, Commissaire," disciplining impatience. "Monseigneur bid me hold myself at your disposition. For whatever use I can be, which is not much at present. We are an order of nursing sisters, with affiliations in most European countries. We work in small groups in more or less any country you care to name. Malnutrition, chronic disease, shortages of food, shelter, basic hygiene, you name it. The house is ours, what's left of it. It is used for anything up to twenty women to rest and refit and even enjoy a holiday after a tour of two to three years in some jungle before popping off afresh to some other jungle as our superiors may direct. A brief tale, quickly told. We've been home nearly six weeks. Some good soul appears to have decided we were in danger of getting lazy."

"The obvious question is whether you have any notion who this good soul may be."

"None whatever nor any reason to suppose of any."

"No threat? Warning? Peculiar occurrence? Oh – weird letters, obscene phonecalls?" She shook her head. "No accounting at all?"

"I must have ripped the elastoplast off the face of some chap who hadn't shaved in a while. I'm sorry if I appear callous. I've lost two of my best friends. It's better if I say that has happened before and will no doubt happen again."

"The whole group was overseas with you?"

"Six of us. The others were from somewhere else. We don't all rush off to jungles. Some women can't handle it. That makes no distinction between us. You will find plenty of poverty right here on the doorstep."

"About the way the parcel, packet – bomb – was introduced."

"I can't be much help there. We take turns with the conciergerie – doorbell, phone and so on – just as we do the housework or the cooking. That girl's in hospital which reminds me that as

45

soon as you're finished I must go to see her. I should explain that there are young trainees, novices as they used to be called. I should also say that if you have questions about finance I will refer you to Monseigneur's secretary, but we depend as much on charity as upon what we may earn. Good people give us things. Parcels arrive and it might be anything from old library books to motheaten blankets – we sort it out and it might well take a day or two." Castang nodded. "Make up a packet, label it medical supplies, it could be anything, cottonwool or disposable syringes, nobody'd pay any attention."

"Were you in the Lebanon?"

"No. I've known women who have been. Why?"

"General supposition. Refugee camps or whatever, a large number of sects and factions, some extremely violent and a possible hatred of Christians. A remark made by one of your women about shellfire." She laughed, heartily.

"Mr – Castang, is it? My name is Annunziata. You can find the conditions you describe in most corners of the world. We were in Nicaragua and got ourselves mortared by some souls who are a great deal more Christian than we are. I'm quite used to being told to my face that I'm a Communist, atheist, lesbian agent provocateur. Your trueblue bible-puncher can be very intolerant indeed. All that surprises me is that it should have happened here. But there's so much hatred in the world that I don't find the time to bother about it. Sure, go right ahead and smoke. You see, Mr Commissaire of Criminal Police, I see much nastier sides of existence than you do, but I would also guess that I see a lot more love."

"True, here in Europe we're rather short of love."

"Not altogether true. I understand you; a lot of chilly apathy, petty egoism, too much interest in over-eating and making money; I could still surprise you. We have a lot of friends, some surprising, and who like to remain anonymous. I'm not going into details."

"You mean the cocaine-addicted movie queen who gives her money to the poor?" He was only being frivolous but she wasn't.

"Oh, if you want to sentimentalise – yes, dirty filthy cock-sucking prostitutes who maybe know more about love than you and me put together. I mean that love appears in unexpected places."

"Mr Commissaire of Criminal Police," with mild irony, "isn't perhaps altogether as barbarically crass as you wish to suppose. We are not much liked. What we do best is shoot people. We are unjust, treacherous and violent. We're trying to better that."

"Yes?"

"We use this tough talk; show how tough we are." She looked at him for some time, gravely.

"I take your point."

"I don't know that I've got a point. I have to ask your pardon for another stupid and insensitive remark."

"I think you're asking me to examine my conscience. We – we go out there at first with a lot of missionary zeal. The idea is to alleviate suffering. Wherever it is found. The illusion is that among primitive peoples there will be poverty, misery, disease, but that somehow it will be purer, simpler, less corrupt than here at home."

"The desert is the garden of Allah."

"Something like that, yes. You get your fiftyfourth ophthalmia of the morning, another eight-year-old, you find yourself thinking of a winter morning in Flanders. A still morning with snow and people going to the baker, seeing their own breath and smelling fresh bread. It's one of the stages you go through. We get it still from time to time. Like malaria," with a short harsh laugh.

"I understand."

"I should be asking your pardon. For my dirty mouth."

"I want us to understand each other. Only this morning a bomb. You know better than I how delayed shock works. I'm not going to press you. Try and think, for me. Brutality, violence and suffering have followed you here and perhaps there's a reason for it. Reason isn't a good word when we're talking about terrorists. Some connection perhaps, very slight, not apparent. Right now, we have no pointers, nothing to go on. The technical people may find some indication but it isn't likely to help much: I mean too many people have access to weapons and explosives."

"I'll try," simply, taking her handsome big hand out of the pocket to hold out to him.

"You come from round here."

"Yes. This is my home."

"Is it long, since the last time you were back?"

"About two and a half years: why d'you ask?"

"No reason."

"'Reason isn't a good word,'" smiling. "It's the men as a rule who try to be so rational. I'm usurping your function. I have to be rational about such things as pharmaceuticals which have toxic side-effects. Apart from that God's not a particularly rational concept and I like it that way. No – our overseas tours last about three years. We were a bit premature but Monseigneur, who is our technical superior, felt that things were getting a bit politicised out there, and we try to avoid all such involvements."

"Isn't any position, just about anywhere, likely to get politically polarised, by somebody's propaganda?"

"That's the way I feel. The Church is supposed only to interest itself in Propaganda Fidei, and all this talk of left-wing and right-wing leaves me cold. Things were getting a bit dicey. Those Contras, you know, partisans of the Somoza dictatorship, malcontents and people who lost cosy incomes when the Sandinista régime got in, ran complaining about Communists to the United States, knowing it was showing the bull a red rag. But we were in an area disputed by arms, and it wasn't very prudent to stay there, we might easily have been kidnapped."

"And you were mortared that time." She shrugged.

"We didn't get a scratch and we come home and three of us . . ." her face working, fighting to keep unemotional.

"And what does Monseigneur think about that?"

"You'll have to ask him, won't you?"

At the door Castang stopped again.

"You spoke of friends."

"Yes. We have many. Women – men too – whose lives have led them into other paths. Married – schoolteachers – shopkeepers, anything; I know an income-tax inspector. But who understand what we try to do and help us any way they know or can."

"You don't by any chance know a woman called Adrienne Sergent?"

"I do as it happens. Not well. She's one of the volunteer aides I spoke of. She keeps a hotel. I've met her a couple of times, no more, but why do you ask?"

"No more than an idle fit of curiosity; she's been in my mind. She disappeared and we'd like to know why. Nothing criminal suspected," shrugging shoulders in his turn.

Annunziata didn't seem perturbed or even surprised.

"Since I haven't seen Ada for all this time there is nothing I can tell you. Anyway, people behave in unexpected ways."

"You might know whether a disappearance – very sudden, abrupt, taking everyone who knows her by surprise – surprises you when you think about it."

She thought about it.

"I don't, or didn't know her well enough. No fool, and a strong character. If she decided something, she'd have a good reason – reason again! – motivation, would you call it? You're the policeman."

"She's been described to me as a thoroughly good person."

"Yes, she is."

"One witness went as far as to say that if there were any guilt, it wasn't hers."

"From what I know of her, I'd agree."

"She was a widow. A man, do you think?"

She broke into a grin. "I'm not much of a witness concerning women's relations with men. I've never had any."

"Perhaps not. But you know a lot about love."

"Ah, that is different. Women love in many ways. If you ask whether Ada had a great capacity for love, then I'll say yes, no question."

49

"Then?" A wry look came upon her face.

"Mr Castang, women seek happiness. They seek it through love. Men seek power. Some women, of course, do likewise but they do violence to their nature. You're asking me a theological question. We make great efforts to attain happiness, think ourselves very very fortunate if for a moment we catch a glimpse. In this world at least, a term of human happiness is going to be very brief – and . . ." she sought for the word she wanted " . . . beleaguered."

"I quite agree."

"Well, you've taken me totally by surprise. She vanished? And you don't know how or why?"

"We haven't really looked yet."

"You might be well advised not to."

"That thought has also crossed my mind," sketching a little laugh, a little bow, closing the door gently behind him, to leave her to her thinking and him to his.

He looked at the sky. Greasy soup-tureen, no pleasure in that. He looked at the street, roily-moily, didn't help either. He didn't suppose that going back to the office would be a source of joy and consolation, but there wasn't a whole lot of choice. The mass of cloud, of a nasty clay colour, would not go away when called upon, nor even back to England where it belonged; didn't even summon the wish he were on a beach in some unvexed Bermooth. He was here, and Good Appetite.

The technicians had buggered off back to Lille, and no by-your-leave about it. The explosive was standard plastic and might have come from anywhere. Bits of detonator and wire were just that, and analysis was not likely to contribute more. Timing mechanism had been a cheap Swiss watch sold by the hundred thousand in all countries. The construction of all this had been simple, competent and professional. This was the one item of information that could be considered valuable, explained Mr Campbell. No sophisticated tricks, nothing you could call a signature. A blackboard demonstration of the textbook method for the portable explosive device, as taught to army artificers. Is that a help, is that a signature? Not a thing to go-off-in-your-hand but a circuit solidly anchored to a stout piece of cardboard. It would resist vibration, jarring, dropping-on-the-deck. It had been packed in a sturdy cardboard box of the sort cans come packed in, to be found and picked up in the throwout section of any supermarket. Sealed with adhesive tape such as is bought by the roll at any stationer's. The opening had the usual boobytrap: the lid would wrench the wire loose and close the circuit.

Almost certainly, said Mr Fabre, delivered the evening before. Time delay thus – if not opened – up to twelve hours, allowing all concerned to be anywhere they chose before the alarm. A small van had been seen, but so had many others of so many standard patterns and colours as to be worthless: on a winter evening in bad weather all colours are black when they aren't grey. Somebody had seen a man carrying a large cardboard box, shown after exhaustive pursuit to be a student who had borrowed an electric drill for some home carpentry.

Mr Louppes' photographs were quite pleasing from the aesthetic angle; not otherwise informative.

Where is Miss Véronique Varennes? Not back yet from Amsterdam, where doubtless she dallies pleasurably, tiptoe through the tulips. Won't she be disappointed just, at missing all this fun! And Madame Metz is terribly sorry, but she must remind Mr Castang that the press has been kept at arm's length only by the promise of a statement and answers to questions at five-thirty precise. Thank you (cursing Monsieur Sabatier) for bringing this to mind. There are no press facilities here. Town Hall. We've just time for a wash, a beer, and to make a few notes upon a piece of paper.

Quite a crowd. There hasn't been a bomb for some weeks and the odd choice of target has attracted attention. The lights are turned on so that the local television station can get a bit of footage for the evening news. Hoping there is plenty else that editors will find more exciting, Castang is as dull as possible.

"I must be factual, prudent and guarded. No responsibility as yet has been claimed for this attempt. Nor have we any findings so far permitting us to ascribe it to any group or

51

movement. No political purpose is apparent. Please do not interrupt, wait till I've finished. Assumptions are futile. We must evaluate. This is likely to be a long job. It will be done on a national scale and in the closest collaboration with other countries. Pending this, the technical findings point to a deliberate plan and method, nothing haphazard, professionally carried out. Why any group or person should choose to attack a house of missionary nuns known for their work among the deprived passes comprehension and arouses understandable outrage. The enquiry has been entrusted to the local services of Police Judiciaire, in conjunction with the municipal police, gendarmerie and security services, under the orders of Commissaire Sabatier in Lille: I understand that the Prefect and the Minister of the Interior have made confirmatory statements. That is all."

"What's your immediate line of enquiry?"

"None established."

"Where were these nuns working?"

"Disparate groups: the house is used as a rest centre."

"You haven't answered."

"Africa, South America, no relevance that I know of."

"How was the bomb introduced?"

"As far as has been determined, in a box labelled medical supplies, which attracted no attention, and was left at the entrance last night."

"Timing device or distance command?"

"Timing, and no further comment on that subject. Material has been recovered and sent for analysis."

"The Bishop refuses to answer questions."

"That's his business."

"Is he answering yours?"

"I'll know that when I ask them."

"So who else are you going to ask?"

"I repeat, no line of enquiry is at present established. My immediate object will be consultation and coordination with every European authority upon terrorist operations. We have to know whether this is an isolated instance or part of a larger pattern and with that I have come to the end of what I can usefully tell you."

"Are you so sure this is a terrorist thing, Commissaire?" A voice with an American accent. "Couldn't it be an act of private vengeance?"

"I've no answer to that at present beyond saying that every possibility will be scrutinised and that right now I'm going home."

Vera, his wife, three or four years younger than him, sees herself as a mossgrown hag. A fine bone-structure means she looks the same at any age, and she has the sort of fair hair in which grey scarcely shows, though she looks for the first threads with tormented glee. Her figure has stayed remarkably slim: the limp, from the spinal injury more than fifteen years before, is only noticeable when she walks. She is not an oasis of domestic tranquillity, and never was, but has much strength of character, known to Castang as her damned obstinacy. Being unable to walk for five years taught her, as she says, to think.

At drawing she has kept her hand in; to be even remotely professional one must do one every day. Her painting ambitions have slackened, though she still works at them, and she reads a lot in an omnivorous anglophil style she primly calls 'eclectic'. Her two schoolgirl daughters, wedded to their loathsome television set, are obliged to indulge furtively, sitting on the floor in their own pigsty bedroom. With them Castang is both over-indulgent and over-authoritarian; proper, he says, with daughters. He complains much about the house being asphyxiatingly full of women: they venge themselves by sarcastically calling him 'Dad'.

Vera's frame of mind is not this evening unusually vile or scratchy, but she has listened to the radio, knows him to be tired and anxious and has made efforts towards a good supper and an atmosphere of harmony. She hates being Wifey, 'bobonne' (has gone through every feminist phase and is still exceptionally fierce on the subject). Male caprices will this evening be indulged, because the man has been greatly abraded. Terrorists, Paris and Monsieur Sabatier make up a hideous sandwich; he has chewed it patiently all day and a reaction is inevitable. She is prepared for anything, from thrown plates to abrupt sexual assault.

He is not so much quiet as oddly still, drinks a large malt whisky without rushing it, stretches out on the sofa till supper is ready, does not roar at the girls about their homework, asks politely for the sound of their little radio to be turned down just-a-scrap, and eats for once without criticising the food, a winter soup with beans in it, vaguely Mexican and the girls complain of too much red pepper, Waldorf salad – Lydia complains about celery – and as a special treat (which stops Lydia complaining) pancakes 'because you had no proper dinner': he had not of course come home at midday; a cop had been sent for a horrible fastfood sandwich, and most of that had gone in the waste-paper basket. He had had an embittered memory of Richard, his former boss who had trained his secretary to cook him nice little things in the office. Delectable Fausta with the hair-down-her-back. So unlike Madame Metz.

"Come over here on the sofa."

"No, the girls aren't in bed yet."

"I said come over here on the sofa." Vera suppresses a sigh and goes to lock the door; they are certainly looking at an unsuitable movie and will gloat at not being ordered to turn it off before doing their teeth. Oh well . . . at least it's less uncomfortable than having one's knickers dragged off in the bathroom.

"A woman today told me that human happiness is a brief and beleaguered term."

"Especially beleaguered," said Vera trying to see that her tights do not get laddered.

4

Marklake is living in disquiet. Forget it, said Gabrielle. So you should just forget it? All this good advice he can do without. Unexpected and surprising the police kommissar yonder had behaved like a civilised man, had promised that persecutions and pesterings would be no more. But this was like a ring he had once had, with a very beautiful opal. It had developed a crack which for months had been a grievance. There was no reason for the crack. Flawed, and now worthless; he had felt robbed: he felt robbed now. Of his peace of mind.

That strange interior, where that woman had lived with her birds – this had stayed with him, vivid and compulsive – visions there that like the vague, indefinable sense of unease he could not get rid of. He was thinking of making a picture out of this (that was the way to resolve this sense of being uncomfortable in one's clothes, one's skin). Boil it down to essentials, it was a still-life. Fruit, and birds. Something that would be somewhat in-the-manner-of a Chardin but would be no Chardin: it would ask questions, to which he had not got the answer. He had made various arrangements with fruit rolling apples about on the diningroom table; it wasn't right yet. To Gabrielle's annoyance he bought a bird – irritated her scattering seeds about but he rather liked it. When let out it stood in unexpected places and looked at him. He looked at it and made preliminary drawings in charcoal. Gabrielle complained it would make messes on pictures, on rugs, on his coat. He didn't care, he would pay no attention to her, he was beginning to see this picture. He wanted a melon. The season was wrong for melons, he would concentrate strongly upon the smell, the feel, the texture of melon; the apples were wrong, summer fruit he wanted and spring even it isn't yet, he found a nice blue and white bowl and saw it filled with raspberries. The bird was yellow, shading towards orange and as well towards broken whites; he must have a melon.

"Obsessed you are becoming with this melon," said Gabrielle.

The very next day there had been a bomb attack up there, some nuns, the world we live in, nuns he had use for like the rough ends of a pineapple up his – but these were good women and were they bad, ignorant, superstitious women a bomb does nothing but make bad people worse. An idea he had had once – an Arab still-life, a flat wicker-basket with lemons, pomegranates, handgrenades – rejected at once for the cheap, theatrical idea it undoubtedly was; a poster that can make (and a poster he made, as a contribution to a disarmament campaign). A picture it isn't.

He was still thinking about this when something else happened, more disquieting, more disturbing because, because – words are not his trade and he gropes. Innocent is not right. For whatever this is it's not, he feels quite sure, innocent.

He had been out, along the river, as far as the bird market. He was not quite satisfied with the composition, it was not quite complete. A second bird is an idea to which his mind as he stumps along, extremely well wrapped up by Gabrielle against eventual but today imaginary March winds, is giving Norman answers: yes and no and maybe but he rather thought not. He caught his bus and wedged himself into the corner reserved for Anciens Combattants, which he was, sunk his big head inside the collar of the overcoat (furry, rather elegant) and became so absorbed in the contemplation of walnuts that he overshot two stops and had to walk back. Walnut shells – and if cracked they open into neat halves, intricate and of interesting texture. So that both the inside and the outside . . . Not quite sure yet because he doesn't want this to be any silly parody of those tiresome seventeenth-century pictures which

56

are Allegorical and are forever nudging you in the ribs with Have you got the message? – nonononono.

Gabrielle is staring thunderstruck at a large magnificent object. It stands there in the middle of the floor and he walks all around it. A heavy stocky old man in an overcoat and with his hat still on cannot be said to look like a leopard wondering whether this goat conceals a trap, but however ludicrous, it is so. He looks wordlessly at Gabrielle who gabbles that two deliverymen came with it, like that in three pieces, two ordinary men in ordinary overalls, and put it together like that in the middle of the floor; they said Sign Here, there's nothing to pay, no formality, just a typewritten piece of paper with the name and address. They had a truck how should she know what truck, a transport truck a remover's truck – ja no she hasn't seen the name, who looks at the names of delivery trucks, she has kept saying a mistake— It isn't a mistake look at that brass plate that is screwed on the thing, it says Marklake. Such mistakes cost fifty thousand francs, she would like to be told who it is makes these mistakes and thank you, shouting at her isn't going to make it vanish, a Djinn she isn't.

The brass plate, small like a cigarette packet, like the matrix for engraved calling cards, has a simple legend: MARKLAKE. FROM HIS FRIENDS.

"This is a joke."

Maybe. Jokes this expensive you won't often see.

Confused memories of Trojan Horses, of bewaring of Greeks who bring gifts, cause him to examine the object with great care. If there is some hidden trap or device then it must be too small to be visible to the eye. Further it looks lovely. Further it has a lovely smell.

"My friends whom I don't know give me a writing desk, I should be a writer all of a sudden, my memoirs is it now I am going to sit down and write?"

"There ought to be a chair," offers the mesmerised Gabrielle, "to go with it."

Utterly discombobulated the old man belts off downstairs to raise almighty hell with the concierge. Put out by his manner she is rather rude; when perfectly polite men from a transport firm bring a new kitchen stove or a refrigerator for her tenants is she supposed to send them away again? Transport firms there are maybe five hundred in the Paris area, look them up if you have time to spare in the yellow pages, she should pick one out and it would be to stick in her stamp collection maybe, does he think?

Gabrielle is running drawers in and out: they go like silk.

"Beautiful workmanship this is, beautiful." There are odder things that have happened to him during his life? One or two. They didn't arrive from his friends, though. Friends! Yes, he has friends. He has also customers. Some are rich, one or two are eccentric. Not like this, though.

It could be of English workmanship. Or it could be French, in the anglophil style beloved by rich Parisiens. Even now in the Faubourg Saint-Antoine you will find traditional workshops which will make you furniture in any style you please and of the very highest craftsmanship the moment you care to pay for it. Turn you out from a Sheraton or a Hepplewhite patternbook or the Brothers Adam a piece as easily as do you a Leleu, an Oeben or a Riesener; or say the word and they'll do you a fifteenth-century Florentine – nothing like that here. Not even late Victorian, but a style that is no style but simply a timeless piece of England, a geometry of simple rectangles, not a curve in it anywhere save in the beautifully finished corners. Utterly simple walnut wood cut in the mass – Spanish walnut seeing it and feeling it. Am I a fool, do you show me a sea-otter fur and I will maybe tell you it is bloody beaver? This stuff you can't fake. It is not old wood neither is it new, and there is not a screw or a nail anywhere, every single element dowelled and the handles cast brass.

Who cares if the English or the French or maybe the Spanish made it, it is made by a man over seventy years old, nobody else can or will do work like that.

It doesn't matter the man who made it I am wondering about the man who paid it.

You stupid woman the man who paid it is some shithouse

banker, Worms and Vernes, Neuflise and Mallet, what have we to worry about such people.

"Marklake!" She only calls him by this name when she is very serious. Or very frivolous and now she isn't joking. "I am thinking too who gave you this.

"And I am maybe thinking Robert?" And that shut his mouth.

Does Robert even exist? Neither of them have ever laid eyes on him. Between them it is not spoken of. Marklake is a survivor of 'the camps'. There were never very many, and there are fewer now.

He speaks freely of this time, with humour, a humour which we others have learned to paste into the category: jewish humour; gallows humour. Berlin humour. 'Robert' dates from this time. Like jokes about Dr Goebbels: did he exist, outside the jokes? Since the day, eighteen years after nineteen forty-four, when they first learned that yes, Robert also survived the camps, there have been Robert-jokes. Two, three, in the early years. Nothing for some years, now.

Robert's jokes are Berliner because his mother was a Berliner. Marklake would say that, since Robert owes his existence to a Berlin joke . . .

In nineteen fortyone Rudolf Hess, a serious man, flew to England with the idea of making peace; plainly a Good Idea. Oh, said the Berliners, what a good idea. But alas, it means that our Thousand-year-reich is only going to be a hundred. How so? But look; we've lost a zero . . . There are only two to go. It is probable that this kind of joke infected Robert as it were from birth.

This one – expensive and elaborate – does it grow out of another? And what does it presage?

The unmistakable silver sheen that cannot be faked upon sea-otter fur. There isn't any any more. Like the giant panda there are maybe a few left in some special nursery but the Russian government will not be very quick to tell you. Extinct, they will tell you; sable you can have if you have the money, you will need a lot, I am telling you and no shit. Robert? No

59

no, there are none left, I am telling you, like the sea sparrow and the Californian condor. There are no wolves left in France.

Maybe you are serious and maybe you are just a vulgar voyeur looking for kicks, or maybe you are even one of those who say it's all bullshit, it was just a typhus epidemic, he is among those who can tell you: there are not that many left.

Maidanek or Sobor or the Struthof, man, they were all death camps. Dachau or Bergen-Belsen, you don't need gas chambers, there are so many economical ways of killing people. There were two death factories, just like General Motors it's a statistical thing, we want you to beat last month's output. Don't frig about beating people or freezing or giving them injections or counting who slings themselves up against the electric wire, just concentrate on stepping up the assembly line.

Two like that; Treblinka, that's where I belong, Poles, the big ghettos, yes, Lodz, all my relations, all the people I knew in my childhood; a remarkable place, the railway station was a work of art.

But I had gone to France to be a painter, I did my service in the French Army, who didn't ask was I a Pole or a Senegalese, so when they put the hook on me . . . that's right, Auschwitz it was; Treblinka I would have felt more at home, maybe?

Like any big factory it's sloppy round the edges. Very efficient, yes. But there's a black market, right next door to the big market.

He has some unbelievable stories, old Marklake, and listening you know them to be true: they are so unbelievable, and almost always so funny. 'His' colonel, not a high rank if you were in the Waffen SS and under the command of that blunt and decent man General Gottlob Berger, who told ol' Traue-Heinrich he didn't care, Reichsführer you may be, no man of mine is going to be concerned with such filth and any man you send me who utters that talk, first I'll bust the fucker down to a buckass private and second think himself lucky if he dies of frostbite, that's a nice easy sleepy way to go.

But his colonel was a mighty man around a camp. Full of ideas too. He was going to save Rembrandt and Rubens for humanity. Jewlovers they might be, one had to Understand, Marklake, d'you follow me, God has put it into my hands to Select.

You fall about laughing. Ol' Marklake there, given canvas and paint and a studio with a north light, the smoke from the chimney blows away in the wind. I don't want, you hear me, any damn portrait with uniforms and medals, I don't give a fuck for the goddamn medals, paint me in the robes of Burgomaster Six of Amsterdam; you have to understand the Duke of Alva, you have to under*stand* King Philip. These sly types, with their artificially low ranks, Schellenburger and such, whores, it's these diplomat bastards like Requesens. I'm a *soldier*, Marklake, Berger told the Reichsführer straight, Heinrich, fuck me about and I'll give you such a stomachache even Felix Kersten can't fix it; I'm stuck with this shitty job, Marklake, and it's got to be *done*. Not you, boy. You're not going up any chimney.

That is to say. Not while you are my Court Jew.

Many have remarked upon the tendency among SS officers of a certain rank to acquire Court Jews. Most were skilled men whose gifts could be put to special use, and Marklake as a painter comes in this category: there were doctors, musicians – and magicians. Some were Jesters. The special flavour of Jewish jokes became particularly exquisite inside the wire. Even non-Jews could enjoy them, and in camps like Mauthausen or Dora or Flossenburg there were plenty of non-Jews who learned the funny side of being worked to death. You would need to have been inside the wire yourself, properly to appreciate them. And you won't find many people left able to see anything funny about Auschwitz or Treblinka, where funniness stopped in mid-breath and the fun-loving camp officials are a very exclusive club. Even old Marklake has no one left with whom to share his best jokes. But even when, as can happen sometimes late at night when he's had a few drinks, he sees his own survival as hilarious, he does not mention Robert.

* * *

61

"Funny little man," said VV. "Very Dutch." There are, however, nine-and-sixty ways of being very Dutch, so that Castang imposes stillness upon himself, and a quiet voice.

"Funny thing, Koopman means Businessman – in the literal sense, I mean." He has also to fight the wish to rend her flanks with great clanking Western spurs. "So I go to this barrack in the Marnixstraat, that's their Police Centre, great crowds of macho yobboes give you a paper cup of coffee in exchange for a hand up your leg."

"Come to what we don't know, Miss Varennes, do you mind?"

"Don't think it was easy, a name like that and all you know is he does business in Northern France, there are about three hundred and when I get there, these goddamn trams and it's pissing down with rain, take a taxi they expect you to pay it out of your own pocket, the fellow starts complaining. My fault the hotel is shut!" A smile twitching at Castang's lip because this is indeed very Dutch: he tries not to let it.

A written report would have given him bare facts, but this way he builds the picture; can see for himself the vast glassy office building on the Weteringschans of the sort that disfigures central Amsterdam, and of all the people called Koopman who are doing import-export affairs this one man who has known Ada Sergent, and is irritable at his comforts being disrupted.

He had not been surprised at the police coming to see him. That's business: all the electronic gadgets in creation don't make up for the personal contact, which is why he goes himself every three months instead of just sending the sales rep. Just as all the business-class bullshit in chain hotels does not make up for the proper breakfast you got from Madame Sergent. She understood her job, by golly. Thing with the French or the English either, they're too damn lazy, too selfsatisfied. The Hotel Caravane was a ridiculous little place, and in it was a woman, he didn't know how to say it, a woman in a million. She didn't chat you, flatter you, fiddle you or ever show the slightest curiosity about you: she knew exactly what you wanted and gave it you. We are 'nuchter', we Dutch, how d'you say that, bare-knuckle? We don't mess about.

Three years, four, he'd been going there regularly. Not even half the price of a Hyatt or a Sheraton, service like you couldn't get in the frigging Savoy.

Véronique had after all been the right person to send. With this girl – herself very Dutch, thought Castang – he had felt at ease, dropped the protective fluster. And become, yes, 'nuchter'. Not 'my wife doesn't understand me'. He didn't talk about love.

Well yes, he used to bring her little presents. Nothing personal; a bunch of flowers, a nice bottle of something to drink. What you'd bring your sister, dropping in for a cup of coffee her wedding anniversary, knowing that to her the real pleasure was your remembering, thinking of her – and that too is a key to successful business. See them as a person, not just an order to fill. A courageous, a meritorious woman, a supportive woman. If she'd gone off – yes, it was a stab, a grievance – with a man then all he could say was Lucky Man and probably he didn't deserve it.

So had Meneer Koopman any idea who this chap who'd drawn such a lucky number . . . ?

Don't know, no. Might hazard a tiny guess, wouldn't lay odds on it, and wouldn't recommend Miss – d'you say Inspector? – to do so either. Chap, irritating chap. No, must be fair: a man of some parts. These evenings – you go out for a meal, you have a couple of drinks, you unwind after a busy day, once you've written up your log, checked your notes and your next day's schedule (mostly he was on the way back from Paris, with people to see in Lille, in Bruxelles) it's a detective-story for an hour and then bed; but he'd got into conversation with this fellow and bound to say, no fool. Charm of course. The English sort. Public-school stuff such as he personally found offensive, but d'you understand charm, Miss? The trick is to concentrate totally upon the person in question and make him feel you are genuinely interested.

I do as it happens, one of these Scotch names, MacLeod, I'll spell it, better I'll write it down, that way you won't get it wrong. Robert MacLeod. Canadian maybe? – lacked that appalling English smugness, that utterly parochial incapacity to find interest in any single thing but their own piddling Tory-party. Being a journalist, conceivably, does it.

I don't know, Miss, how I come to know things. One picks stuff up, one has impressions. He behaved well, not that Brit act of strolling about pretending you're a habitué. And nice manners. But he called her Ada, which I wouldn't do. Knew his way about too. Certainly wasn't the first time he'd been in the town. Now I'm sorry, you've come a way, I've played fair, I've given you time and my undivided attention and told you what I can, but this is work time in a work area, so . . .

Just one thing, Meneer – I appreciate it, believe me – could you pin down any item in Madame Sergent's behaviour which might lead one to believe . . . ?

No, Miss, I'm sorry, I'm not going to start imagining things. If I had noticed anything I'd have told you, and being honest I haven't. I'll bring you as far as the elevator? You've no transport? Well, over that way, the Frederiksplein, any tram will take you back up towards the station.

"Like a sister," concluded Véronique. "You're fond of the old girl, comfortable with her, she understands you. You don't see an awful lot of her. Somebody has a birthday, or it's New Year. Love? – I suppose that's the word you'd use."

Castang wrote down: Robert MacLeod, pronounced cloud. Scotch or conceivably Canadian, but educated accent. A journalist, mm, or described himself as such. What would, assuming an English newspaper or even the *Toronto Star*, such a one be doing our way since we aren't exactly headline-makers around here? Yes, there might be something there, check on it when an opportunity arises, this stinking bomb enquiry isn't offering many.

It is getting us nowhere, bits of it fast and the rest slow: not one single damn thing of any use appears upon our little green screens and our dim grey minds. Castang who has been too busy to think about the bishop – these ecclesiastical connections don't appear particularly fruitful – was jogged into remembering him by (of all unlikely irritants) an American stringer for one of their news magazines: Madame Metz always reads it at the dentist's and had been impressed enough to let him chat her up into letting him in – a languid soul but skilful enough, dropping into the chair opposite Castang's and letting the jaw fall.

"Hate to bother you, Commissaire. Isn't interesting anyhow, is it? Filed a bit of colour, editor puts it on the spike, back to Paris to see if anything's moving there but just thought I'd drop in before I go, see how your sodium leaks. Not exactly an explosive mixture, is it now?"

"Need oxygen; I'm short on oxygen. I haven't a damn thing for you except that I'm in bad trouble for forgetting my wife's birthday, and now there's a hot story, you could be filing three thousand words on that while I wonder how I'll ever dare go home."

A lazy chuckle. Americans are the only people left who chuckle. This and their strange devotion to yellow legal-pads. Still, thought Castang fairminded, we put yellow headlights in our cars. Maybe they have a good reason.

"Seen the bishop yet?" The journalist was sitting on the base of his spine. He actually had a yellow legal-pad; was idly making drawings on it.

"My ears are still ringing from the blast."

"Just wondering what those nuns were doing in Nicaragua." The idle tone alerted Castang. He remembered too the American voice (had it been the same one?) which had queried the motive of the bomb. Some notion about a 'private vengeance'? The American government had interests in Nicaragua. Antennae twitched: as an experienced cop he knows one should answer only factual, technical questions.

"Oh, you mean it might be something political?" with rather overdone innocence. "I suppose all acts of terrorism are, if it comes to that. We'll ask the State Department. I'm only a technician: my concern is the who and the how."

"Not likely to find out either, are you, until you ask why?"

"Ask the gangbusters; I'm just a flatfoot."

"It can't be that you're beeing stoopid, can it?"

"I mostly am," said Castang mildly, "but I've no comment on that." They are good at wheedling. Come on, a nice little exclusive for Johnny. But he could hear Monsieur Richard's sarcastic voice. 'And before you know where you are there's the Foreign Office ringing up in outrage, are you the silly prick the source on that kite being flown in *Newsweek*, and the week after you've a posting to French Guiana.'

"I'm disappointed in you, Commissaire, bright as you are. Nice little bomb like this is exactly the leverage you need to get out of this hole where you don't deserve to be, and over to that good job in Versailles." This is the plum regional service of the PJ, with responsibility for the whole Paris area outside the city itself. Richard himself, not a 'political' cop, had never got it.

"It sounds as though there's something you should be telling me," woodenly. "In the interests of justice." He has some scrap of gossip, thought Castang, that he doesn't dare print, without an attributable source. But the American shook his head, clicking the switch on his ballpoint.

"Tat only for tit, friend," and got his legs out of the chair. "Too bad for you."

He was halfway out of the door when Castang thought of something. Cops' minds are full of these obscure cross-references.

"Know a journalist called Robert MacLeod, do you?"

"What was that again?" His back was turned but Castang could have sworn it startled him.

"You people all know each other."

"You're asking me for information?" mock indignant. Putting on a small-boy act, swinging on the doorhandle.

"Oh Jesus, is it classified?"

"Seem to have heard the name." Little eyes, watching Castang. "He's some sort of Brit. Don't know him. Any other little favour I can do you?"

"People claim to be on papers, half the time they've no proper press card."

"You want me to show you mine? You disappoint me, Castang, you really do. You get your mind clear. Then if you should think of something, you got my number. Something to get you an official commendation."

Never never never let them suck you in, Richard used to say. Their act is always flattery, trying to make you feel important. Tickling vanity is the way they work, throwing out a speculation to get leverage some place else, make you believe you're Deep Throat in the underground parking garage; to them you're just another silly big fly. Resist the blandishments; it takes a politician to know how to work the press. Like Sabatier.

Even if he has no Yellow Legal Pad he makes notes. What he has is a French schoolchild's exercise book; two hundred pages ruled in squares, a red line margin: Thoughts. It hasn't helped him remember his wife's birthday.

The nuns were in Nicaragua. While there, were they involved in some dodgy deal, hankypank of political nature? – a) nuns b) bishop. Thin, but just conceivable.

If so, is there any connection connexion (a moment's pause since both spellings looked wrong) with Americans? Source, very dubious, a lousy journalist trying to build himself a story.

There might have been a story, but the kind heard/told over a sixpack of beer: gossip in the sergeants' mess, certainly nothing printable. (Any chance of verifying this? Serious Paris papers have South American correspondents: have any of them been in Nic. lately?) It hasn't been much in the news. There will certainly have been some *American* journalists, on the other side of the frontier. (Map? What is the frontier? Honduras?) Perhaps Sandinist gov. refusing facilities in frontier/combat area?

Or is it just editors finding this not-very-interesting? Public doesn't even know where Nic. is – not sure I do either.

While on the subject of Journalists, who or what is Robert MacLeod?

McCloud?
MacLoud?

Oh Jesusgod, what the hell am I to do about Vera?

5

Nothing at all except take stick because no number of biblical ejaculations nor expletives is going to help you being viewed with cold fury by your wife and an extremity of hot indignation by your daughters. They aren't speaking to you again ever. Vera gave him his soup with the glacial politeness of a hostile headwaiter: he was something the cat brought in and *Basta!*

The situation was one in which saying or doing anything whatsoever gets you in worse. Like perhaps most men he didn't set much store by birthdays, occasions of meaningless jollity and tedious reminiscence. A bit perfunctory when given presents, which too often one neither needs nor wants; an enthusiastic giver of presents, whenever it came into his head, which was quite often, he is just a normal Thing-minded male. Then, too, he has never had any family, so that the tradition is lacking. She had a family, privately by him considered (ignorant and backward) stalinist peasants, who took her leaving very hard: it wasn't only the local authorities who had gone on a great deal about treachery and ingratitude. A proud lot, and with their own dignity. They don't speak about it and neither does she. Area of mind and heart marked 'no entry'. She is a private woman. Birthdays are times when she is to be found shedding silent tears in corners, burning candles in churches. To forget has not been a negligence but a desecration. There is now nothing he can do. This is ludicrous. Also it is tragic.

It is hateful to have this consciousness of being a barbarian, a giver of pain to helpless women, and there being nothing he could do about it.

In evil frame of mind, next morning, he was disagreeable to his staff for no good reason and stalked out of the office in the direction of the Episcopal Palace, with the general idea of beating that bishop (reactionary obscurantist cleric) round the ear until he found out what nonsense these nuns had been getting up to out in the jungle. Madame Metz had made an appointment. He had looked vengefully forward to being told that Bish was very busy. A polite, no a warm voice said please come over any time he liked; Monseigneur would be delighted.

Nor was he kept waiting. A faded but kindly woman with tired eyes said Monseigneur didn't want to have Monsieur Castang stuck in the office but in his private apartments, and guided him through a diplomatic-sounding set of titles like the Administrator and the Librarian into a small neat sittingroom: no pious pictures but a good Mantegna copy over the disused fireplace; sofa and armchairs covered in dark blue corduroy, a worn but nice crimson Afghan rug. And inside a minute the door, good plain oak, this was a nice honest old house, whisked open and Bish whisked in. Same hardwearing grey suit as last time, same warm crinkly smile under a severe paratroop haircut, small episcopal cross of plain wood: Castang commented on this.

"Yes, it's nice," said Monseigneur simply. "Olivewood. Supposed to be from Jerusalem. Though I'm a bit dubious about that. The Mount of Olives. I'm not at all sure how many olivetrees you'd find there – one or two, d'you think, kept for pious tourists?"

"You've never been?"

"I've sometimes had the time and sometimes the money but never both at once. Politicians are forever going to show how proJewish they are, trundling about in skullcaps. I'd like to, I get on well with Jews; nicer folk than most of us, can be awful but surely never more so than Christians."

"I suppose, if I were to suggest that most Popes have been gangsters, most cardinals politicians, most curés the tools of the rich, obsequious about keeping the people in superstitious ignorance – you'd write me off, I daresay, as a typical third-republic backslider?"

"Of course not; I'd quite agree. I'd answer of course that men are bad but this does not prove the badness of institutions, or what would I be doing here? We'd have a long enlivening discussion. Leaving ourselves out of it I'd suggest that there were a few better curés than there used to be (now that there are so many fewer) and maybe even better bishops, a source of much scandal past and present. You might suggest that commissaires of police, likewise a source of scandal, are also better. But it's not," briskly, "what you came for, is it?"

"I wanted a base of understanding and agreement, and I'm happy to see we've got it, so that we don't find ourselves at crosspurposes. I do have to admit that it's the celibacy that sticks in my throat more than anything; women not just half the human race but separating the sexes divides, weakens, impoverishes: you need both to get anywhere and I'm not just speaking of biology." A lot more vehement than he meant to be, because of Vera's bloody-birthday.

"Again I'd agree, though I'd ask you to be flexible. There are men and women too to whom celibacy needn't be crippling. We need a healthy attitude – nothing worse than some prurient old man crossquestioning girls about sex in the confessional: but confession can also do a great deal of good, without going all freudian about it. You've met Annunziata, haven't you? – now she has a very robust attitude towards sex even though totally celibate."

"Ah, you mean the sisters of mercy and the wounded chinese sailors?"

"Yes, exactly," bursting out laughing. "I think it deplorable, personally, but it's a highly tricky concept. You have also a vow of obedience to the State, and there are doubtless moments when you're unhappy about it – though please absolve me of any wish to pry into your conscience."

"We do understand each other," feeling much happier, "and on that sound footing I have some awkward questions."

"Shoot," said Monseigneur. "We do incidentally have a bit

71

of the demon-drink hidden away if you'd fancy some, or my kind woman makes cups of tea or coffee."

"Tea'd be lovely. It amounts to this, basically. We haven't got any motive for this attack. Nobody nowadays goes blowing up nuns, even if this were Spain it's no longer nineteen-thirtysix.

"I can't see any social reason. I can't see any personal reason either. These women are humble, poor, chaste and obedient. Fraudulent behaviour in either financial or sexual relations is the generalised mainspring of crime, in the legal and technical sense that concerns my office: theology is your affair. Remains the political."

"To terrorists of whatever obedience, the political motivation is certainly also theological. We're looking at the two sides of the same penny, there." And into this opening Castang dives headlong.

"Reverend Father, Monseigneur, ach, tja."

"Dutilleul," tolerant of these splutterings. "Mr Linden Tree, a good peasant name I have pride in."

"Ah. I'm a chestnut tree, we're brothers."

"We are indeed."

"Then I don't need to fence. Terrorists come every flavour Heinz ever thought of and fortyfour more and to stop swimming in this soup I've got to find out who what 'n' why. Something happened with those women in Nicaragua."

"Now what can have led you to draw such a, I mustn't say far-fetched, but surely arbitrary a conclusion?"

"Listen," choking it while the kind-lady brought the tea . . . "There's an American journalist. News magazine. Now you and I can say anything we please about such things, call them tuppenny-ha'penny crowdpleasers, be as contemptuous and dismissive as you like. But they're intelligent, they've their eyes and ears everywhere, they might not choose to print it and they might not dare to print it, but if they get hold of something we better listen." His tea was too hot.

"Castang," said the bishop. "Since we're speaking candidly. These women are brave, simple, and quite rightly pay no attention whatever to political affiliations. Right? They only ask, who is suffering, who is poor, wounded or diseased. I'm no Alabama bible-puncher but you are not going to deny me the basic tenets of the New Testament. I was naked and you clothed me. I was thirsty, and you gave me to drink. You do not contest that," putting fierceness into the bisyllable of the verb. "I'll fight for these women."

"Hey," said Castang. "Hey. Aren't we getting into a wrong attitude? Confrontation, that's the last thing I want."

"If there is a misunderstanding," stiffly still, "I beg your pardon. You aren't then giving me to understand that you ascribe some degree of responsibility to – ?"

"No no no, but some causality perhaps, however accidental. We've done a lot of work on the possible sources and reasons for this bomb, without a lot of result. I begin to look at the improbable."

"I fail to understand you," pushing his hair, which has already a shoebrush cut, into spikier shapes. "How can you talk of causality?"

"I want to be allowed to test a hypothesis, even if it is far-fetched, without it sounding like crude anticlericalism. If I speak of missionaries I don't think automatically of the mission-ary position," wanting it to be a disarming smile.

The bishop lowered the bristles but was puzzled.

"I've heard this joke about the missionary position but I've never known what it meant." This was a move towards disarma-ment but managed to embarrass, out of innocence.

"I spoke out of turn. It's an old joke; I suppose that in origin it was anticlerical and I should ask your pardon."

"Tell me though, or next time I meet it I may make a gaffe. Sounds as though I've made one already."

"Describes the commonplace attitude of sexual intercourse, woman supine and man on top." It got a smile if only a very small one. The brow cleared, at least.

"I see. The idea would seem to be that the missionary played the witchdoctor by abusing the credulity of the superstitious savages, is that it?"

73

"Broadly, I should think. I'd say it was more a colonising mentality than anything religious, which has the bad name nowadays." The bishop thought about this.

"You reassure me. I'd like," earnestly, "to reassure you. I'm afraid that undoubtedly there were people like that. Even literally I fear, as well as in this rather crude metaphorical sense. Much abuse, in the name of bringing the Gospel to the heathen. Leaving aside the claim that it's less relevant nowadays, you've met Annunziata, you realise surely that she's not in the least – "

"Of course not. Please understand me. We do have a few colonies left even if they're now called overseas territories. Reproach to our conscience. The majority would surely vote in favour of getting altogether out of New Caledonia, these odd few islands there are left."

"I'm relieved to hear you agree," a little tartly.

"Pretty tough rearguard action though, by the reactionary element with investments to protect. But I was thinking about Nicaragua."

"I fail to see the parallel."

"Look, Monseigneur. Americans didn't colonise the way we did or England, but they acquired a strong habit of thinking about South America as their back yard. Money to be made there. United Fruit Company or whoever, happily plundering the natives. Nowadays they get over their bad conscience by claiming they only intervene to prevent communist takeovers, which is a polite cover for protecting commercial interests with powerful lobbies in Washington."

"Not to speak," dryly, "of this communist peril being the direct result of colonial plunderings in the first instance."

"Now we're in tune," said Castang. "I was wondering whether people over there would take the view, however mistaken, that missionary activities were linked with this neo-colonial kind of mentality."

There was a silence. The bishop rubbed an eye, while thinking.

"It would be more likely," he said at last, choosing words

and guarding them, "to find the shoe on the other foot. There would be an element inclined to think – even quick to think – that missionary activities, which nowadays are medical or educational, with no emphasis on the antiquated line of handing out prayerbooks and enrolling the Children of Mary, were in danger of comforting – perhaps even encouraging – the spread of various marxist tenets, such as collectivising property." Castang found himself listening carefully.

"So did anybody take a dim view of these particular activities?"

"But this is a wild exaggeration, Commissaire. To say that these women, by no means an isolated case, often met with incomprehension and even hostility, that's one thing. To say that I – and other authorities – judged it more prudent to withdraw them from areas where there are perpetual guerilla flare-ups, that's another. But to suggest that violent destruction – in some spirit of malice or vengeance – could follow these women home here to Europe, that's something else again and I can't follow you on the path of so remote a hypothesis."

"I did say it was improbable," said Castang. "You aren't able actually to exclude it though, are you?"

"I'm not able to suggest a reason why I should find violence on my doorstep, or of those under my care – no."

"Not quite the same thing. You refuse to tell me lies, and perhaps too you refuse to tell me truths of which you fear the consequences?"

"That's tendentious, Commissaire. I can't accept any such conclusion and you must not ascribe to me sayings or thoughts I have not expressed."

"No. That's correct. But you must not seek to prevent or hinder my interrogating these ladies along any lines I choose, because that could turn out to be an obstruction of justice."

"Explain yourself," haughtily.

"Monseigneur – you're their father, the authority. I don't know much about vows of obedience but I do know that if you were to forbid them to talk about a particular subject they'd be likely to take that as a command."

"You mustn't seek to influence my conscience."

"No. I'm trying to redefine the distinction I read about as a boy, giving Caesar his due as well as God."

"I bear it constantly in mind," wintry, "but I too realise you do the work given you, and I respect that, and on this note I suggest a lighter one, which is obeying the rules of hospitality and offering you a drink."

"With pleasure," appreciating tact.

The bishop led the way through to an older and more formal part of the palace, a library where an old priest in a soutane who was working at a desk, got up with a smile seeing them and went to a corner cupboard, where he produced a tray with glasses and a decanter of port.

"Librarian doubles as barman – we're poor here." Well-worn joke but the courtesy pleased Castang.

"You've some fine pictures here," looking around. Only the 'best books' were kept here, in glassfronted cases, and in between were hung historic portraits in ornate old frames.

"It's a historic building," said Monseigneur. "Cheers! It's a historic see. Some of my predecessors were notable, even if one takes a critical view nowadays of their political activities – that gentleman there is the younger Granvelle, who became chief adviser to Philip the Second upon the government of the Spanish Netherlands, that sorely vexed question."

"It's a tradition," said the old librarian, enjoying another well-used joke, "that the occupiers of the see should have their portraits painted – there are a lot more in the gallery beyond. Monseigneur isn't looking forward to the chore of sitting for his likeness."

"Most of them done by dreadful academic hacks," agreed the bishop gloomily, "and I'm not sure whether even having three green eyes and no nose wouldn't liven things up." Castang was struck by an idea – that rarity, as Hanaud says.

"I'm acquainted with an old gentleman in Paris who is said – I'm no judge – to be a quite remarkable portrait painter in a traditional style, but nowise dreary academic either. Might that be an idea? – I could suggest to him that he get in touch and you could see for yourself."

"By all means. It has to be done alas sooner or later and I keep putting it off. As long as he's not too expensive!"

"I've an idea he'd be accommodating. Sort of thing he'd fancy, I believe, it's worth trying. But he's Jewish, would that be a difficulty?"

"Quite the contrary – chance for us to be ecumenical in a small way: I call that a recommendation."

"I'll give him a jog," said Castang, who wanted jogging himself, not to forget old Marklake. He had a lot more on his mind, though, stumping along the pavements towards his home. Divisional Commissaire Sabatier was getting restive, and cross with it, and Subscrub Castang was due in Lille, on a mission of – heyhey, don't use that word. If we get into the missionary position I'll always be the one underneath.

And that afternoon off he went, conscious of the fact that he had not achieved a lot. Lille isn't much over a hundred kilometres, and that on the autoroute. The same one goes on to Brussels, and on northeastward into Germany, but on this occasion Brussels was as far as he wanted to go.

Monsieur Sabatier was in his office, morose, which made him more human. The recurring line 'What are we to tell the Minister' (sounding indeed like the chorus from one of those operettas dear to the Edwardian public) is all too familiar to senior police officials: parliamentary democracies have always this farcical side, and the Chamber of Deputies in Paris is every bit as Gilbertian as the House of Commons.

"One or two lines of enquiry beginning to look a bit promising."

"Heard that one already."

"Yes, but tell him divulging it is not in the public interest."

"Wants results." Ministers never can understand that evidence is a jelly-bag. Squeeze it, try to hurry it, and the juice comes through cloudy.

"Tell him it's the CIA."

"Look, Castang, I'm serious."

"I'm not at all sure that I'm not being serious." Since as we know there is a favourite dream: that of an intelligence service that will not be answerable to Congress, that will not have a budget depending upon the caprice of parliamentary democracy. It's the only way to stop those tedious Elected Representatives nagging, and we won't tell the President either.

"They do a lot of funny things but did they come all this way just to blow up nuns? Is he going to believe that? I mean, it wasn't planned just to pester you and me."

"No, but however many twists there are in the corkscrew it still ends in a sharp point. And we're like an old bicycle tyre. Clap a patch over Iran and Libyans come bulging out: tie them up with a bit of string and it's Bang, right in the middle of your Syrians. We must be given time."

"Abso-lutely. Can only hope that any day now there'll be Basques to distract him. Or Corsicans. But I must have something concrete."

"I'm not kidding you at all," said Castang heavily, "when I say I think I may have a pointer to a konspiratsia, and I believe the local bishop might have some light to shed on that, and how am I to get it? Seal of confessional, they'll say. You want the Cardinal here on your neck?"

"Oh dear Jesus."

"But if you like you tell the Minister that – under the seal of the confessional – and see how he likes it."

"Less bad," said Mr Sabatier, cheering up: the last thing the Minister wants is the Religious on his back, be it the Cardinal or the Chief Rabbi. You can't post a bishop to a village in the Vaucluse like a recalcitrant schoolteacher. To a politician the power of religion is that altogether too many voters believe in it.

"And when he asks what you're doing?"

"That you've engaged me on a delicate confidential mission."

"Where to?"

"I don't know, but I'll sure as hell try to find one."

"Just remember, Castang, if he should turn nasty, the amount of protection I can give you won't hold the dike for long."

"Yes."

That's the one certainty in the whole affair; that Monsieur Sabatier will know how to make it clear, to Paris, how he is responsible, but that Castang is answerable. Some synonyms are more synonymous than others.

Like Brussels is a good name to call this city, because Flemish Brussel is not synonymous with French Bruxelles. It isn't the same city, since 'Innovation' burned down in nineteen sixty-seven, but Castang didn't know it then. However many horrible buildings they put up, there abides still the faint flavour of civilised architecture, of Horta and Van der Velde, of delicate bridges between art-nouveau and art-déco, of before the Bandar-log.

Castang's informers have provided him with the address of a bar; in fact of two or three, but this is the right one. The Press has stamping-grounds, follows tribal patterns. Furthering the Jungle Book metaphor, the bandar-log are here in quantity at all times, clutching their coconut-shells of whatever may be this month's fashionable drink. Vodka, tequila, white rum, all over-refined to taste of nothing – a move again into Czech gin and adding almond syrup to pastis? Fertilise the soil heavily enough and he gets at last to Wise Old Baloo who sticks to Chivas. This time it's not Americans he's after but Brits. They've colonised Brussels too. Not of course that he wants the twits, loudly indulging in Maggie anecdotes and how Jaguar are really going to pull the pants off Porsche next time round. And WOB, thanks-be, isn't trying like that ghastly Australian of a former generation to get immortalised by both Ian Fleming *and* John le Carré: he's not Sir Jocelyn Hitchcock. He listens, and when he speaks it is in a rusty voice with terrifying pauses before the next word: he's the old Obadiah and he's Praise-God-Barebones.

"Robert MacLeod? You won't find him here. Oh yes, he has been here. But not any more. Robert is not exactly constant as the northern star. What's your business with Robert?"

"It's one of those very long boring tales of a friend of a friend reputed to be a friend of Robert. He seems well known so he seemed a good starting-point upon the long trudge."

"Oh yes, he's well known. If that's a recommendation. You're a cop. By the sound of you a Paris cop. You are wheedling, cajoling and otherwise snowing me. I repeat, you won't find him here. He's done gone."

"All right. I'm not trying to pierce the secret of the great pyramid. I want a few basic reference points for Robert and I pay my way with expensive drinks: that's fair enough, surely?"

"I've no complaint, within these parameters. Robert-public or Robert-private?"

"I'm trying to situate an elusive personality so I would think both."

"You're quite right because he is both and they're hard to disentangle. I'm not an authority on the private because it's elusive, secret, and sometimes entertainingly eccentric. Others, notably editors, appreciate the eccentricity less since Robert is notoriously brilliant and equally unreliable. There would now be few willing to give him a job, he's been in pawn so often. He can't stand boredom. Send him, say, on one of the world's dimmer assignments, say the secretary-general of NATO, he'll come back with an exclusive on the Reverend Moonie, it might be good but it isn't what you asked for. He's gone out and got pissed with everyone from Leonid Brezhnev to an ulema in Saudi Arabia who doesn't drink: that's the point. Send Robert – at vast expense – to Washington, let's say you want a sober piece upon the floating vote inside the Supreme Court, what Robert cables is the about-to-be-named new director of the FBI is Bob Hope."

"So he's out of a job?"

"If he's in a job he's just filed ten thousand words on the Bundes-Chancellor had lunch with Henry Kissinger and did they have green peas or grapefruit-flowers with the roast duck, for the *Hotel & Caterer*."

"To get a sort of terminus a quo, when was it you saw or heard of him last?"

"Thinking – Christ, when did that last happen? – about a year ago in Central America. Probably representing the *Exchange and Mart*. Heard of, strictly not saw, since Panama, Salvador und so weiter are assignments I'm not in competition for."

"Could it be Nicaragua?"

"Conceivably, since Robert is always friends with the kind of foreign minister who holds his press conferences in paratroop boots and a keffiyeh."

"And dropped out of sight since then?"

"Sight, sight, don't go pinning me down. If you want the worldwide authority on Robert MacLeod try Hughie Hamilton."

"Who's he?"

"You're in the wrong town, should have stayed in Paris and cultivated smart society." So it wasn't altogether a waste of time and whisky.

The Islands-in-the-Seine are oddly contrasted. Only a little bridge separates them, across a small passage of dirty water, and they could almost be in different hemispheres. True, the Ile de la Cité is twice the size, and hits you in the eye, full as it is of vast hideous monuments (that is Castang's eye; he finds them all ugly as well as too big). He is prejudiced, because the western side of the Boulevard du Palais is brimful of his hierarchical superiors who make his life burdensome: as for the top end, grand medieval masterpieces, Hotel-Dieu and Notre-Dame, well, he just hopes he never has to go inside, and especially not feet first.

The Cité too is stuck between particularly depressing features of central Paris: on the one hand the crockets and pinnacles of the Hotel de Ville and on the left bank smelly ol' Boul' Mich'. Pity the conscientious tourist from darkest Pannumjon, wasting simply reams of Minolta and quite unaware that the Ile Saint-Louis, at two minutes' walk, really does look like Paris.

Ringed by sombre, quiet quays looking dull and concealing enormous but unostentatious wealth, inside it is a little village of only half a dozen narrow streets, on a scale which magnifies the noise and animation, full of dark, cool little shops selling bread and fresh vegetables as well as Chinese art and silk scarves. Some of these houses are genuinely old. Baron Haussmann had no reason to knock them down to drive a huge straight boulevard through the Ile Saint-Louis because it doesn't lead anywhere. The rents are among the highest in Paris.

This was a house between two bigger ones, etiolated and stunted by growing up towards the light as though in a black forest of pinewoods and held up by the neighbours. It had been very difficult to get in: Mr Hamilton was fussy about new acquaintances; extremely by-appointment-only, and even with a powerful introduction from a *Monde* journalist he had known from his own Paris days (cool smiles and 'You'll find Hugh quite a character') it had needed many phonecalls and secret passwords.

It was still difficult to get in. There was an evil-looking door of medieval thickness, knopped and studded and barred with forgework like something out of the Bastille, and inside that there was one of the nastiest concierges even Castang had ever met, and then there were five flights of crooked stairs, waxed till every uneven tread was its own separate deathtrap. At the very top would be the sanctum of the QueenWitch, alchemy and acqua tofana from the materials supplied by Ruggieri the Florentine poisoner. When at last he did get in, it was a lovely surprise, as of course it was meant to be.

The whole loft or attic of the house had been left entire as a studio apartment, very large, certainly a hundred and thirty square metres, very high under the steep-pitched roof with the Y-joints showing of the old wooden frames. Three big skylights flooded it with light and sun (there were french-windows too, on to a balcony full of flowers). Castang didn't ask, but could deduce that Mr Hamilton had been dug in since before nineteen fortyeight, and doubtless paid a rent calculated in the francs of that epoch, nowadays amounting to about threepence. Mr Hamilton didn't mention it, but he doesn't speak about this to anyone. For all anybody knows he owns the goddamn house. He has been the permanent Paris correspondent of a most respectable London daily since the war. This isn't the only place where he's well dug in; he should have been retired long ago. He belongs to the charmed world which existed in Nancy Mitford's imagination, of Gaston Palewski and General Spears and Diana Duff Cooper, and he is flavoursomely redolent too of all the Fourth Republic politicians. And he is also 'very-Saint-Germain'. He speaks that exquisitely-pointed French and probably has his place permanently reserved at the Brasserie Lipp.

He is old, of course, he must be seventy if a day, but in excellent preservation, slim and upright. He won't need any fitness machines; those stairs, which have Castang buggered, are quite enough. His movements show a practised conservation of energy, and his voice is quiet. He has flat silver hair, a face bleached to extraordinary whiteness, further contrasted by a dark suit.

Even the most observant cop does not get far with further observations – it is a very comfortable flat, full of beautiful objects, and there is no sign of wife or mistress, let alone boyfriends – because Hugh Hamilton is not just a very private person but a most skilled and practised interviewer: he's the Ancient Mariner, has Castang riveted in thirty seconds, and indeed the discreet commissaire finds himself telling more than he learns. For the old boy wastes no time. No whimsy-flimsy anecdotes about Bérard and Cocteau; Jacques Fath and Christian Dior – or even decidedly fruity characters like Monsieur Le Trocquer, the sometime President of the National Assembly who used to – not a bit of it. "So you want to know about Robert MacLeod. What? And why?"

In this position Castang has only one procedural rule of thumb; to tell as much of the truth as you can, and nothing else. Judgment as he will find does not lead him astray on this, for Hugh Hamilton is not just extremely shrewd and alarmingly spry: after an entire lifetime among the most polished insincerities he's not to be taken in. He is also the most discreet of men.

"That's an interesting tale. Have some claret, shall we?" That's all: he wants time to think about this, and how better than with the Pichon-Longueville. And Castang has also the sense to say he knows but nothing about Bordeaux but is not so debased he can't give praise to the Bordelais gods. He's not a namedropper, Mr Hamilton. Neither in the childish, oddly innocent style of James Bond nor the vulgarities of the footman's 'I said to Winston'. The tie is certainly Sulka, and doubtless for suitable occasions there would be clubs and regiments, but Mr Hamilton doesn't go fingering it.

"Very well." He has made up his mind. "I can give you some help – and a mise-en-garde, we won't say a warning. England for French people is a trapdoor world like the Vatican, and you will swim there as best you may; I judge you capable of using your brains.

"I do want it clear that I take no responsibility for Robert, his doings, friends or anything else. I don't know where he is nor how to find him. Saul Carstairs may be able to help you there and again he may not." Mr Hamilton was also a man of economical, elegant movements. He crossed the room to sit down at a writing-desk, uncapped a pen, put on reading glasses, considered the wording of three or four brief sentences which he put down on a half sheet of paper. He addressed the envelope, licked it, tucked his glasses back into his pocket.

"This will get you a hearing. Perhaps better." Castang had stood up. It wasn't a lot, but he understood. Mr Hamilton did not often go this far. A hand was held out; he got a sudden warm, amused smile. "I don't know what you're going to make of this. Go on the way you have begun. Do be careful of these stairs – they are treacherous."

Obediently, Castang made his way down with prudence. The concierge came out, on the bottom landing, with an eye to his having any little silver spoons stowed away in his pockets. He looked at his envelope: what would that tell a detective? Excellent quality, a small and very legible handwriting, a script like classical Greek, a medium pen and black ink: yes, that gave an accurate picture. He could of course look inside, but decided that going on as he had begun meant trusting Mr Hamilton. Was that superstitious?

No telephone calls? Having been summoned, this lordly way, meant only that Hugh didn't want to be seen with a PJ cop in a public place. Engaging, to carry discretion so far. Little notes, to be presented personally. Perhaps it simply said 'See that the bearer of this goes down the oubliette, obliging'. All very urbane and eighteenth century; Talleyrand and Fouché. He spluttered laughing while crossing the bridge; he had recalled a typical Talleyrand wisecrack. 'Monsieur Fouché is like a book, gilt only along his top edge.' He looked for a bus-stop that would take him down towards the Porte d'Italie. 'The moment that people stop talking about him, Monsieur de Chateaubriand believes he has gone deaf.' That journalist had been quite right; Hugh Hamilton had character. 'Tongue like a cobra. But if he gives his word, it's kept. As for contacts, there's no journalist in Paris with better. Because, you see, he can be relied upon, and you know how rare that is.'

It did rather look as though he was getting a secret mission after all! And to a grandish sort of chap, an Important-Editor; yes, that would impress Monsieur Sabatier. The left hand didn't always have to know what the right hand was up to. Mr Hamilton wouldn't be interested in discussing a squalid subject like bombs. Just as the Divisional Commissaire in Lille would have no time to listen to stories about an old biddy who kept birds. The world has room for both, one would like to think. Paris too is large: it contains people like Hughie, and like old Marklake. They wouldn't be likely to know one another. There had been a couple of promising-looking watercolours on Mr Hamilton's walls which he hadn't had a proper peek at. Something the English went in for; perhaps he'd painted them himself.

6

Castang didn't have any ulterior motives here: a generalised police belief in touching-people-up-a-little. Since he was in Paris anyhow . . . He had even a pretext for a 'friendly move'.

"Thank you, I'd like a cup of coffee very much. No, I'm no nearer solving that little puzzle. Very likely I never will. I've other worries. I had business here, and an hour to spare before my train back. You don't mind? I was talking to the bishop, there at home. In the palace – tja, the way things happen. Nice old house, classified monument I should think. Historic diocese from very early times, gallery of former incumbents, the present man has to have his likeness taken for the record. He was agreeable to my asking you, where's the harm. Striking head, not that I'm a judge of what's paintable but it crossed my mind."

The old man was sitting there, massive like a figure by Maillol. When young he must have had great physical strength; the chest and arms were those of a legionary farrier-sergeant. The eyes shrewd – was that the right word? Not like Hugh Hamilton's, a man who has spent his life around the court, a diplomat. But these eyes had seen the deportations; the round-up of the Vélodrome d'Hiver, the camp at Drancy, the trains. He dislikes the word 'Holocaust' – it is cheap – say only that these eyes have looked at a great deal of death as well as a great many pictures. In comparison, Hugh Hamilton has seen nothing worth mentioning, nothing worth remembering – his memoirs would be of trivialities, of Wally's diamond clips and Edward's cufflinks.

"But yes." Motives he doesn't look for. Slyness and smartness he has no interest in. Let people be slippery, clever: it is to him indifferent. He is a man who has crossed the Atlantic in a small open boat. No radio, no chronometer, no compass. A little pot of the crudest, coarsest food to see him on his way. He slept on the boards, under an old tarpaulin. Never once warm, never once dry. What water he could collect, in a sail. Great cracks open in the skin, and salt in them. Sailing, sailing. There will be land, or there won't. That will be as God decides. There had been moments of extraordinary beauty. Sometimes the sun set, and sometimes the sun rose. Noises in one's head. One hears voices, one hears trains. You don't put this in memoirs, either, because there aren't any words. And now here we are sitting, in this room with its wall of glass, smelling rather pleasant and homely for these materials are those too Vera struggles with.

"But yes," repeated Marklake. "This I like. A bishop, yes, I make of him a Fénélon, a preceptor, yes, for a young king. When he has a good face, I paint it."

"I think the money'd be right."

"Ach . . ." brushing away flies, "something we work out. But you tell him I'm a Jew? Bad Yid."

"No no, he's a powerful Zionist."

"Zionists!" It didn't sound like a category the old man was much thrilled with, but no matter. Castang drank his coffee, strong, delicious and came in a beautiful cup: when like a cop he looked underneath there were the Dresden crossed swords. Maybe a fake: there are lots of Dresden fakes. Who cares whether it is a fake, when it is such a lovely shape?

"A portrait I don't do in three days. I have to have some base."

"No problem, he'll put you up. Madame, too."

"Prime, tierce, none," rather enjoying the idea. "Vespers when the light fails."

"You'll come?"

"When he makes me a little agreement in writing, to rank as contract."

"An honest man, I thought him."

"So are we all, within our limits," said the old man. "Mama! Somewhere we got some cognac?"

Clinging on to reality by the fingernails, you could call this. True, Mr Hamilton's warning had sunk in, and stayed with him.

It's the High Society that's the trouble. To be sure, some Foreign Parts are more foreign than others. Looking at it with a police mentality, through Castang's eyes: it's not so much the language barrier although this, in England, is worse than in most places.

Assemble facts. Castang is drinking tea, English tea, that powerful stimulant: he likes it. Central London; what is roughly called the West End. Ten-thirty of a blowy March morning. It is cold, wet, draughty: that doesn't worry him, he's dressed for it. There are lots of clouds; nice clouds. Gleams, too, of sunshine, surprisingly hot. And showers, surprisingly cold, the characteristic March rain the French call *giboulée*, a good name. Spring comes to England earlier than to Central Europe, with England's characteristic spring flower: daffodils in the squares, in window boxes, in bunches outside Victoria Station, and he likes daffodils very much. He is lucky; in April the place would be full of tulips which he dislikes with strong unreasonable prejudice.

There isn't any real language barrier; Castang has better than a smattering. He has been here several times. Neither the French nor the French police are any good at other people's languages, and since he is quite good, he has often been chosen when a need arose to send someone to foreign-parts. He has a fair grasp of Spanish and a bit of German, and elsewhere he will work his way with astute combinations: in Italy, say, a muddle of French and Spanish gives him the illusion that he is talking Italian. Men do not understand this speech, but women and children have no trouble with it. In the other countries where he has set foot – few; he is not a Travelled Man – there is the advantage that they do not expect one to speak Hungarian. Whereas England is like France: they look at you with amazement, hatred and contempt. Here he is more of a foreigner than in Poland: it puts him at a disadvantage.

The rich ought to be tolerant about this. After all, they are the Travelled folk; been to uh, Japan'n'everything. And they're educated. Castang knows very well that they aren't – on the contrary – but still clings to a pathetic belief that somehow they ought to be.

Castang used to work with an excellent cop called Orthez, who looked like a treetrunk, had apparently no brains whatever (a great advantage in police work) and spoke no language, not even his own. But understood the poor, wherever they came from.

"Awright, mate, shunt it along then." A black biddy clearing away teacups. What was it she said? Now Orthez would have needed no translation.

Castang saunters; interludes of pelting along, darting about; up, or maybe it's down, Fleet Street. He admires Carmelite House, doesn't think it likely there are Carmelites there, admires the black glassy thing which looks more oldfashioned than any Victorian façade and so appropriately contains the *DailyEx*. Gets buggered like many before him with so many Fleet Street addresses that aren't on Fleet Street. Wonders – ditto – why so heavy a religious atmosphere canonises journalism. White friars, Grey friars and what kind of friars are Austins (are carmelites brown? Dominicans are black-and-white, or has he got that wrong?)

"Like t'see Mr Carstairs." Like t'see, Want t'see: which sounds rightest?

"Got a pointment?"

"Sure." Is sure more sure than yes?

"Awry, upvere 'n' along, asksseckry."

"Fankyou." Practising th- th- th-, up several theres and more alongs.

"Oh yes," with a look saying oh no. "Mind waiting just a moment then, Mr Er – " Not a bit. In French too, just a moment means three-quarters of an hour, but in fact Mr Carstairs is organised, so he ought to be, he's a very grand editor indeed. He has bewildering numbers of secretaries. Some have that distinctively never-washed look peculiar to English women which poor Ian Fleming complained so about, but nearly all are pretty in a slummy way. They pop in and out, and in five minutes one pops with a very pretty smile saying, "Mr Er – ? Would you like to come with me?"

Mr Carstairs' office was very large, which was just as well because removals seemed to be going on: furniture standing about everywhere and chaps as well as girls milling, floating or just dallying. In the middle of much inexplicable activity an island, large, a sort of Sargasso Sea where weed and treetrunks and plastic cups came to rest; at the centre of that a large table and behind it a big barrel-chested bloke made more so by a beautiful shirt and the most extravagant crimson braces Castang had ever laid eyes upon. A large square pale face and some curly fair hair. Politely he stood up, showing a solid, hard belly, shook hands beamingly, sat, disconcertingly pointing a finger, first at Castang then at his nose saying, "Yes. I remember. You telephoned."

"True." Fearful job it had been.

"You're a friend of Hughie Hamilton's."

"Not a friend, I'm afraid, but he did give me a letter for you." Castang had religiously as any carmelite avoided any steaming-open. Mr Carstairs ripped at it with a kukri or something curved and vicious, read the note frowning, put it aside, and said, "What's all this then?" One of the cleaner girls distracted Castang with a huge beam and a monstrous brimming mug of something: he struggled, said, "Fankyou. Robert MacLeod."

"Thank you, Thelma." Or was it Velma? He was reading the letter again with more attention. Castang stirred and sniffed. Nes, rather thin in immense quantity.

"Now I see." The unwritten no doubt, between the halfdozen short lines of that lovely Greek writing. "Mm." Mr Carstairs looked long and hard, not rudely, Englishly at Castang, who had decided not to attempt the brew. "Robert, mm." He looked at his watch, a tremendous great gold chronometer under the splendidly ironed shirtcuff (plain onyx links) and bellowed, "Stephanie!"

"Yes?" A nymph was there like lightning; dirty maybe, but disciplined.

"Get me a table at El Vino in maybe a quarter of an hour." And then very politely, to Castang, "Now I hope you're going to forgive me, this will be an early and rather hurried lunch but at least we'll have a chance to talk. Will you think me hideously rude if I ask you to stay right where you are and possibly read the paper for say twenty minutes paying no attention to this uproar while I get disentangled and then you'll have my undivided attention and no further nonsense."

Castang found himself lowered into a chair with a plaque screwed to it saying that it was Lord Northcliffe's, and sat in some unease lest Lord Northcliffe should come in and say 'Out of there, you.' However, there were compensations. A bottle of champagne appeared in front of him.

"Sandwich all right? Try the smoked salmon." Yes of course; it's like Cooper's Oxford, tea, and Melton Mowbray Pie. Peculiar pub; seemed to be full of lords, with loud voices and Havana cigars. Mr Carstairs explained that these were lawyers, doing a roaring trade in the gothic elephant down the road: there weren't quite that many press barons. We're used to them but they're damaging: people like yourself observe these antics and ask how on earth the country can call itself modern. One of the last but most tenacious of Dickensian survivals, explaining to the Court that one shouldn't leave immoral literature lying about because the servants might see it. They're the Notable British Trials Series, he said brushing crumbs off his shirt; Is this wine dry enough for you?

Very nice, thank you. I know; we have them too, being theatrical: mm, they make good television.

"Robert belongs with that crowd, really. Classic manic-depressive – could have been a remarkable advocate. Could have been a remarkable anything but for the tendency to come to pieces in one's hand. What's your real interest in Robert?"

"Simply to find out more."

"Committed a crime, has he?"

"Can't say. There's certainly been a crime. No evidence whatever that he had anything to do with it. He seems to be part of an unfinished dossier on something else entirely. I come across the trail of this comet: it's a circle, everything is in circles," drawing them on the table. "I try to enlarge my circles. Sometimes they intersect and sometimes they don't."

"Good, I'll enlarge your circle. Robert's a contemporary, my friend – he has a talent for making friends and perhaps a better for getting rid of them. Distinguished academic beginnings, like Winchester and New College or Eton and King's, sort of thing holds out much promise and he's all the brains you'd wish but he does everything arsewards. I've made job after job for him and now I'm reduced to throwing him a leftover sandwich here or there. He's a swashbuckler, yes, I agree – a good word, we here like a bit of swash and buckle – but he does make his imitations of the Rake's Progress a little too enthusiastic."

"Do you know where he is?"

"In fact I don't, but if I did you'd hardly expect me to put a cop on his heels, would you?"

"No. My trouble is that I can give you my word of honour I'm not pursuing him, and who the hell believes a cop's word? Counting you that's three efforts to get the mythical Mr MacLeod into concrete terms. You all whet my curiosity but I get nowhere. Sometimes he's Mac Loud but mostly Cloud."

"Have another sandwich, said the White King – or was it the Knight? Or some hay: sorry, being English again. Look, no now I'm serious, Hugh Hamilton suggests I send you to the source. You've been through three witnesses, plainly you're not going to give up easily. I'll take a gamble on it – we like gambling – and let the old man decide. I'm not to know whether I'm doing Robert a good turn or not, and no doubt I never will. If you're ready we'll go back to the office and I'll ring him from there. No no, these are on me. Because last time I saw Robert here he paid for the drinks. Leave it – you'll get nothing else out of me."

Except a phonecall. Mr Carstairs reappeared half an hour

92

later in the cubbyhole where Castang had been left in the edifying company of the *Times Literary Supplement*, with hisjacket off again and an air of I have Done my Duty.

"Old man wants to see you. I tried to be fair, give you a good mark. Don't mind saying I'm surprised, mm, funny old man, maybe he's going gaga down in the country, thinks a French cop might be a change from the ghastly neighbours. All right, now I'll make you a little drawing, my turn, got a car? Now this is a place called Burwash, down in Sussex, handy for you on your way home, but there are three Burwashes, so here's the Key, you take the Heathfield road and then a sharp left turn opposite the pub . . ." Niederhasslach, thought Castang, and then Oberhasslach, but don't ask where Hasslach is. "Thank you a lot."

"Not certain you'll thank me nor I you but let it pass. Expects you tomorrow at lunch, tonight you're out in riotous London, what'll it be, the Folies Bergère or the Garrick Club: mm, comes to much the same thing."

Not certain we'll thank each other, thought Castang, rolling along the drunken English road made by the rolling English drunk, a scary performance, with the hired car, no more horrid than usual and instructions just to leave it at Dover, expense account is dented, but not calamitously. Not certain Burwash exists, nor the road, nor the pub; but when in England one has to learn to enjoy gambling. These English; Mr Carstairs, Mr Hamilton . . . but Robert is like that too. Meet the unorthodox, Monsieur Richard used to say, treat it in unorthodox fashion. I do; I do . . .

Surprised that there really was a place called Heathfield, and there was a pub, and a road, and – this was barely a track, up a steep hill in a complicated sort of hobbit-country, but there were human beings – that is recognisably a girl with a dog. He drove very slowly. There was a big yew hedge. There was a wooden notice. He pushed the car into some bramble bushes and got out to look. Yes.

Scarcely a Cottage, he'd call that, but what did the English call a cottage? – well, it had only one storey whereas hobbit-holes had round doors. Nice garden, very private, lovely view from top of one down over to another. Wooded valley between: here, rosebushes, lots more bushes. Pretty isolated. Not afraid of burglars. Why were these English doors so very low? He jangled at a bell, and an old man too tall for the house came out and said, "Come in."

Old but tough, and far from gaga though certainly around eighty. "Tiring at the end, and tiresome throughout, that drive." If cottage it was, then well stored with all the right cottagey things, wood smoke and old prints and many books; Persian rugs, fine china, polished brass. Even a bit too much of everything for Castang's austere tastes: the homely clutter, definitely. A bright sapphire eye caught the circular cop look.

"Thinking I make it rather too easy for the light-fingered brigade? But you see, I didn't live in Europe all those years without learning a thing or two, and despite the mild exterior I'm a Desperate Character." A bubble of giggles. "A notice saying Explosive Boobytraps, which is naturally false, and another saying Guard Dog, which is true. Woof woof," and a deep grumbling noise came from the kitchen. "A light rumour, carrying like dandelion seeds around the countryside, that I sleep with a twelve-bore. All this is profoundly wrong, bad, immoral – except for the dog. What would you like, some sherry? I find the world in which I still live and which I still like, a detestable one, but was there ever an old man who did not say the same?" The first guess is that even now he is a fundamentally shy man. The second that he conceals fear and worry at what, perhaps, Castang has come to say. The shadows which you fear, you march straight at. "Get our business over before lunch, shall we? If we can."

"It's as they've told you. I'm a criminal brigade cop, I'm interested in Robert. But there's no criminal enquiry afoot. Or let me get this straight – first, there was an incident, which seems to involve Robert, though I've virtually no direct evidence of that. Nothing criminal. A woman disappeared but there's no reason to suspect foul play.

94

"Secondly, and some months later, we did have a crime and a grave one, a bomb attack which we'll call loosely a terrorist outrage. We haven't shed light on this, and at the present we don't look likely to. In consequence, we're casting out far afield. A hint, itself vague, arrived that this might originate in the confused politics of a South American country, where the victims of this bomb, who are missionary nuns, had recently worked. My casual interest in Robert produced the information that he had been working in the same country at around the same time, and that is absolutely all. A very loose, minute thread. Either I disregard it or I try to tighten it, but I must beware of wishing or hoping that it may provide me with a lead. To find out what I can, to broaden my knowledge, that's legitimate. Mr Hamilton went as far as to say a journalistic instinct: one tries to find out enough to apply a true-or-false test. And this has brought me to your doorstep."

"Smoke by all means," himself taking a pipe out of his pocket. "That's clear. I've been a journalist myself. And I dare say you've already found out that Robert is an irresponsible character, has several times been mixed up in shady or at best questionable doings, has had brushes with the law in various countries, and is in general something of a black sheep. Yes?" Puff, puff.

"Hints and rumours, but it isn't evidence. Interests me little or not at all. I would like to know some real truths about Robert."

"And you've come to me. Well, that's the right shop. Robert, as you may have realised, is my only son. Very dear to me. I am an old man, I have few illusions. Too old to have much grasp upon reality? Still, a lifetime in journalism leaves traces and I'm not a dotard. Plainly, too, Robert has been the source of my greatest disappointments, a cause of some embitterment, and also a reproach, forcing a continual re-examination of my own mistakes, follies, griefs, quite possibly crimes.

"I want some time to think about this – lunch will give me that. I have thought of it already, forewarned by phonecalls from Carstairs there in London – and, as you guessed, from

Hugh Hamilton. But now you're here, and now that you've stated your case of conscience, I want to marshal exactly what I have to say to you, so I ask you for an hour's grace. We'll have the other half before going in to lunch. This woman who disappeared – she sounds interesting." So that over the other half, Castang told what he knew about Adrienne Sergent, which was little. "That's remarkable," was all the old man said, putting his pipe in the ashtray to cool. "Well now – lunch. She sounds like Mrs Bathurst," which conveyed nothing.

Lunch was simple, good, and English. A round table, china with dark blue and red dragons, heavy, plain old silver. Soup of early spring vegetables, tasting of garden. A sole Colbert with peas. "Deepfreeze, I'm afraid. Too early for the real ones." Served by a silent, middleaged countrywoman. Castang exclaimed at the sole.

"A Colbert, good God, it has disappeared from France." MacLeod was delighted with this.

"Mrs Roberts agrees with me that it's among the very best ways. Hardly anyone knows how to do it. Real butter is the trick. There are terrible people here, dreadful little economists and such – Oxford of course – preaching the virtues of margarine. How d'you expect an economist to have a sense of taste?"

And then there was an apple charlotte. It was caramelised crisp. No cream.

"One mustn't either with a Tatin," said Castang who was by now slightly drunk, in a contented way. This went straight to MacLeod's heart: Castang couldn't have got himself a better mark in a month-of-Sundays: good English phrase.

"My dear chap, when I lived in France a tarte Tatin was my favourite pud. Naturally, she doesn't know about Les-demoiselles-Tatin but her local equivalent is just as good, you agree. She'll be thrilled. Mrs Roberts!

"Our guest wishes especially to compliment you upon the charlotte and that of course there must be no cream, isn't that nice? Don't go because a thought has occurred to me.

"We have some complex business to discuss and I am going

to propose that he spends the night. Now for this evening have we a bird? – freezer, I'm afraid," aside.

"No partridges left, I'm sorry, and I haven't seen a woodcock since last autumn. There'd be a pair of grouse."

"Only third best but no matter because they don't have them in France: we'll call that settled then.

"Now this is very fortunate. May I prevail upon you? A walk will do us good, you've the right kind of shoes and a hat, I'm delighted to see, do you like a stick? – splendid. Come on, dog."

"Who's Mrs Bathurst?"

"You couldn't have asked a better question. The writer Kipling – know him? – much liked in France – lived along the valley, the stream down here is his Friendly Brook. He wrote an extraordinary story about physical passion, and quite rightly left it enigmatic because no writer can really convey physical passion. A later novelist of considerable reputation wrote an amazingly silly passage to the effect that Mrs Bathurst was a hotelkeeper in New Zealand beloved by a lot of sailors and he couldn't see what all the fuss was about. Of course he couldn't; homosexual of course, what the devil could he know or guess about the subject?"

"Really? In New Zealand? Sorry, that's remarkable but I beg your pardon, I interrupted."

"No no, that was all. The fact is, Castang, I know just a tiny bit myself about sexual passion. Nobody knows what happened to Mrs Bathurst. It is possible that you will find out. It's also possible that you may wish you hadn't."

"I've been told that already. But it's my job, you see."

"Yes. So I am going to tell you a few personal things. I'm not drunk, nor am I gaga. Whatever bright boys like Carstairs think. You see – look, there's a rabbit. After him, boy – Robert is not my son. But I was deeply and calamitously in love with his mother.

"German girl. Something of a Nazi too, I'm sorry to say.

"Now that I shouldn't have said. I'll withdraw the 'sorry to say'. She refused to deny opinions honestly held and I owe it to

97

her to respect that. She was true to her principles. An interesting piece of theology; do we condemn a human being for holding principles we know to be false and to have led to extreme evil?

"But in our criminal courts we condemn not only for active commission of crimes, but also for complicity, for being accessory, for giving aid and comfort. Which she did. Being a nurse in a military hospital; we can argue common humanity. No civilised person refuses to alleviate the suffering of either enemies or criminals. The Germans blurred the point in that infuriating way of theirs by failing to distinguish clearly between Wehrmacht and SS units.

"I have lived too long with these questions. Enough water has flowed under that particular bridge. Odd to be telling you this. You have to know. The English, it's understandable, are quicker to feel kinship and liking for Germans than for any Latin people."

"It's taken us forty years," said Castang, "to come to terms with our own hypocrisy during those times, and it's not at all certain the process is complete."

"Ah. How do you stand, on this matter?"

"In the matter of war crimes, I'd say we were all tarred with the same brush. Speaking of crimes against humanity, we in France do not come out of it well."

"Then you can see clearly enough into my evasions of the time. As a war correspondent I held a privileged position; the power to manipulate. All sorts of highly-placed friends, pals, drinking companions or just good-ol'-boys in the military government – one could pull a string nearly anywhere. I could have married her, for example."

"She refused?"

"She refused. I could have kept her out of prison. Forgive me; this is still painful to me. Come on, dog, it's time to turn back. But she asked me to save her child. Which, as she said, was innocent."

"Which you did."

"Yes. That is Robert. I pulled the strings. Mm, pride, vanity, arrogance. I took pains in the matter. Upbringing, education, oh, fine dreams I had."

"And her?"

"She died. They sent her to a prison camp. It wasn't a Belsen but we won't try to argue that conditions or treatment were all they might have been. Tuberculosis, probably. It was not easy to find out . . . the network had worn a little thin by then. I tell myself it would have been too late."

"Robert knows?"

"Oh yes, he knows. It is more damaging, not to let them know."

"You think – uh, want to avoid jargon – there's something of a split in the personality?"

"I want to avoid every kind of facile judgment, Mr Castang, and so, I hope, do you."

They walked on in silence. Before reaching the house,

"This has shaken me more than I knew," said the old man. "I'll ask you to excuse me for an hour. I incline to the siesta habit anyhow. Mrs Roberts will give you some tea. You don't mind entertaining yourself awhile?"

"I'll do some thinking."

But the old man had recovered on his reappearance. The dinner was as good as the lunch. It was futile to wonder whether Mrs Roberts slept in the house.

"I've thought," said MacLeod, "of one or two literary allusions. My friend Mr Kipling wrote a passably terrifying little tale about a middle-aged virgin who is companion-help to an elderly lady and forms a maternal attachment, we must not go further, to the son of the house, a young officer in the Air Force who is killed on a practice flight. This is in the 'Fourteen war, you understand. The day they receive the news of his death, a German plane on its way home drops a bomb which kills a village child, but the plane crashes and the pilot, badly injured, falls in the bushes, where she finds him. She refuses his appeals for help and watches him die with feelings of pleasure and satisfaction. It is made quite clear that she feels sexual pleasure. This, rather than her revenge, shocked the reading public of the time, but one would have found

99

a consensus of opinion that she did rightly. Is she or is she not a murderess?"

"It's absolutely clear in French law," said Castang. "Non-assistance to a person in danger, when the danger is of death, amounts to culpable homicide. A jury would of course find mitigating circumstances and any good lawyer would have got her off on the emotional appeal."

"Quite so." They were eating Stilton cheese. Castang is chauvinist enough to find it inferior to a good Roquefort, but says – which is only just – that it's an arbitrary sort of decision.

"While resting," MacLeod broke a contented silence, "I refreshed my memory of a criminal case that was famous between the wars. I don't suppose you've heard of Alma Rattenbury? Well, she was a middle-aged woman in comfortable circumstances; a kind, jolly, vulgar soul who had the misfortune to combine powerful physical impulses and a supine husband who drank a bottle of whisky a day. She fell violently in love with a boy of eighteen.

"He was passionate enough for her, got overwhelmed and clonked the husband with a poker or something while the poor old chap was snoring in his armchair. No evidence that she in any way incited this. In fact she was greatly shocked, being genuinely fond of him – he was a harmless soul, a retired business man. But in shock she said a lot of silly things, got tremendously pissed and accused herself of the death. So they were both tried for the murder.

"The other interesting factor is an upright, highly moral Victorian judge, who cleared her of guilt in law but crucified her with talk about adultery. So that she was freed under a black cloud with every finger pointed. They chopped the boy of course and left her feeling the guilt for two murders.

"She went off and stabbed herself through the heart four times. Which is said to be an impossibility. The journalist writing the account points out that the physical shrinking from such a death is such that a disgraced Roman general had to wedge his sword to the right angle and fall on it. She drove the knife in steadily four times; can you believe that?"

100

"I've neither seen nor heard of such a thing," said Castang, "but in police work I've learned that the impossible happens and the improbable melodrama that would be thought extravagant in the crudest fiction happens every day in fact.

"She was, of course, a woman. I don't see a man capable of what you describe."

"That same journalist had rather a neat aphorism. 'There are, at least, reasons for a great crime: for a mean one there are at most excuses.' Which sounds as though he'd been reading Gibbon but I take his point."

"So do I," said Castang who had never heard of Gibbon.

The old man got up to look for his pipe. Studying the tin box that held his little cigars, Castang noticed that it said 'Guaranteed Tobacco'. Now that was a weight off one's mind. Especially written in Spanish.

"I can't see Robert as a criminal for this very reason. Whatever his faults he's not mean-minded. He doesn't care a damn about money. Odd, oldfashioned notions of chivalry. When he was a boy he made his mind up to be a gentleman like Allan Quatermain." He's forgotten that I'm French, thought Castang, which is good.

"You don't see him planting a bomb?"

"Heavens, no; too much imagination. Just as he'd never commit suicide."

"You're a good witness."

Mr Erskine MacLeod was suddenly bored with his pipe, put it in the ashtray, which was a sort of stone mortar or quern. Perhaps someone once ground corn in it.

"I'm old. I've lived too long and not much, in my life, has been worth doing. 'Plus habet hic vitae, plus habet ille viae.'"

"Sorry."

"You boys learn nothing any more. That is the Roman poet Claudian, about the Old Man of Verona, a peasant who had never been outside his village. Admirable translation by Helen Waddell.

"'You'll have seen life, but this old man has lived.'" He looked at Castang, suddenly very old. "Robert has twice my talent," he said.

7

Marklake of a fine spring morning and in a sunny frame of mind, in the studio which was filled with sunlight and the Double Concerto of Brahms, conducting bits with a paintbrush, singing the grave and noble phrases of the cello, pursing lips and muttering when he peered forward at the easel. He was supposed to be cleaning up the studio, prefatory to going north for a few weeks to paint the bishop's portrait. Negotiations for this had been satisfactory. Behaved like a gentleman; more than you could say for some bishops. Or rabbis either. The only snag had been Gabrielle, who said she wasn't going to stay in any palace. A small furnished flat – well, partly-furnished they called it: probably meaning nothing, but it wouldn't be the first time he and she had gone camping together. Indifferent to discomfort. Even something quite primitive; but no dependence: no beck-and-call stuff. The Diocese had been helpful about such eccentricities, and magnanimous about expenses.

But he did want to finish this, first. Properly to celebrate the arrival of spring; tardy as usual, cold and rainy until of a sudden the city of Paris was illumined. Horrible as it is. The colouring of the Ile de France at the precise angle of sunlight in the very last days of April – ah. *Fluctuat nec mergitur*, from the City's coat of arms, which has a lovely little ship. We Float and we do not Sink. Right, he said. And Gabrielle brought a bunch of spring daffodils and put them in a bluey-grey faience pot that usually held salt, and looking at them he had to paint that. To celebrate the spring.

Gabrielle came pottering in with the morning's post. He muttered and jabbed with the paintbrush. Put it on the table and don't distract me with the rubbish: what good to man or beast is that? Junkmail it is; poor devil of a postman bent double under a flood of worthless nonsense. Shall I buy shares in the Paribas Bank? Shall I subscribe to the *Reader's Digest*? Should I live to the age of Moses I – what was wrong with the woman standing there making faces? Bah, she wouldn't budge, the tiresome female, until he reacted. He came and poked at it with the wooden tip.

Junkmail does not come in heavy expensive envelopes. Nor printed by that sort of typewriter. Computers they have which cannot spell, write backwards, do not punctuate, scatter meaningless dots and zeros across their stupidities.

Filled with suspicion he looked at the back. A raised oval seal, embossed. Embassies they should be. The Helvetic State is chock full to the brim of important, rich, impressive Bureaux and not a one of them a face you could paint. A portrait of an Atomic Commission you are asked to make? Of the Red Cross? Of UNICEF? Not a little ship, but theirs wasn't likely to sink either, thank you: a Swiss Bank.

As Georges Brassens so justly has said, Beware Of The Gorilla.

"Open it and you know maybe what it says," said Gabrielle.

"Too strong it isn't to be ripped by the human hand."

Turn off Brahms. Not the moment for Brahms, Siegfried you could do with here, to understand the language of the birds.

"There isn't a cheque in it." But a sheet of crackly watermarked paper like nothing more than a prewar five-pound-note. Which looked, indeed, like money. Today's paper money, Marklake has been known to exclaim, in public toilets it comes off the roll.

Dear Sir,
    Pursuant to the instructions of . . .

But here he had all his trustiest old friends writing to him! Pierpont Morgan and the Lehmann Brothers. That most seductive of all financial partnerships Kidder and Peabody. A tombstone it must be: the shares are oversubscribed in Saudi-Arabian Desalinisation and just look at the chance you've missed. Instead of printing them on the back pages they send them out now like the free issue? To read the second paragraph he put his glasses on, which helped somewhat.

We have thus the honour to inform you that under these dispositions this sum is held at your convenience and that your Contact Officer will be Herr Josef –

Josef! A bank is now my fine new Swiss Uncle Seppele! . . . Not one other word can I understand.

"Mama!" He sat heavily, pushed his glasses up and rubbed his eyes with the backs of his hands. Mafia money! He should paint the portraits of every casino in Las Vegas and throw in Mr Sinatra for free. Wiedergutmachen money from the West German government no doubt. For sure they pay you in gold eight hundred thousand pounds, ja. Marcos money. Duvalier money.

"A fraud," said Gabrielle. "A hoax," feeling the paper between her thumb and finger. "Paper they stole from the security printers in Melun, an engraver's plate, a big joke someone is making for you to fall into."

"No joke," he groaned. "Give me my pill, mama, I am feeling a migraine." He looked with great sadness at his daffodils. This sort of worry at his time of life: some peace at last he had a right to, no? Rich men who didn't pay for work executed – he was used to them, and Gabrielle shouldered the infinitely tiresome tasks of pursuit. And they were French, not Swiss. As for jokes – no, Peabody is not a kidder. When the Swiss owe you money they pay you sensibly, promptly, reasonably, Bank Vernes, yes, people you have confidence in. This is . . . the only word he can think of is sinister. He is frightened, yes, frightened as he has not been in nigh on fifty years. He remembers the time – only too well – when you paid large sums of money to the Emigration Office: the price to get out of the Third Reich. Money he does not like, trust, nor understand. When frightened, he had learned that lying low is a no-good answer.

"Mama, pack the bags."

"The bags I can have packed in an hour and the Gare du Nord is a taxi-ride." The easel, the paint-tray, fold into a wooden box which he has carried throughout Europe.

"The Gare de Lyon is a shorter ride."

"We are going north."

"First we are going south." A train-de-grande-vitesse goes to Geneva, for those who want to, and at this speed you haven't time to change your mind.

Not so long ago, the Banque de Paris et des Pays Bas felt the need to be loved. Borne upon the wings of television cameras, the potential lover was wafted through the carved double doors and tantalised with vistas of elegant living in a palatial eighteenth-century style. One had only to turn the corner to fall upon Casanova and the Cardinal de Bernis chatting up a few lecherously-minded ladies. Swiss banks are unlikely to promote this impression. There's a shortage of lovely tall windows, built artfully of small panes to make them look taller still: you tend to wonder where the daylight is coming from; whether, in fact, it's daylight at all. Lacking too are the shimmering textures of chiselled stone and wood and corners by Caffieri, and you don't look at the ceiling to see if it was painted by Tiepolo: the ceiling is more likely to be looking at you.

Everything in fact is deliberately dull, of a dullness expressed in terse statement and the colours of a psychiatric clinic; and the pictures, if there are any, would not be described as erotic. The very names, the Union, the Corporation, are designed to be as dreary as is consistent with good management. Paribas by comparison appears raffish; one would almost say Gaudy.

Marklake, bulky and splendid in his overcoat with the fur collar (the streets of Geneva are treacherously draughty), Gabrielle with a disapproving expression and a little sealskin toque, are not ridiculous figures: nobody will be impolite – nothing could shock the staff more than to be thought anti-semitic. Uncle Sepp is summoned and appears, murmurs an invitation into a little room, where it is so hot that Marklake takes his coat off, appearing in his richly sombre Good Suit.

105

Sepp's colourless eye rests a second on the scrap of ribbon in the buttonhole which tells one the old man has been There, and come back again. No need for him to bare his arm to show the tattooed number. It's a club rather more exclusive than oh, say White's.

There's the money, you will say; Sepp knows about the money, and it is a sum you or I would go Wow at, and this surely conveys respect as well as a golden shower Danae-like upon the beneficiary. Not a bit of it: Sepp never goes Wow at anything (save maybe a new model of Minolta camera for which he has a secret passion) and in these circles this much is thought of as just adequate. The old man would need to be a lot weightier before they'd find him substantial.

As well try to chip away at the granite foundations with a plastic pickaxe as shake Sepp on the provenance. His bland face, apparently of aluminium, a slight polish on the nose and cheekbones, neither laughs nor frowns. His eyes, brownish and expressionless as the bottom of a coffeecup (the coffee served is excellent, and in Limoges china; Gabrielle looked), do not approve, do not disapprove. His accented French is less thick and less comic than Marklake's own, and when the old man mutters in Yiddish he shows understanding in academic German.

The matter is very simple, he explains, patiently defining every bristling technicality. The title is good. Previous title does not concern him. Mr Marklake is identified, to his satisfaction; confirmed in his title. The item in question is a liquidity, which simplifies matters further. There are no coupons to clip; provision of dates and dividends and – no, not even like a bearer bond. Certainly it is real. It is even visible. Should you wish to be satisfied upon that point, as Swiss law has been satisfied, he, Seppele, can summon the dog-headed Cerberus that guards nether regions. It is at your disposal, which is not to say we should recommend your walking out on to the street with it. Your instructions concerning its disposal – but that is what we are here to discuss. Shall it be poured (being a liquidity) into an investment account? Sepp would be happy to summon a

Portfolio Adviser. Shall it not be? – then he must explain a few points of banking law. Certainly it can be held in liquid form to be poured wherever the entitled owner shall choose, and there is no hurry, no hurry at all, decisions are things which must ripen but there is a little consideration called negative-interest he feels bound to mention. These are simple number codes, it suffices to respect the procedures as outlined in this little book here, and he, Seppele, is your willing slave. Very well, then specimen signatures please, and these forms, Le Roi le Veult, Le Roi s'avisera, and then we need trouble you no further. A few stamps, a few seals, what seems a great deal of money to pay for having Sepp's autograph initials in the countersignature corner, and lo, he is your new, kind, if severe and a bit stalinist Uncle Joe. Do you want some money?

"You mean to say you've got money here too?" But nobody laughs. Courteously, Sepp goes with them to the street. Mark-lake stops to shake his head at a piece of abstract sculpture, a piece of porphyry which would have been nice before it got tampered with.

"Mama, what I want first is a quiet, peaceful crap." Gabrielle unperturbed casts her eye up and down the street and says, "There." In this sort of Swiss street, a Konditorei is never far away. The very best kind of coffeeshop, smelling delicious. The lavatories smell delicious too but of lavender, have pale-yellow tiles and a mossgreen throne, paper to match, flowers as well as plants, everything bar the *Neue Zürcher Zeitung* to read, even a tray for your cigar. When you pull the plug the airconditioning comes on automatically and a new cosy swans-down wrapper grows magically over the seat. Delighted, Mark-lake does it twice and goes to tell Gabrielle to run quick try it too.

Nowhere is she more Jewish than in these surroundings: it is worth coming to Geneva just to eat cake, just as when, finding herself in Lyon, she would make a beeline for Bernachon's chocolate. The girls' black frocks, starched white aprons, and hair washed that morning, have passed her inspection: there is something to be said for Switzerland and it's the magic word 'frangipane'.

"Mir ein Schwarzwalder," says the old man, whose favourite cake is that classic marriage of choc'n'cherries and Both Black, "and I want a glass of tea." And gets irritable with the tiresome girl and her pest of a list of fortyseven different kinds of tea. "Gingerflowers when I want I'll ask for."

"So?" Gabrielle, revived.

"So nothing. Money they give me and they won't say where it comes from. They don't know, they don't want to know. Ask, they say Morgan; ask Morgan they say Chemical. It's not mine, I don't take it. It sticks to me, I unstick it, blood on my hands – I only want my own."

She eats her cake and bides her time, accustomed to these tirades and to weathering them. The bank was very large and has made him feel small. The man is not only diminished but feels cheapened in his manhood. The petty have power, and use it to bully those larger than themselves, but He will cast down the mighty from their seat and exalt the humble, says the Psalmist. Marklake had not wished to have anything to do with this money, had come here determined to refuse it, and has been manoeuvred into accepting responsibility for it, giving away a part of himself.

"We will make a very fine walk," she says, "along the lake shore. A grand gentleman and lady we shall be, and in consequence you will give me lunch at the Hotel des Bergues."

He glanced sideways at her. Serpents, these women. Undeniably, the idea is attractive.

"A sensible man will head straight for the railway station to get his ass out of here quick."

"So I should get a horrible sandwich, one slice of pig and no butter? There are trains this afternoon."

"There are pictures I should look at."

"Pictures we look at when it rains."

"The Hotel des Bergues is very expensive."

"And we are now very rich."

"I should pay, with money doesn't belong to me."

"Why not? Is there one single customer does not do the same? Allons, allons, I know all about this."

"You have been drinking tea with Kidder and with Peabody?"

She deflates these heavy sarcasms with a teaspon pointed at him.

"Robert it comes from."

True; whether you are sitting upon a bourgeois Swiss lavatory surrounded by flowers or whether you are holding on to a rope with your ass out over a cliff, both the principle and the result are the same.

"In no sense at all," Castang was saying, "could one call that a waste. For the first time, a coherent theory, and we can pursue it. No wonder the bishop was so cagy."

"National Front," said Monsieur Sabatier, holding the idea at arm's length and examining it. "Could make sense."

"He makes no secret of being left-wing. To the traditionalist faithful, and you get them round our way too, he's a target. There have been the usual squabbles about churches occupied by the reactionary group. You know, bust the doors in with a battering ram, banners and statues of Christ the King. No business of ours, but I know he gets a lot of abusive anonymous letters. Movements to have him shifted, make him Bishop of Belle Isle en Mer: the hierarchy refuse to condemn him but are halfhearted about backing him up."

"Yes, but a bomb."

"Much the same as when King Philip decided he wasn't going to stand for any more goddamned heretics spitting on the Holy Catholic Faith. The Party of God gets very violent indeed, very hezbollah altogether."

"I take your point. Very well, go into it. But be careful. You know the Ministry. They are very sensitive about getting votes from the National Front. Keep a low profile." Castang promised he would be a mouse.

At least Annunziata could not claim any longer that the

ringing in her ears stopped her hearing properly. He had the form made out, saying please to present self at the office, for hearing in connection with a judicial enquiry. It was not only a tactic, to get her out of the ecclesiastical atmosphere. He didn't want anyone, such as the local press, still hanging about, to have any notion of a conflict. Police Judiciaire Investigating the Communist Bishop – this might please the National Front no end, but not Commissaire Sabatier, and pains must be taken to make this clear. The telephone is sometimes a useful instrument. A personal call, he told Madame Metz.

"Monseigneur? Commissaire PJ, good morning to you. Thought I'd ring, make sure of avoiding any misunderstanding that might crop up. Evidence has come my way to strengthen – put it to give substance, to the supposition that something or other which happened out there in America . . . yes; Sister Annunziata . . . ah, she mentioned it to you. Yes, I sent her a chit. What did she say?"

"She sought my guidance."

"Very proper."

"Naturally, I have told her that obedience is also owed to the civil authority."

"I hope, Monseigneur, that you added, also to the judicial authority. Because I must make it clear, the indications I have received are of a serious nature, and make it impossible to be magnanimous if I should meet with evasions and denials."

"I'm glad you rang, Castang. I'd be grateful too if you could give me a similar assurance."

"I'm like you, I do believe. That is, I will promise to do what I can, provided that this is not contrary to the interests of Caesar."

"Oh," laughing, "I hope I know better than that. I seek only that you should not treat all corn as good when it comes to your publicity mill. Simply, that you do not use the right to interrogate to bring the affairs of the Church into disrepute." Now is that an admission?

"I would certainly want to guard myself against anything that could possibly be interpreted in any partisan light."

"Well, Castang, that would be a weight off my mind. Annunziata is dear to me, in human as well as divine terms. As you probably know, my conduct of the see's affairs is criticised by many. I don't believe you seek to add fuel to any fires."

"By no means. You have my word on that."

"I'll send her over this afternoon. That suit you?"

"Best," said Castang, "when it comes out suiting both of us."

So here she is; tense and prickly, but respectful. Not scared. Got her orders. Quite ready to quarrel about interpretation of same, and easy does it. They are also strongly feminist. Accustomed to receiving orders from men and to obeying: obedience is important. But apt to get decidedly narky over these bad habits of the Pope, that the woman's first duty is silence. She's a hard-mouthed horse, and must be ridden with a gentle hand if she's going to be ridden at all.

Suppose let's say that Commissaire Sabatier had a mandate to interrogate Vera? How would that turn out?!

Castang has a range of interrogation techniques; from the half-witted look and effortful typing with two thumbs to the 'You've just contradicted yourself'. He often does 'I've forgotten what all this is about'; prefers the over-friendly to the over-hostile, though does the Nasty on occasion; uses irrelevant telephone calls and meaningless pieces of paper to intimidate, as well as walking about, roaring, and handcuffing people to the central heating; but the one he likes is the no-technique-at-all: simple and spontaneous. Being polite and being patient shouldn't take all that much effort.

"You see, I want to feel it, to enter into it. Physically. Look – " Annunziata is not used to this sort of imaginative projection "is it malarial, do you have to swig away at the Mepacrine or whatever it's called, sleep under nets? Is it hot and humid even in the highlands? Muddy underfoot? In tents, are you? Make a shelter with branches, a ramada, or do they thatch? Tell me about the ants, the flies, the – the – butterflies? What clothes

111

d'you wear, and on your feet? The smell; is there a characteristic smell?

"The table where you have your dispensary, is it wood,
metal, what? Are there termites? I want to see it, touch it and
feel it. Mostly women, are they, who come? Gynaecology for
the most part? Parasites, jiggers in their feet, bilharzia? – my
medical knowledge is limited.

"A thing which interests me; how much use do they make of
local plants? Would there be just a few household remedies
everyone knows or would they go to someone with a wide
knowledge and range of sophisticated plants, a herbalist? And
how would it fit in? I mean, if someone was using a decoction
of flowers or berries to treat an infection would you scrap all
that and rely totally upon synthetic chemicals? The point I'm
trying to make, does the one exclude the other?

"Had a generator, did you, for electric power? Worked off a
truck or how? Yes, I see, I was being real boy scout, building
my own steriliser out of old cans soldered together.

"Who did the cooking? Share that among you, or have a
local woman to help – have your own spoon to dip in the pot,
huh? And what about your supplies, I take it you have a field
telephone – no, it would be a shortwave radio, am I right, to
some sort of headquarters: but how should I know, I've never
set foot in a place like that and would be singularly useless if I
did. I've got a junior inspector, a woman, who might be some
use to you.

"Do these populations have a specific local problem like
tuberculosis, or is it just chronic malnutrition and low resistance
to infection? No, indeed I'm not wasting my time, though I
apologise for wasting yours. Without basic reference points I
have no idea about states of mind, behaviour patterns – the
framework for existence.

"This is now getting clearer. Tell me also about your relations
with the administration; all right, as far as there is any. Is it
purely military or is there a civil authority, over and above the
village headman?

"And the Americans? One hears a lot about interference –

112

these advisers, so called – and they seem to have a vast amount of money to spend, and I presume a sophisticated organisation of logistic support.

"Quite apart from the Protestant missions and the charitable organisations, did you find reality in the sinister man from the CIA encouraging them to be anti-Communist with large bribes?

"Good, and in the areas under military control, however vague that would be? And we've heard a lot about mercenaries, on both sides. Former Vietnam veterans who've gone over to the other side through protest or even idealism, or is it only for money? Well, I've read hardly anything. My own daily paper in Paris have people in South America, turn in an article; but I mean *Time* and *Newsweek*, uh, uh, the *Christian Science Monitor*. There are always journalists knocking about, and people on the spot like yourself find them a great nuisance, but if they didn't exist how would people like me ever get to hear anything: did you have experience with people of this sort?

"Sorry, would you like some tea or? – that was rude. There I am, crossquestioning without stopping. No, I have some myself around this time, I have a kind lady who'll look after us, we are a tiny bit civilised here when we think about it, which as you notice isn't very often. Madame Metz, haven't we a ginger biscuit? Well, get someone to go out and buy some. And I'm out of cigarettes while you're at it."

This cuisine was not easy. There were many barriers, some formidable. That of the discipline, modesty, discretion of a woman trained in a religious order. That of the 'them and us' mistrust of the police which does not exclude nuns. That of a wider them-&-us, between imbeciles who say they are interested in bull-fighting, and someone who has been in the ring. The basic conviction of a working woman, that men do not, will not ever understand a single damn thing. As well as the intelligence, obstinate character and general bloodymindedness of this particular subject. If she thought him a perfect fool, then so much the better.

But he did get answers in the end. Fragmentary at first, filling intervals, like rainwater spreading from puddles into rivulets under a downpour, connecting and spreading.

"When the military area came our way, that was the time we had to get out. Not so much the danger; there's a certain level of sub-chronic danger that you accept and live with. There are plenty of hazards and this is one. It's the disorganisation. Military area means refugees, means a breakdown in the pattern you are trying to build up, of getting people to care for themselves and get above the poverty line, the substarvation level. Military area means disruption; harvests aren't gathered, harvests aren't sown, homeless people are physically deprived and psychologically destroyed. Fear and insecurity and bewilderment. You are tearing old people and children away from their house, the village, the society which they know and trust. You have degraded and infantilised people so that the men don't know how to work, the women don't know how to care for their children. It meant that we were overwhelmed, there wasn't any way we could cope.

"But it took time, and painful decisions: you can't just pull up sticks and climb into the jeep. We stayed for some weeks where we were. It isn't a firing line, there aren't any trenches. You might get mortared; we did, once. What you're frightened of is someone creeping in at night and rolling in a grenade. You might hear some sporadic small-arms fire; they enjoy letting off ammunition.

"I'm not going to talk about Contras. I'm not a politician. The rights and wrongs don't concern me. They exist on both sides. They're given a lot of money, they do a lot of damage. If it's a good thing to reduce corruption, to break up the big ranch estates and start setting up basic land reform, then I'm a Marxist, a dirty Commie. It's exactly the same as in Brazil or Haiti or anywhere else: the rich have everything and if the poor try to band together they are shot up by the Tontons Macoute, a private army financed, armed and encouraged by the rich. Before you give a peasant medicine, or education, or law, or even a road, you've got to give him a field he can work and grow things on. No different to China and I've had to learn not to see bright red hearing this eyewash about Communism. Every one of us who's ever been out there is a Communist; can't be anything else.

"So yes, we found ourselves treating military casualties. You can forget all the crap you've seen on television about field hospitals, drunken doctors screwing all the nice willing nurses. They often abuse red-cross markings and you have no immunity – we had to get out in the end in a hurry because we couldn't allow ourselves to get tarred with combatant status. Some of the American-led Contra groups were fanatic, out to stamp on us. We were wicked, you see.

"Yes, some of the mercenaries are dangerous. Often psychopathic, often yes, stoned, and irresponsible, throwing money and arms about. No, none of us were killed – we had to come home for that – and none of us were raped, though that has been known; the most we got was abuse and intimidation. But it could only get worse. One of our village helper girls was beaten: we could have been next.

"There was a journalist once, and yes, he did cause trouble. I never did find out exactly, I mean piecing it together, I'm not a policeman – I don't wish to be rude – I mean I had better things to do. That sounds rude too but I know that you are trying to understand.

"There was a helicopter, those people had lots of them. I don't mean an armed one, what they call a gun ship, though they carried guns, everyone did; I mean handheld things – I'm sorry, I know no more about guns than you do about medicine. They used them for spying, for observation, as well as carrying their big chiefs around, people who couldn't walk a mile on a trail, overfed, meddling, fat people, the ones who do all the damaging things because they know nothing, see nothing.

"These machines didn't come our way much because of course the people on what I mustn't call our side shot at them. They didn't often hit them.

"You see, those things go fast and are difficult to hit with just an ordinary gun, you have to have some special thing, a missile they call it."

Something of Castang's amusement must have shown through. Annunziata, accustomed to talking to people as though they were slightly backward.

"I really know nothing about it. What happened, one came close by, which they didn't as a rule. Of course, the mercenaries took a pot at it and must have hit a rotor because it didn't crash but it was forced to put down; not very far away so they went to look. They weren't supposed to. A sector occupied by the fascists, though one never really knew, so they took risks with it. Gleeful, shouting like children. The journalist went with them. It would make a good story, you see.

"It ended badly. The plane bumped, landing, and the people in it were hurt and stunned. But there was something very valuable in that plane. A big fascist patrol came to rescue it, or them, and arrived at the same time as the boys. Two of them were killed, and more wounded; they got back to us, and we had a lot of work and were attacked soon afterwards so I never had time to find out exactly.

"But what I heard was, that group got hold of some valuable piece of loot. The boy I was treating gabbled about a briefcase, and I think there must have been somebody senior in that 'copter, planning documents and orders, you know, valuable military information, because why otherwise would the other side have been so frenzied to try and get it back? There were the wildest rumours flying about as to what it could have been. I think the journalist got it because he disappeared. It would have been a tremendous propaganda coup, from his point of view."

"Did anybody mention money?" asked Castang blandly.

"Oh yes, the wildest rumours, but frankly, I had other things to think about. One boy had a lung wound. We weren't supposed to treat any military injuries. Compromised you see not just our non-combatant status but our avowed neutrality. So I got into trouble, with a big telling-off from the area superior and he gave orders to pull us out, and when it got back here the Provincial said for us to be sent home. I'm sorry if now I've got you into trouble. Monseigneur told me I'd better

116

– of course there's no proof, but maybe they thought we'd – and so this might have been a sort of vengeance?"

It could only have been a paymaster, thought Castang. He had no idea how such things were done. Would they pay, those CIA people, mercenary troops in the field? It would be more likely that large sums of money – liquid – would be available for solving local difficulties in a hurry, for bribery, for compensating damage, for greasing headmen and local percentage men. A piastre war it had been in Indonesia and surely the same everywhere. You greased everybody. Or the petrol failed to arrive, the rice disappeared, the guide mysteriously took a mistaken path and your jeep suddenly broke down.

An important Mr Somebody. A briefcase, and perhaps a sealed ammunition box. What would they use? Gold? Or more likely plain good-ol'-US dollars in used bills and smallish denominations. But that would be bulky, indiscreet, vulnerable. It didn't much matter – not his problem! Robert would have found an answer. No wonder they were furious. An important semi-secret grease fund disappearing under their noses. Presumably the 'copter pilot, in broken awkward countryside, made a navigational error. One per cent on a compass course could make a nasty gap at a hundred kilometres.

"Would you recognise this journalist, if you saw him again?"

"I'm not too sure. I couldn't promise to."

"Anything like this?" languidly producing his joker. A photograph provided by Erskine MacLeod. A Robert from, though, some years earlier.

She looked carefully.

"Like, perhaps. This seems a younger man. But perhaps it's an old photograph. No, I'm sorry, I can't be sure. I have scruples anyhow. I might be getting an innocent man into trouble on a completely fortuitous resemblance. And anyhow I don't think one can recognise people from features. Movement – there is character in a walk, but somebody smiling into a camera . . ."

"I'm not trying to push you."

117

"It might or it mightn't and I can say no better."

"No, you've done your best."

"I'm a nurse. A boy was injured and in pain. I refused to be ordered not to treat someone because their ideology's frowned upon. A fascist soldier would be the same. It was my conscience. One never does wrong to obey that."

"I completely agree."

"There are anyhow Americans on both sides. The boy was from Dayton, Ohio, I remember. He showed me pictures of his mother and sister. Go ahead. Call me a sentimental ninny. Monseigneur did. I only wish," sticking out her bony chin, "the bomb had got me, instead of a girl who had nothing to do with this."

"Stop being a sentimental ninny," said Castang.

8

"So Annunziata's a horrible Communist," said Castang laughing. "Not so bad for her, though she nearly got chopped for it. Worse for you, perhaps." The bishop was smiling too. Sad? Thin? No, just a smile. Tired, perhaps.

"You know the celebrated phrase of Dom Helder Camara?"

"Who's he? Familiar name, but . . ."

"Archbishop. Northeastern Brazil. Large area. Notoriously poor. He was conspicuous too. Should have been a cardinal, and even more obviously wasn't. As the phrase runs, 'When I worried about them being poor, everyone said I was a saint. When I asked what made them poor, everyone said I was a Commie.' Land and money, all of it, is in the hands of those who own the big estancios. If the peasants form a co-op, make any protest, wonder aloud where their next meal is coming from, the estancieros send in their private army. Who will break a few toes and fingers, shoot a few knee and elbow joints, blind a few men, rape a few women, set a few huts on fire, disembowel a few children. Pour encourager les autres. Clerics who have the impudence to suggest that these are not perhaps the ways of divine justice will be frowned upon. You might recall the name of Monseigneur Romero. Salvador: I have trouble myself sorting out these American countries. Shot him in his own cathedral, for obstinately shooting off his stupid mouth in persistent disregard of counsels of Prudence from the Vatican and the United States Ambassador. I don't think anybody's about to shoot me, don't get the idea I consider myself that important."

"And the landowners," said Castang lazily, "are excellent

Catholics, go to Mass every Sunday, their daughters are all Children of Mary, and they make big contributions to the Pope's private exchequer."

"Castang, I don't want you to view me as some sort of disgruntled malcontent. I think, too, we should be careful, when in the back line, to avoid too much critical lip about those in the front line. I don't care much for many of the Pope's viewpoints, but recall I'm bound by vows of obedience, loyalty and discretion. Just like Annunziata. And I'll give you a short lecture if need be about Vatican finance. There are a lot of misconceptions."

"My wife has taught me a poem. It's very short and I've still managed to forget most of it. Written by an English boy in the nineteen-fourteen-eighteen trenches. Right here, almost. Educated, sensitive boy. He asks himself questions, about the heroes of antiquity. 'Was it so hard, Achilles? So very hard, to die?'"

"'Stand in the trench, Achilles,'" said the bishop softly, "'Flame-Capped, and shout for me.' Patrick Shaw Stewart, one of the most gifted of his generation, a partner in the house of Baring at the age of twentyfour. I know the poem, and it comes often to my mind too."

"It is always the best who die. And the mediocre who survive."

"Indeed it is often said that the decadence of France dates from this, and that in England it accelerated the decline. The blood on this land . . ."

"All right," briskly. "We'll judge nobody. There are far too many aspects of this, still, which are obscure. Mine not to reason why. My duty is to make what I know known to my superiors.

"Let them wonder, for instance, whether any intelligence agency, overt or covert, American or Russian or any other, is really going to plant explosives in a French convent. Sounds to me far-fetched. Even if both you and I know that these clean-living American Marine colonels are all ayatollahs in their fixation: they have all had direct messages from God. I don't know, it seems a little too mean-minded and trivial, to bomb Annunziata because she treated an American soldier for bullet wounds. Even if he was to their eyes a despicable traitor."

"Money, Castang, money. Even if she knows nothing, and she's telling the truth as you realise, rumour there was talking about a million dollars in gold. Now discount for rumour, discount for the greasing to get away with it, the weight and bulk, discount for changing, for laundering, for bribing a great many people, two things strike me. One, this would be a lot even to those fellows you mention. The other, that there would likely be a lot left. Even if it's all funny money from selling dud missiles to ayatollahs and buying dud missiles for Indians, it's still a lot.

"As for the silliness of intelligence agencies, I don't think we need point our finger at Americans or even at colonels who think they're Joan of Arc. Do you recall a singularly intelligent French operation aimed at putting a bomb under a pacifist organisation, in a harbour in New Zealand?"

"Very, very vividly."

"You know, too, that we have a rich and powerful political group here which thinks itself Joan of Arc and Bernadette Soubirous rolled together. Sacred Heart, Save us from the Arabs, the Jews, the Freemasons, the Communists, and the vernacular Mass."

"Oho," said Castang.

"I don't want to get paranoid about it," said Monseigneur, gently. "They have after all confined themselves hitherto to abusive anonymous letters. I think I might have scruples, Castang, at your making known to your superiors some of the things which occupy my mind, my fears. Could we make an agreement about background, as journalists call it?"

"We could," said Castang.

The bishop was wearing a soutane today, new, and looking to be well-cut. Nice little cloth-covered buttons all the way down, a good sit around a starched and gleaming Roman collar, a flare over the hips suggestive of gunslinging Western toughies, Gary Cooper, or John Wayne, with that delightful intoed walk.

121

No, not John Wayne, he was a great supporter of the Roll-Back-Commies brigade.

"What's this soutane act?" asked Castang. "Being sexless in a skirt, a bishop has to be a whole man, balls out, as Richard Nixon put it if inelegantly." Monseigneur got the giggles at this.

"My painting costume," he said. "In just five minutes I've a session with your portraitist, delightful old man. He agreed. A bishop can't be painted in a business suit as though he were a Swiss bank."

"Quite a lot of bishops seem to be the next best thing."

It was a frivolous remark, but it changed the expression of Monseigneur's face.

"Yes," slowly. A distinct drop in the temperature.

"I feel envy," Castang went on. "I could do with a uniform like that. Scarlet I think, rather than purple. Grosgrain sash, little cape lined with satin, mm, must get my Military and Ecclesiastical Tailor on the job."

"You can have mine." He was thinking. Looked again at his watch. Made his mind up. "You had better come with me, Castang. We have to have a little talk. About Church finance. I won't have time later on. And this is something I have to be done with."

Surprised. "Won't it upset the painter?"

"No. He likes a conversation to be going on. Helps prevent the subject going stiff and wooden. He talks himself, when there's nobody else." He led the way through to the gallery, where the light was good.

Marklake was there already, examining the light, highly concentrated, professional. He looked keenly at Castang, gave a brief nod of recognition, went back to his easel. The bishop took his pose, already practised at it, composed and controlled. Castang found a chair at the side, out of sight-lines.

"Head up a little more," laconic. "Turn the jaw just a scrap – so. That will do well," picking up a brush.

"The problem," said Monseigneur calmly, as though the conversation had not been interrupted," is to get past the capes and sashes, while not compromising their reality. We aren't

122

looking for any study-in-scarlet, mm, Meissonier cardinals having a whale of a time with roast beef and bottles of Bordeaux. While also avoiding a lot of symbolic crap."

"Kitchen tables with skulls on them," said Marklake, amused, "Correggio Saint Jerome. Large book, learned commentary upon pious subjects."

"Don't want to be stuck full of arrows either. Saint Sebastian not my thing at all. However, not to be frivolous," sharp eye swivelling momentarily –

"Keep your eye upon the picture of Fénélon."

"Right, and back to finance. A short boring lecture, Castang, but you understand the structure of flow charts. The Vatican is a complex subject. Separate three different things for a start.

"First, Vatican City itself. A state like any other. Very small, of course. Around four hundred citizens, mostly ecclesiastical bureaucrats; something better than a thousand employees. Kept in fair financial balance, income from the post, selling stamps and medals, from tickets to the museums, quite dear. Further aided by clever tricks, like getting cheap electricity from the Italian State. It's of no further interest. Okay?

"Secondly, the Papacy itself, as an organisation. Large, complicated, expensive, a point I'll come back to. Can be subdivided, roughly.

"Into, foremost, the Curia; a multitude of commissions and committees, all with their own secretariat, plus tribunals, all the diplomats too, the nuncios in every country, a whole Foreign Office, you're with me?

"And the big communications office; Radio Vatican; the newspaper, the *Osservatore*. These two massive organisations cost a packet and are in chronic deficit. This has all been greatly enlarged and modernised, the days of little memos on the backs of used envelopes are gone, full of computers now. Around two thousand five hundred employees, badly paid but still a big charge in salaries.

"So how do you finance this? The Vatican isn't in fact very rich. Owns a lot of real estate, but most is apartments in Rome let to clerks and typists, their own people, so biting your own tail there; can't charge high rents when they're anything but highly paid. Even a cardinal is only pulling in around ten thousand francs a month: it's not a lot even with the black Mercedes.

"The third major element, but totally distinct from the other two, is Propaganda Fidei, which runs all the missions, and since we are keen on missions, and make large contributions to same, they have pots of money, more than the other two put together, and are in nice financial balance, thanks. Clear so far?"

"Yes. If I've understood, that finances Annunziata?"

"Quite so. To be sure, between my local finance and their central bureau there's a considerable hugger-mugger, but in practice it is lucid and distinct: no problem."

"The hands at rest," said Marklake quietly.

"We return to the Papacy itself. So they're in deficit, spending about double their resources, and in order to bridge the gap, they make massive appeals to the faithful public. This is done by a commission of fifteen bishops, three from each continent. As you can readily imagine, the two queen bees in that set-up happen to be the bishops of Köln in Germany and Philadelphia in the United States, who are the two richest in the world. Either of them has far more money than the Vatican itself. All still clear?"

"Perfectly," said Castang, who had realised that Monseigneur wasn't telling him all this for fun. He might, like Jesus, be speaking in parables, but Castang better sit up and pay close attention.

"Right. We come to the naughty bit. The Vatican Bank is separate from everything hitherto mentioned. Their capital is composed of the property, investments and liquidities of all the religious orders: put together that's quite something. It was always a cosy affair, run by one or two extremely urbane cardinals and a few sophisticated gentlemen from old Roman families with a good network in the banking world. Turned in a handsome dividend and the Pope himself took a pretty cut in the profits.

"But some twenty years or more ago it was decided that

Italian finance was both too narrow and too rocky: they widened out into international waters. That needs a high-class professional in charge. Instead, they put in that Marcinkus, who played golf with Rockefellers – just like Eisenhower. So he kept his brains in his bag, and got caught in the squalid fiddles you know about from the press; Ambrosiano, right, Michele Sindona. Lost a great deal of money, had to make good a deficit of two hundred and forty million dollars which is a lot but they did it from their own reserves.

"Listen intently; this has nothing to do with the Papacy as such, but causes consternation in the ranks of the faithful. Contributions fell off badly, thirty per cent down in a twelve-month. They're in deep trouble because they've huge outgoings. So where are they to turn?

"Everything I've told you is known, public. Beyond that point I know no more than you do: I'm a small unimportant local officer in Transmissions. My population is loyal, often fervent, and mostly poor, and when I send out the word on the twentyninth of each June to cough up cash for Saint Peter, all I know is that like everyone else I'm thirty per cent down, and that would apply too even in Köln and Philadelphia.

"So what goes on? Guesswork. Does His Holiness cut down on lavish voyages to Chile? Apparently he doesn't. Money's coming from somewhere.

"Your guess, Castang, is as good as mine. You can afford to be indifferent. I'd feel unhappy, myself, about contributions coming from sources whose political ideologies and motivations I cannot share. Not even in my worst nightmares."

"Don't frown, Monseigneur," said Marklake. "Makes a bad line. Relax the muscles."

"The bank's official name," obeying at once, "is the Institute for the Promotion of Religion. I fall foul of these euphemisms. The Committee for the Reelection of the President. People give money for the Cause, glowing hearts and eyes aflame, and one's not too sure what the Cause is. Opus Dei, the Work of God. I have fewer certitudes, fewer dogmatic persuasions."

125

"Schutz Staffel, the work of God," suggested the old man colourlessly, cleaning a brush.

"Onward Christian Soldiers," tried Castang.

"One has also the Word of God, the Will of God, and numerous other divine attributes, frequently fertilised by gigantic sums of money from God's private accounts in Salt Lake City."

"Wasn't it always the same? The Rose is in the name of the rose."

"Yes, indeed. People murmuring that Franciscans were supposed to be poor got into some very hot water."

"Jews got likewise into hot water, for their deplorable habits of desecrating hosts and poisoning wells, thereby occasioning the Black Death. A little rest, Monseigneur? For myself," said the old man. "Pause. Peepee."

"And I've been playing truant," said Castang, strolling over to look at the canvas: large areas were still blank. Others were undercoated. There were strong nervous lines of drawing. Illumination began to underscore traits of a remarkable character. Or two, since the subject and the painter were both ranging about this field. He glanced up. The bishop was frowning over some papers the secretary had brought in for signature. Castang left quietly.

"This much is clear," said Castang, wishing it were. "This chap MacLeod got hold of a large sum of money, while playing front-line war correspondent in an obscure corner of South America. Plain looted it. A wrecked helicopter, an officer with a briefcase, could have been carrying operational orders or confidential this or that, they went to look.

"We can't begin to understand how, but he got away with it. Must have been laundered through several filters, leaving title with the bearer somehow. Nor can one make out the origins. I thought at first it must be secret-fund stuff, used to finance these innumerable anti-Commie crusades. The bishop thinks it more likely to be Catholic money, the Virgin of Guadeloupe telling the faithful they must give lots and lots of dollars for Nice Pope against Nasty Stalin."

"Couldn't care fucking less," said Monsieur Sabatier, impatient with this rigmarole. "The essential is that it's nothing to do with us. I still haven't made out who bombed the nuns. Was that the goodies or the baddies?"

"The fascists rushed to the scene. Doubtless they knew the helicopter was full of lollipops. There was a firefight. Some mercenaries were killed, but MacLeod got away with the booty. There may have been few left to stake a claim to it. The obscure part, which doesn't interest you, is that he came back here. I think myself that he wanted to give some of that money to the nuns, and was looking for a discreet way to do so. I think the fascists picked his tracks up and followed him here. They seem to have missed him, and out of sheer spite bombed the nuns anyhow – blow for freedom, quoi? Or thought the nuns were in the conspiracy to steal the money, or had profited from it already. Who knows what goes on in the muddled minds of the Gott-Mit-Uns brigade? They'd like to get their money back and zap MacLeod. Zapping nuns might not have been part of the deal. Missing MacLeod, zap nuns, just for apple-pie; they're all dirty Commies."

"Just a minute! I don't want any CIA death squads over here zapping anybody."

"I don't believe that for a second. Much more likely their local pen-pals in the Nat. Front. Who have a strong dislike of the local bishop. Zapping him might alienate the local population, but busting the nuns would give him pause. I can tell you it does."

"I'm not interested in nuns and bishops," bawled Monsieur Sabatier, "I'm a law-enforcement agency. The moment we've got a political motivation for a criminal act we're out, Castang, we're clear. A nice shitty dossier to turn over to RG, I make a confidential report to the Minister and we're home." The initials stand for Renseignements Généraux or General Information. Behind this bland euphemism lurks the political police, and nobody in the criminal-investigation branch wants anything to do with those creeps.

"Splendid, Castang, splendid, that's very good work." Monsieur Sabatier is a good Catholic. The Cardinal-Archbishop of Lille has been known to make his life a misery. A bit of proper detachment, and on the whole one can feel much cheered-up. There may be a few insignificant details not entirely clear, but hell, that's what one has Castangs for.

Vera gets impatient too, with the persecutors of her patient Worrier. From her Czech peasant granny, she has carried into adult life a taste for rustic turns of speech.

"Monsieur Sabatier," she says, "I paste on the wall, behind the paper." Phrase in use amongst Dutch and Flemish ladies irritated by the menfolk. She has also, upon occasion, fluent grasp of platt-German obscenities.

"Am Arsch g'fikt 'n' zum Mond g'schossen." A radical solution to Bores: screw them up the ass and shoot them at the moon. Castang, who knows a few in Spanish but likes to enlarge his vocabulary, is greatly admiring and slightly shocked, that his virtuous spouse should command these earthy expressions.

"But I don't understand," giving them both a second beer, "why your boyo Robert conceals himself behind the alias of a Jewish painter."

"If I knew that," said Castang, "I too could make the fruit machine come up with a bucket of silver dollars."

Perish the thought, that one should screw bishops up the – but one uses any leverage one has.

"Monseigneur," said Castang gently, "I don't want at all that any unfunny fascists should put pressure on you. Neither the Work of God, nor the Will, nor the Word. I am here to prevent crime, what a hope, still, let's pay some lip-service to a good idea once in a while."

"Now what's all this about, Castang?" in the tone of a busy man having his time wasted.

"I want you to do some detecting."

"If I am to take you seriously, I must understand you."

Castang had put the telephone down to drink half a cup of stone-cold coffee, but the effect of pregnant pause was achieved.

"Monseigneur, the Police Judiciaire has no remaining official interest in the events which have been disturbing us. That remark, by the way, is unofficial."

"Noted. You have a motive in telling me this? Thank you, in passing."

"I have several. If the authorities have found grounds for isolating the explosives attack as committed for political reasons, it becomes part of policy, maybe foreign policy. They don't take me into their confidence."

"I follow you."

"You might or you might not get a call from a very pleasant fellow called Commissaire Morosini. He's not a close colleague of mine. We have a nodding acquaintance. Bit of a breach of confidence, but thought I'd mention it."

"Thank you, Castang." The bishop cleared his throat. "If that should take place, I'd regard it as a matter for my ecclesiastical superiors."

"Quite so. You see, I'm only concerned with quite a narrow and technical definition of what constitutes crime. A bomb isn't a crime, in that sense; it's an extension of somebody's political statement. Similarly, if somebody said to be a journalist commits unauthorised acts on somebody else's territory, it doesn't come within the criminal code. In fact in my book there's never been any crime at all."

"It's nice to have this so clearly stated."

"So you could say that there are one or two little obscurities that continue to perplex me, on purely personal grounds. Signing some name which isn't your own in a hotel register is hardly even a misdemeanour. By coincidence, the name of the old boy doing a job for you. I notice he likes a chat, while working."

"He does indeed. Theology, exegetics, biblical controversies: we have interesting discussions. He's well-read, has a curious, wide-ranging mind."

"In the light of what I've been telling you, no crime, thus no legal grounds for interrogation. Just curiosity, you might say, about personal history. If you led the conversation in that direction – this was the meaning of my frivolities about detective work."

"Rather thin grounds."

"Not perhaps as thin as all that. This fellow did a vanishing act, and round the same time, too close perhaps to be coincidental, the woman who kept the little hotel vanished too."

"You aren't suggesting anything criminal there? Even of a uh, political colouring?"

"Quite the contrary. By every single account a good and honest soul."

"I see. I have one reservation, which is that if anything did happen to come to my knowledge, it might be expressed in confidence."

"You'd have to make up your own mind about that," said Castang. "Jews don't go to confession, do they? I'm a bit vague on their theology. Small breaches of confidence can sometimes be justified when they're likely to lead to good. We had a minor example a few moments back."

"True," clearing his throat again. "Shall I say I'll do whatever is within my capacities, to render service?"

"That's a kindness. Nothing to do with Caesar. Only personal, for the centurion, that other biblical figure you're acquainted with. Give me a ring, any time." Po-o-oh: expelling a long breath. Castang has a healthy dislike for this sort of conversation.

9

May – it's a good, and a bad month, in the North. Good since at least everything is green, birds sing, maybe even nest if one looks carefully: there will, presumably, be some summer vaguely in the offing. Bad because it seems to do nothing but rain.

Nothing worthy of comment, there. Isn't that the case with any month of the twelve you care to name? Right, but around May one gets an obscure sense of dissatisfaction; the feeling that it's gone on raining long enough and that this would be a good time for it to stop. One has had this feeling in April; one will have it again in June. It leads the peoples of northern Europe to behave in silly ways, in the months of July and August.

Castang is feeling staled and dulled. The young, bright greens of tree and hedge are a weariness instead of a solace, for the blackened old brickwork, lighting the dimmest plant into brilliant green flames, tells him that men age less well than bricks. The lengthening days seem to him too short, and the chronic twinges of pain in his smashed arm are harder to bear. He is irritable and so is Vera. They nag at one another in a foolish, boring fashion. Damn it, he had no holiday last year.

These old, battered provinces of Artois and Picardy, with their many rusting skeletons of mineshaft and steelworks, their innumerable reminders that for nine hundred years the invasion routes of Western Europe – the sunset land – have lain along this path, have an astounding vitality. Townsman that he is, he forgets too easily that this is farming land, strong and deep, and absorbs the torrents of blood, the stupefying rain of fragmented bone and splintered metal.

At least he can look at trees, taking a roundabout way to work; perversely, since of course it is raining, and his arm feels put through the mangle. How the hell, Castang, are you going to understand anything about human beings without learning (as Vera has taught him) to look at trees? It is not the much hacked and demolished oak-ash-thorn of the Artois country-side. Desk-bound senior officers have not much opportunity to look at that.

These are municipal trees, as recommended for resistance to car exhausts, acids, salt in winter, draughts, small boys; the long list of municipal hazards. There has been, thanks-be-to-god, a diminution in Japanese prunus. Tulip trees; rowan trees. Ginkgos. Sugar maples, a variety that will never produce any sugar but has pretty, lanceolated leaves.

Castang feels much cheered, arriving twenty minutes late at the office, taking his hat off and shaking it; good, that'll lay the dust on this vile staircase.

"Madame Metz, good morning and ring my wife will you, there's something I've forgotten to tell her." The holiday roster is on the wall. He jerks at the phone cord which has become entangled. The two senior inspectors have by tradition and sacred right the two months of July and August. Those he doesn't want anyway. Young Louppes must wait until September, and Varennes consequently must go in June; silly girl saying she was going to the Sahara so that she would enjoy the rainfall when she got back . . .

"I'm going to take a break. Where would you like to go on holiday? Yes, I know about the children's schools. The hell with them, they never learn anything there anyhow. Yes, I know it's too late to book anything much, we'll just have to trust our instinct and hope we're lucky. Yes, of course there's unfinished business, always is and always will be. Bored stiff with it and shove it up Paddy Campbell. I don't know in the least what I want. Don't much care. One can only hope the flood of Dutch and Danes has not yet reached its maximum.

Very well then, think about it, and so will I think about it, and we'll see by lunchtime whether these two shrivelled minds can produce an idea. No, I don't want to go to Jugoslavia. Or maybe I do, I'm going to make an incantation against discontent."

So that a great whirlwind of activity stirred Madame Metz into frenzy, and since she was going in July that made two whole months he wouldn't have to – now come on; stop moaning. There are several highly wearisome enquiries which have been dragging on for months; what, if anything, has been done about the Fiend of the Autoroute, who rapes hitch-hikers? By eleven o'clock he felt refreshed. There weren't quite as many people in jail as usual, either. Nothing he can do about people in jail, since much of his job consists of putting them there, and pushing them out is the job of the Judge of Instruction. But jail is less funny than usual in the summer months, when the prison built to house six hundred goes past the three thousand mark and the daytime temperature reaches thirty degrees and there's no way they can have more than two showers a week. July and August, in a prison, are worse than the other ten months together.

He'd had no time to think of his own affairs, and decided upon a pub and a beer as an aid to meditation.

The rain had cleared. Tja, that sharp dazzle of sun through water vapour. Suddenly it is extremely hot; the hotter for the high humidity. Want a cool, dim pub.

He sits dreaming over a lovely south-German beer, dark and not too sweet, of beaches where judges and deputies would stop judging and deputising; just sit on the sand and be human beings: of lovely girls with naked breasts, few of them lovely but on the beach they *look* lovely: of going swimming even though the stupid arm cannot really swim any more: of – who was that vaguely familiar figure who has just caught his eye and given him a casual nod? Sharpen your wits, Castang.

Delaunay, Monsieur Delaunay of the railways. Yes, and there too is some unfinished business. In this same pub he had brought old Marklake (more unfinished business) to meet

Delaunay and yes, Nelson Walter. By now, he presumed, gone home to New Zealand. Those two men who had – rather like this sunshine – shed a light, more dazzling than illuminating, upon an enigmatic figure which went on popping up at the back of his mind; a sharp small stick.

Delaunay had turned his back, seemingly wishful to avoid him. Well, he was the Polizei, a character many people prefer to avoid, whether their conscience is bad or not. But the fellow took a sidelong glance back over his shoulder, for reassurance, and Castang smiled and beckoned. A solid man, and sensible. He hesitated for a second, shrugged; brought his beer across, offered a thick warm hand, sat down. Castang drank in silence, signalled for another for them both, offered one of his little cigars. The broad pale face, careful if not hostile, relaxed a little.

"I go, every now and then, through the street. The Hotel Caravane still shut and shuttered. Pity, that. I must try and find out one of these days what can be done about it. Doesn't look as though she is coming back."

Delaunay looked at his beer for a long time, making his mind up, stirring about in an ashtray with a burned match. Without looking at Castang he said at last, unwillingly, dragging the words out,

"I saw her."

"You did?" surprised. "Spoke to her?" Was there some banal explanation, after all? "Where was that?"

"Spoke to her, no. She turned her back. Dodged me. I wasn't going to chase after." It had hurt him; he brought it out painfully.

"It was along the coast," he began to explain, reluctant. "Not a Madrid train but the border, at Hendaye. Afternoon train, gets back to Paris about midnight. We've had trouble often on that stretch. You know, the Basque independence movement. Protests, blockages, derailing threats. There was a cop hit by a train, chasing a girl terrorist, you maybe saw that in the paper. Our people were nervous. The line was blocked, derailing attempt, they broke it up between Anglet and Bayonne, train

134

was delayed two hours. Well, you know Biarritz station, out there in the bloody countryside. There was nothing to do so I went down to the town to kill an hour while they cleared the track. I was having a coffee with a taximan I know." Castang listened while the scene was laboriously reassembled. No use hurrying him.

"On a terrace, there in the middle. She walked past me on the pavement. Close as I am to you. She saw me! No way could she not have recognised me. And she made exactly like dodging someone you don't want to meet, got to cross the road you know and terribly busy looking out for traffic. Well, I wasn't about to get up and go running after her."

"It was probably someone else," said Castang indifferently. "I've been caught myself. Uncanny resemblance, you get up and oh so sorry, and afterwards how's it possible to make a fool of oneself like that."

"No!" irritable at that much obtuseness. "No mistake. Look, Commissaire, you've maybe not thought of it, but railway controllers are trained to see people. We go down a train, believe me we look. We know whose ticket is what, over long-distance we ask once and that's it, you're for Poitiers, you're for Paris. We know who's trying a fiddle, who's sneaked into first class and is pretending to be asleep. Who is a potential trouble-maker and who's a drunk. I saw her, she saw me, she didn't want to know me. All right, she's reasons of her own. Still gave me a little pinch, inside. She was a friend, and she was straight, and would never have acted that way. But she did . . ."

"Yagh, like you say, reasons of her own. Who knows? In Biarritz, eh? We're not officially interested anymore," said Castang. "It was decided to let that side of it slide. No evidence of criminal act or intent."

"Business takes me down to Irun often enough," said Delaunay, "but I've nothing to do in Biarritz. It's a dump, anyhow."

* * *

135

"You smell of drink," said Vera in a vinegary voice. Going through a puritanical phase. But she hasn't had a proper holiday either since lord knows when. Going moreover through a difficult phase; that of the woman who, herself forty, still has children under ten. Nor can one park them for the day. There are the times known to all when in-laws are a bore and a burden; and the times when one is grateful for them. Vera suffers, profoundly and secretly, from the reckless moment a lifetime ago when she cut herself loose from country and family. And Little Orphan Castang has never had any family at all since his auntie in Paris who brought him up succumbed to cirrhosis of the liver while still in her fifties.

Vera goes out for the day. She has not spent a night away from her children since they were born. The sense of security thus given to the little darlings is of profound psychological importance, but one mustn't be surprised when Mum becomes a bit acid.

"True," said Castang comfortably, "I smell of drink. But lo, a great clarity of mind tells me that the Atlantic coast will be our best bet at short notice. I'll get Adrien Richard to find something for us. It will do him good, to do a bit of work for once." Monsieur Richard, formerly a Divisional Commissaire in the PJ and for many years Castang's immediate superior, had retired a few years back. From being a good friend, he had entered the category of friends one has rather-lost-sight-of. It was the right moment to mend this. "I'll ring him this afternoon. Be cheaper on the office phone." Richard has become a golf-playing bourgeois swine. Tja, he always was. But he has other sides too. His skill at not letting the left hand know what the right hand was getting up to made him a chief more difficult to get on with than Monsieur Sabatier; a lot more present, but also more rewarding.

Vera has little to say, and for once little to object to. She is secretly pleased, and more secretly relieved, because without telling anyone she has been working herself up to the announcement that she was going to be an August Widow; a well-known category in France of wives married to busy-busy business men whose affairs are too important for them to leave Paris; and who in reality as well as legend gambol and gamble in dangerous-living upon the August beaches.

Overstrain has not demolished her humour. She finds these adulterous biddies boring, in or outside the pages of popular fiction, and hasn't the least intention of safety-pinning the wedding ring to the lining of her purse. But she has bought herself (in darkest secret in Bruxelles, glancing uneasily about in illogical fear that Castang might suddenly pop in, doubtless to buy a sexy nighty for his new mistress) a snazzy bathing suit. Not a bikini; this particular mutton is not kidding itself it's lamb: but well cut, audacious as well as expensive.

Likewise après-beach clothes, the sort you can add bits on to as the sun goes down. Likewise shoes. Hats. Earrings. Ecological but expensive cosmetics made of plants. Nice bags to stow these goodies in. The glee and terror inseparable from all this has done her a great deal of good. Hiding these treasures in obscure corners of the apartment has been more satisfying than adultery, if almost as nerveracking.

She might have known it. A family party after all, with the little dears clustered close. Put your hat on, darling; no, you can't swim so soon after dinner; don't go out too far, the undertow is treacherous this time of tide. Making goddamn sandwiches. And all this in Boring old Biarritz, glued to one's tedious husband. But she's relieved too. She'd been thinking of Dubrovnik (since it's a socialist sister-state, full of Fucking Czechs), or ghastly Corfu stuffed-with-Brits, or . . . or . . . she'd been too tired to think: let him do the thinking for her.

Good, thinks Castang, who knows nothing about the secrets in the bedroom, being a bad detective, but observing the brow unknitting a wee bit. The girl needs a holiday badly. I must try and make it worth her pains. Hell, I'm paid enough for that. I'm not going to peep a syllable about Madame Adrienne Sergent (nor, I have hopes, Robert MacLeod). Hell, she has her secrets too.

As for Madame Metz, eavesdropping upon my private telephone calls, much good may it do her.

"Richard? Aha. How's my old mate then? How are Judith's camellias doing?"

Richard, initially, is very tiresome.

"Delighted to see you. We can put you up. Nonsense; plenty of room." This won't do at all. In fact nothing could be more destructive of friendship.

"I don't know any house agents. Yes, of course, every single goddamn inhabitant. Well, yes, there are the people who acted for me. That's years ago; they're probably dead." Not so much egoist as plain bloody lazy. "Outside a way would cost you less. Say twenty minutes in the car. Suit you better. Less noise."

"I've lots of money." So he has. A PJ commissaire is not badly paid. True, he doesn't invest in nice little stocks, of which he has a holy horror, to the despair of his bank-manager. He has a few small savings accounts. Vera conducts her housekeeping as though they were penniless. He likes to be silly now and then. Egged on by a friend, a university professor who buys Lancias for his wife, he wouldn't have been averse. Or a dear little Alfa-Romeo? Vera refused, horrified. The spare parts are a shocking racket. And I could never climb in and out. No no, the tiny Volkswagen. Might as well drive a coffee-mill all the way to the Spanish frontier. And with two tedious little girls in the back.

The children are unspoilt. They have been dragged about a few times to odd corners of Europe but have not been accustomed to – Ooh, Biarritz. Can we have a surfboard? A sail-plank? Don't be so mean; everybody's got one. Castang, utterly nineteenth century, worrying about the Dreyfus Case, totally thunderstruck at the price of the two square centimetres of printed cotton that make up a bikini for little girls of pre-pubescent age. What! Three hundred francs to cover that ridiculous bony little bottom of yours. Oh Pa, you are so goddamn mean. Poor old medieval remnant. Conspiring with Vera in corners, a deathly hush falling when he entered the room. Poor old Pa; somebody ought to tell him the Facts of Life. One would deal out a few slaps to restore discipline: in fact Vera, ragged from fatigue and recalling a Czech upbringing in which adolescent girls did *not* show their breasts, did deal out slaps, causing exaggerated howls. Lydia Has Tits, said his jealous youngest, aged eight. As for the coffee-mill, Castang and Vera in turns drive this vile invention across the longest diagonal that can be managed inside the Hexagon. A tired – and cross – quartet agrees upon arriving that there is something to be said for the barbaric South after all.

Judith – the Spanish Gardener – kinder, and if anything slightly dottier than when last seen, has made a nice supper for them. The Divisionnaire-in-retreat appears later, with the keys to a bungalow thing, whose roof is said to leak when it rains. But cheap. Well, fairly cheap. All cottages let furnished are the same. The children are hustled off to bed, with the promise of yes yes, they can be on the beach at the crack of dawn.

"Now what is all this?" asks Richard. It sounds like an English policeman, in some nineteen-twenties detective story. Biarritz is like this too.

"Well, you know, I wasn't going to tell you over the phone." Castang looked at him with affection. Richard looked exactly the same and he himself felt rejuvenated by ten years, back in the SRPJ office saying 'Well, you know', with Fausta, Richard's utterly beautiful secretary, making china tea next door.

Not quite the same. A hairsbreadth thinner and greyer, and more English. Biarritz had always been full of retired colonels, in burberries and highly polished shoes (just like Castang himself) and even the French ones got to look English. Richard had an open-air tan, and the polished nose had taken on a high-bridged, elegant cut. Like the 'twenties detective, negligently hinting where the local inspector ought to be aiming his great flat feet.

"You're going to have to do some work."

"I'm not here to do work. I refuse categorically."

"Well, you don't, you know. This is going to interest you."

"I can feel my eyes glazing over." Richard had always hated listening to 'long complicated stories'.

And now he kept saying mm, mm, until Castang suddenly cross shouted, "Stop going meuh meuh like a demented sheep," which was exactly the kind of remark Richard would have made in the days when he was still the Divisionnaire.

"What you need," very calm and staring at Castang with damnably clear grey eyes exactly like James Bond's M who turned out to have been a Russian spy all along, "is a holiday, decidedly, so tomorrow I'll buy you a bucket and spade, and find you a nice bit of beach out of the wind. Right now all that whisky before supper has simply served to make you irritable, and we'll have something soothing and Victorian like mulled claret." Judith had gone to bed, because gardening is so strenuous, and Richard pottered with the saucepan. "I dare say something can be done," was all he would admit.

Some years since he had been here but it didn't seem, thought Castang, to have changed in any real sense. There were still quantities of English about, looking as weatherbeaten as ever. The hotels, neo-renaissance dinosaurs, seemed even to have taken on a new lease of life: that pretty colour-scheme of cream, pale grey and the characteristic Basque indian-red looked fresh and smart; and the icecream Casino incapable of anything naughtier than dear-old-boule. The Russian Church far from moribund, ready for baptisms as well as funerals, and the Avenue de l'Impératrice had still a sneakingly raffish, rastaquouère look beneath heavy suburban respectability.

Some of the monstrous mansions had gone, replaced by horrid little condominium 'residences' but climbing up the hill towards the lighthouse, the slide-area Santa Monica feeling was as strong as ever: the huge villas still and shuttered, the ghostly feel becoming creepy and downright sinister. Loony Tuscan, California Spanish, gothic Hatters-castle; Pickfair and Theda Bara.

Castang was giving happy rein to the imagination, for this is Chandler, RossMacDonald country. This sort of house is for indigent old ladies, about to be devoured by their famished borzois. Where there are signs of occupancy it can only be

140

phony shrinks, criminal astrologists, sects invented by Aleister Crowley.

One can come out here on the leafy, jolly, golfclubby side of Biarritz, of lawns and copper beeches and silver teasets, where the worst you will encounter are the 'hard-faced men who did well out of the war'; but there is another and more truly sinister Biarritz where the hollow trees, twisted and warped, are rotted to touchwood with still a green shoot, surreal survivor; where coarse cement, hideously rusticated to imitate bark, has crumbled to the rusted iron skeleton; where the very word 'Basque' becomes grim and cruel. What can 'Itxasgoita' mean? Castang was not at all convinced he wanted to know, even if the house next door was called 'Belle Rose' – those sawtooth railings, stylised wrought-iron sunbursts, reeked of violence and Aztec bloodshed. And the hispano-gothic of 'Prinkipo' (ex-King Zog, presumably), which looks like an unsuccessful sketch for Albi Cathedral, will be as piled within by heaps of skulls and bones as a Roman catacomb. And even on a sunny June day one does not forget the wind. Crouching bungalows named 'Sous le Vent', 'Au gré des vents' – who needs reminding?

Sometimes he went to the beach with the children, and was duly astonished by Vera's new glamour: some immoderate laughter too, vexing her slightly. Sometimes he went to swim, when it was calm enough for his crippled arm, surprising himself how much he could do with it and astonished too to find Lydia, clumsy child, deft with a surfboard, and Vera's pallid body tanning like an apricot; hobbling ungainly in soft sand above the tidemark but in the water agile as a seal, so that he regained the long-dimmed memory of the young, swift gymnast. Nor, to feel sexy, was there any need to leer round the edge of parasols at young girls with naked breasts. 'Sticking out a foot,' said Vera austerely; 'must be all the shellfish you're eating.' But he was not wholehearted yet, complaining of the sea for moving about too much, critical of the children's nasty playmates. One must be grateful, he supposed, that it was not yet July: German children, while certainly badly-brought-up, still infinitely less offensive than the French who would shortly be piling in.

The restlessness of fatigue showed still in long solitary walks to Anglet – rather low, especially the racecourse end: too many twee little bungalows one and all called 'Chien Méchant'. And throughout the hinterland. Wild gardens full of rank grass and overgrown tamarisk, rambler roses gone woody in great loops like blackberries, hydrangea bushes the size of the ramshackle cottage behind, flaky cracked terraces with aloes in pots waving their arms in submarine menace pretending to be giant octopuses. Tame gardens swanky with camellia and magnolia, deodar and Monterrey pine, English gardens full of bumblebees and wallflowers and the inevitable rockery. Simple, pretty Basque houses and stucco-smeared monstrosities with great bulging wrought-iron grilles to help the Naughty Dogs defeat burglars intent upon stealing the garden swings, Hitashi barbecues and all the other pretentious claptrap. And whereabout in all this would Robert MacLeod be enjoying – what, an idyll? – with Mrs Bathurst?

Were they here at all? They had been here; Delaunay was a good witness. Would seeing him, and his hurt amazement at the snub, and the certainty that he would tell others, be sufficient to make them pull up sticks and whip over into Spain? No way of telling, and he had only Richard to rely upon; an unwilling and disbelieving Richard at that. After the first days of enjoying reunion and gossip and jokes, they had not seen much of him.

The little town is in itself conventional. It would be boring but for a touch of mild schizophrenia formed by the contrast between the little area in the centre pretending to be English and the larger Basque surround claiming ostensibly to be French. Neither are very convincing. The first is only a street or two of shops selling dubious antiques, copies of English furniture, blazers with crests on the breast pocket, expensive little games, and could just as well be in Dinard or Le Touquet. Whereas the natives, gathering in the Aguilera stadium to cheer on the rugby team (an attacking team, with a characteristic tearaway style), are French superficially, reluctantly. You will hear some Spanish spoken on the stret, but these are as likely to be tourists as the Parisiens. The tricolour flag, kept waving on the town hall or other fortresses of officialdom, has a defiant, futile look, as though aware that this is all a waste of time. Whether in the teashop, watching the bourgeois reading the *Herald Tribune* on the buttoned black leather seats, or in the stuffy, pastis-smelling little bar, one has more than usual the feeling of ignoring the other's existence.

There is a segment in between, and perhaps cleverly Robert MacLeod chose it as a meeting-place. Castang did not know, and almost certainly never would, how this had been brought about. Richard-in-retirement was a golfing anglophil bourgeois; this had always indeed been one of his favourite personae. Likewise, as a member in good standing of the French administrative establishment, he would know and to some extent frequent the educated class of people, of any nationality, who have intellectual pursuits, as bored by bridge-playing as by television-watching. It would be thereabouts that he was likeliest to have got wind of Robert. Certainly he would have nothing to do with the local band of police informers. But in retirement or out, he had always known how to keep open eyes and ears, and a discreet guard upon his tongue. He had dropped in last night at the 'cottage', accepted a cup of cocoa, admired Vera's nose now turning from red to brown, and given Castang the name of a bar as though he'd read it in the local paper.

This segment is the world of the demi-sels, and is to be found wedged into pockets of the twenty or so dingy, narrow side-streets which slope from the town centre to the harbour; the little fishing-village of the place's origins, straggling out to a rocky point midway between the two big beaches.

Demi-sel means half-salted; the midway grade of unpasteurised butter. Metaphorically, the generalised term of contempt for those who are too vain and lazy to do any work, too cowardly and incompetent to be real criminals. They haunt seaside towns in summer, with a vague idea of combining easy pickings with a free, prolonged holiday. In a place such as

Biarritz you might find fifty of these grubby, parasitic little nooks: bars whose barmen are all ponces, restaurants whose cooks have never been in a kitchen, waiters who have been walk-ons in some movie's crowd scene. There are little menus outside, and within – if you are an innocent tourist thinking to get a meal – you will end up with an amateurish copy of one or two of that year's modish dishes, after a delay while the 'cook' runs out to buy the raw material and the 'waiter' tries to sell you a bottle of plonk at a fantastic price. Come a bit earlier, looking perhaps for a cup of coffee or a beer, and the only customers are cronies, people just like themselves, come in because they have nothing better to do, sniggering together in their cheap, smart-shabby jargon. There is always a husky, bisexual young man in a beach shirt, with his newest acquisition, who mixes some part-time hairdressing assistance with a bit of prostitution.

It was clever of Robert because the police are not interested in this company – pathetic patchwork of petty trafficking and cheating, drug-passing and whoredom and much swaggering. The police shrugs and doesn't bother: a flabby balloon which if squashed at one point swells out at another.

Richard had said it at the start. 'Can't have any cops involved here.' Not, of course, the municipal police of Biarritz, a well-turned-out and smartly uniformed group of men preoccupied with parking infringements and keeping the beach clear of beercans. Nor, equally certainly, the regional service of PJ in Bayonne, Castang's cousins from the criminal brigade with, as in all casino towns, an eye on the gambling. Nor Security at Home, the DST, nor Security Abroad, which keeps changing its acronym but which is the same old *Rainbow Warrior* shoal of muddled shark and absentminded codfish.

The ones who count, in this instance, will be Commissaire Morosini's cousins of the RG, rather thick on the ground about here. Fortunately for Robert, they are obsessed with the Basque Independence Front, and the franquist terror squads who make war on same. They have an eye out too for fishers in these troubled waters, as it might be Corsicans, or Libyans, or naughty IRA men. Not to speak of the Peculiar Persians, disjointed and wildeyed young men in need of a shave, and persuaded that a holy war is a fine idea, by a mad-ayatollah back in Qom, whose turban could sorely do with a wash and an iron.

They aren't likely to take much interest in an eccentric Englishman, familiar figure everywhere, of literary tastes and negligent habit, speaking fluent conversational French in however homecounties an accent, with unmended shoes and driving a very tatty old Mercedes – this attracts no more attention in Biarritz than it would in Holland Park. It has, too, visible means of support: a journalist with a genuine press card, even doing nothing, is like a 'resting' actor. He may be making a fly-by-night living in soapflake commercials or porno films but he's a recognisable and harmless type.

As long, of course, as Commissaire Morosini hasn't made a big deal of it, with a lot of urgent argy-bargy on the telex. He might get around to that. Depends rather on whether there are any more unexplained bombs going off. Otherwise, the odds are on – say ten to one, reasonable – Monsieur Morosini leaving it till after the holidays. Very likely, he too thinks of his wife and family, and is looking forward to nice Sunny Days in Split.

And it has been clever too of Robert to pick a place less negligent than most, where the lavatories are likely to be clean and there is a good chance of a cold beer.

For this is a gay haunt, quite a smart little bar-restaurant freshly painted, in a nice scheme of basque-red, that lovely rust colour, and the pale greyish-pink you can find on the underside of a fresh mushroom. The waiter has gilt hair and minces, the cook (glimpsed) is an old butch with a beard like King Edward, but they are polite, smiling, clean, and the place smells nice. One should not underestimate Robert's skill, experience and immense charm.

Very English.

Perhaps yes, just recognisable from that old photo. He is in normal wise that much more aged and faded but still a tall, slim, even handsome figure in faded jeans, a madras shirt, old unpolished loafers, in need of a haircut; a knobbly shapeless set of features but alert amused eyes, limp hanging hair and a long lippy jaw.

Something about the way he moved . . . Robert had 'slipped in'; it was noiseless, unobtrusive. But not in the least furtive, no hurried scuttle. The carriage of the body was assured, the face calm. Castang was lucky enough to think of a joke.

"There ought," he said, "to be a zither player. Little touch of Harry Lime." Robert's laugh, free and full of sheer enjoyment, was Englishly loud, so that the waiter scurried out from behind his screen in alarm changing to a delighted beam at a nice couple so plainly contented.

"We'll get on well," holding out a frank hand. "I was a little nervous. PJ – it does have an ominous ring."

"They told you who I was?" That was like Richard. Always tell the truth where possible. "We vary widely. Like people."

"I don't remember Harry Lime in any detail. Except for that art of slipping in and out without being noticed. A crook though, wasn't he? Something black market?"

"Something unscrupulous." The waiter was sidling about looking for a drinks order. Whisky, they agreed upon. Some Canada Dry to take away the taste of bar whisky. Some ice to take away the taste of that, added Robert. Pleasant harmony of thought.

"So if I've understood, the Policía is breathing heavily, but you aren't."

"You've done nothing criminal that I know of as yet," agreed Castang, "but you see when we got rid of the dossier, way up there in the north, it got turned over to the Stapo, and it doesn't take long to say English journalist of dubious anteced-ents. So it might be as well to think about that. They've no evidence that I know of, but they're pally, one must remember, with people who've been known to fake evidence."

"You mean they come looking for illegal weapons, and lo, there's a big packet of cocaine in my suitcase and oh oh."

"Something like that."

"Cocaine fresh from the factory in Langley, Virginia."

"I'd say it was conceivable. Whatever happened to make you unpopular in British Guiana. Stirring natives into subversive action, mustn't let the niggers get uppity."

"Janey, you've been detecting," said Robert with admiration.

"To finish with the clever enigmatic stuff, I know a nursing nun. She's a sensible, discreet woman. But candid, and of course innocent. I tricked her into becoming talkative. No names are on the file but inevitably, some of the facts are."

"Mr – Castang, isn't it? Cheers, by the way, and the drinks are on me. I appreciate this very much; it's not just a kindly thought – it's really generous. Is it low and dirty-minded of me to think it alarmingly generous? I haven't met many PJ people since I used to read Maigret at school. But I can't see you coming all this way just on account of disliking fascists."

"Give me a minute to think," said Castang.

Perhaps the Harry Lime gag was not stupid after all. He had been a friendly crook, of great charm. And a cold-blooded vicious bastard.

"Why did you trust me?" he asked abruptly.

"I took a gamble." Brilliant blue-eyed smile.

"This is a good place for a mousetrap. I could have two large cops staked out in the gentlemen's lavatory, waiting for you to go for a piss. Car in the street, nobody would notice a thing, the two ladybirds there wouldn't utter a peep."

"The message I got," said Robert in a quiet voice, "mentioned a woman's name."

"Two things are true. One is that I haven't had a holiday in two years and I'm pretty tired, and nothing I want more than to sit idle on the beach and look at the pretty surf. The other truth is that I crossed the whole of France for a chance to meet this woman."

"Why did you feel so sure of finding her here?"

"Helped purely by luck, there. You see, I'd more or less made up my mind not to look. I couldn't see her pinching a diplomatic courier's briefcase." Robert's shoulders shaking at this, with genuine laughter. "But I know a fellow on the railways. Long-distance controller whose schedules bring him this way. Did you hear about a scare a few weeks back – the Basques had a bomb on the line or something – that was his train. When he saw her he knew her. I'll tell you something else funny: he loved her."

Robert's turn for silence.

"Everybody loves her. Including me . . . How did you get on to me, by the way?"

"Journalists' gossip led me to a man in Paris called Hamilton." Robert nodded. "And he gave me an introduction to your father."

"My father!" An exclamation that came out as a shout and had the waiter popping out. Castang ordered two more drinks and wondered why Robert should shout at the name.

"I liked old Erskine very much. He gave me a bed for the night and a marvellous dinner. He's very loyal towards you."

"I know," said Robert, with lines showing on his face. "But Ichabod, O'man, there's no going back to things like that. Quotation from the classics, pay no attention."

A further silence.

"So in return for the kindly warning, you want the woman, is that it? Friendly bargain? Exactly what are you proposing? You've got me in a hole, here. You may not have cops in the shithouse but there aren't many roads out of this dump, and gendarmerie on all of them."

"If you trusted me this far why not go a little way further? I promise no interference. No force and no blackmail. I want only to see her and speak with her. I'll give you any guarantee you want."

"She's very shy," said Robert heavily. "Not criminal-shy, not Harry-Lime-shy. Wild animal shy. She'd never agree to anything squalid like this. The most that would be possible would be something formal, out in the open, with me there. Like a lunch? Not perhaps the Café de Paris; too grand and pompous."

"Too expensive!"

"Langley money paying," with his irresistible flicker of humour. "But a country place suit you better?"

"No. I want to see her without you."

"No way and go blow your fucking whistle. You think you're so tough and it's your poxing gun. I walk out of here you've only one way to stop me."

"Keep your voice down, you silly prick. I don't have a gun, I never wear one. Even on holiday. You're a romantic, Robert, and it's a grave flaw. You get into these silly situations out of attitudinising. Piss on the Bogart stuff. Be like Peter Lorre the stinking coward, it's safer. Round up the usual suspects," in his Major Strasser voice. Robert could also laugh at himself.

"You see," said Castang, "I like your keeping faith with her. I've a proposition. Any morning, I can be on the beach. In my little bikini. Red and white striped umbrella. Two little girls, a woman with fair hair, walks with a bit of a limp. She's my wife. You can watch from the terrace of the Café de Paris. With your binoculars. Plenty of dirty old men, focussing on the tit-show. How's that for a deal?"

"And suppose you decide then that Oh, sorry, you were mistaken, there are after all grounds for arrest."

"Robert, stop being childish. What does she know, and what has she known? She decided, I think, that she would change her life. We all want that, but do we have the resolution to do it? But don't go swimmy-sentimental like Ernest Hemingway; spare me the schoolboy talk about liberty being one's own thing.

"I'll give you three days. If she doesn't show I'll assume you've Harry-Lime'd it off to nowhere. See? I'm like the children; keep my eyes tight shut and count to a hundred; give you time to hide."

"Have another of these, shall we? For the road?"

"Hard road," said Castang, "all that soft sand."

149

10

"I am comfortable," said Vera happily.

A silly remark? she asks herself. Comfort is not that important to her. She does not seek it to the exclusion of all else: just as well, because she does not often enjoy it. But sometimes . . . 'Dear Fanny is back,' said Lady Bertram. 'Now at last I shall be comfortable.' Jane is a favourite writer of hers, and on the whole she likes *Mansfield Park* best. The word 'comfort' recurs in it oddly often. Perhaps Jane was herself particularly uncomfortable at the time?

Comfort to her is not, as it would appear to many of these others, the disposal of one's idiot body: Brother Ass, supine upon a beach-mattress, in order to 'bake' – hardly, indeed, can she imagine a pursuit more futile and ignoble. She sits cross-legged; she's 'comfortable' that way . . .

Biarritz is a good choice for that unambitious performance. The climate is mild, rarely hot, and very changeable. It is often blowy, sharp, and perversely rainy at short notice, to the noisy rage of the children and her own secret delight. There are huge noble cloudscapes and racing, chasing, playful cloud-shadows. A place of much gaiety, and Vera thinks that the Empress Eugénie must have been basically a kind, if often silly, generous and 'comfortable' woman.

Henri goes nowhere without binoculars. A mercy he is not a camera addict (quite enough of a snoop without that). Birds he says he's looking at: mm, birds mostly with a thirtyfour inch bust, hopefully bared. Vera prefers to trust her own excellent eyesight. Which, enlivened and ennobled by her imagination, shows her women in long frilly frocks, with a lot of petticoat and bustles at the back which get blown about and ruffled (exactly like hens just after the cock has jumped them). They have small pretty parasols and shallow, saucy hats tilted forward; open sailor collars and soft cravats. Sometimes she sees Eugénie, not being conventionally languid (as though Spanish women did nothing but fan their silly selves) but a sweaty Eugénie, flushed from running and laughing. No Winterhalters here, but Boudins and Tissots. And Winslow Homer; she sees peasant girls from fishing villages in New England, sitting on cliffs and shading their eyes with an anxious and workworn hand; their hair knotted in the nape, their sleeves rolled to above the elbow, their forearms and ankles tanned, their toddling children tidy in clean white aprons (as her own, decidedly, are not!). There is nothing quite like the Cobb at Lyme, though one sees plenty of Louisa Musgraves screaming and threatening to tumble into willing hairy chests, but on the jetty leading to the rock whereon stands Biarritz's tediously pietistic Virgin, brave about getting her skirt wet, Vera would not be at all surprised to see the French Lieutenant's Woman.

And she loves to watch the springy boys surfing. Now that the water is warm enough for them to take off the black rubbery jerkins she draws lines on her sketchpad, brief patterns of wave and sharp little swordfish, tight patterns of abdominal muscle, stylised patterns of hand and wrist and elbow; a ripple in her own muscles, the acid, painful, sweet memory of a gymnast's jump, the lash of a trainer's sarcastic words, sharp as a whip on the calves of her legs: 'Keep those soppy thighs together' (if the body's turn is not fast enough the knees gape in compensation and the points go ticking off).

Now who comes here? A grenadier? A pot of beer? Not the French lieutenant's woman . . . Perhaps Fanny Price – was Fanny fair or dark? Does Jane ever bother saying? Anne Elliott is fair, surely, and so is Emma Woodhouse.

Not 'dressed for the beach' – why is the woman walking about like that, dog wondering where it buried the bone? But there's a sharp northwesterly breeze; the children have been told three times to put tops on – look at Lydia obstinately going back in the water, bright blue! Vera has her little cape on, Pyrenees wool, such a comfort! Hardy Henri has put his shirt on – what *is* that woman up to? In her forties. Long dark hair, pinned up and knotted in the neck, but not a Winslow Homer fisher-girl, though her sleeves are rolled up and her legs are bare. She is carrying her shoes, as though she wants to wade: not very clever, since the tide is high and the wind has kicked up steepish rollers.

The circling has attracted Henri's attention. And lo, he knows all about it, adopts a social air of extreme politeness.

"I'm Adrienne Sergent – have I got it right?"

"Yes and please sit down, I'm Henri Castang and this is my wife, Vera. I'm very pleased to meet you." The tortuous, sly old sod! One had known, of course, that there must be more in all this than met the eye. One couldn't think what, and there was little use in either asking or speculating. So now one had to swallow several grass-snakes all together without gulping; and smile sweetly . . . And in fact Henri has brought off a terrific coup: no wonder he too smiles so sweetly.

"Please!"

"But I don't like to intrude."

"But I asked you to intrude! Vera, you'll forgive me, I promised this lady I would respect her confidence, even with you." And Vera, burned up with curiosity, makes a gallant effort towards professional and personal loyalty.

"Please don't be embarrassed. I know you want to talk, so will you excuse me and I'll go swimming." It is pretty gallant since the last thing she wants is to swim and the police even have the orange flag out saying a bit perilous and you do so at your own risk. It'll ease with the ebb tide, they're telling anxious tourists: the Germans of course swim out boldly.

"Please, don't go. Least of all on my account. I have nothing to say I don't want heard." With everybody multiplying pretty-please Vera unwraps the thermos and makes a social offer of nice-hot-tea. Everyone accepts, save horrible Lydia who makes faces and goes Beuh! and Henri interposes swiftly with pennies for ice-cream, which was what the cow was after all along, but it will get rid of her for a quarter of an hour, little pitcher with the long ears.

The woman sits, wrapping her skirt in with commendable modesty and loses no time coming to the point.

"Mr Castang, please tell me the truth; we have to go away quickly, don't we?"

"It would be best, and safest. I'm sincerely sorry."

"I knew how it would be, I think. I've been frightened of this moment." She looked him in the face. "I've been frightened of you. But you'll tell Monsieur Delaunay I felt dreadful, avoiding him? With Ada's warm love?"

"Certainly. I wanted to see you, for uh, a piece of business. I'd like to know what to do about the birds."

"That's been worrying me. The place is mine, you know. Can I give it to them? They've always helped me. I don't owe any money."

"You can," struck by this simple way out. "Put it in writing, make it short and simple. Give it to me then – or make sure that I get it. You won't need any lawyers, then. One advantage of being a Commissaire of Police is that I can authenticate documents. A court," seeing that she had not understood, "will accept my word that you are you, and that you mean what you say."

"That is a very great weight off my mind," with the sun coming out from behind a large, black cloud.

"Then I have nothing else to worry you with. One or two details, since we're here. Annunziata – you know who I mean? – says she knows you a little."

"That bomb!" closing her eyes. "I used to know her, not very well. I envied her. She could do all the things I couldn't." Ada thought about this in silence.

"And Nelson Walter?" Castang prompted softly.

She smiled; she has a lovely smile, thought Vera.

"Then you know Nelson too. What should I say? He was in love with me a bit," with colour in her face.

"It doesn't surprise me."

"Perhaps I was, too. He trusted me. We weren't – I mean we

153

didn't – I admired him," getting out of the tangle as best she could. "He's – he was everything I'd been brought up to admire. I was a – an innocent child. Nelson has such perfect honesty. Candid? – is that a word? Honour, I don't quite know what honour means."

I do though, said Castang, silently.

"Courage which stops at nothing," abruptly. "I used to drink in – oh, hope, and strength, and determination from him. Good things to have. He's like the boys in the First War," she said, as if screwing herself to an admission. "In Flanders, where we lived. The ones who all got killed. Not like people now. Who are so devious, and have crooked minds. I used to say," laughing, "I should like to live in New Zealand! And Nelson used to laugh and say I wouldn't like it."

Vera's imagination, ever lurid, has thrown up another example. Captain Scott! He set out from New Zealand in nineteen hundred ten. To be the first to get to the South Pole. He would win. He was a Captain in the Royal Navy, and the Navy always wins. He was surrounded by the best people in the Empire, and the Empire always wins. He was a Briton, and Britons always win. Also they never never never; so unlike Czechs. To their immense and lasting surprise, this half-assed crowd of amateurs didn't win. A Norwegian called Amundsen, who being Norwegian understood dogteams as well as ice, he won.

They got their own back by all dying, heroically, stupidly, on the way back. A blizzard, and muddles over supplies. A relief team found them all the following spring, in their poor little igloo. Nicely preserved. One leaves them there. One makes a big cairn, with their skis set upright. One adds a rhetorical epitaph such as the splendid English language, pity the poor Czechs, is capable of. To strive. To seek. To find; and not to yield.

Good, Henri, who has understood something basically English. Bravo the Aquitainian bastard. He came home from England, that time, after studying the tomb of the Black Prince in Canterbury Cathedral. 'Odd. I'd always thought of the black prince as just another bandit, apart from being an upper-class super-shit.' And this half-Polish Jewess, she has ideas too above her station. Little Czech girl; keep quiet. She is fond, too, of telling Henri to remember another English quotation: 'blow your nose and avoid lechery'.

Castang could not see inside Vera's mind, where all this was going on. He could see innocence, not only in the technical, the police-sense. He wanted to find a kindly word, and stiff police jargon came out.

"I've no restrictions to place upon your movements. Or anything. I see that I can trust you. To stop Robert acting the bloody fool."

She got up. Made a sort of bow to Vera.

"Thank you for the tea. And let me apologise again for disturbing you and your family. For me and Robert thank you. Jews are always the same, never anything but a pest." And runs away, stumbling in the soft sand above high-water mark, hopping awkwardly when the ball of her bare foot met a sharp edge of broken shell.

"You're not going to take any official action, I hope?"

"Of course not: I'm on holiday."

"I suppose this was all that horrible old bastard Richard's doing."

"Very likely."

"Henri – where – is – Lydia?" A controlled voice still, and not a scream, but had him on his feet like the cut from a sjambok.

"You go up. I'll go down."

Walk don't run. Save the running until it's needed.

He was aware of his crippled elbow as never since the hour it had happened.

Professional instinct had sent Vera the short way towards the point, because she could not walk fast. He had the whole beach in front of him.

A little girl in a green swimsuit. With a surfboard. Maybe. A little girl with long brown hair – no – Vera had knotted it up.

155

What colour was her swim cap? She hated it, and was always tearing it off.

Direct vision. Peripheral vision. The swimmers at the edge of the water. The fewer swimmers tossing up and down further out. Surfers standing or crouching or having fallen off heaving, arms and chest on the board.

The sea in this much movement, things visible only in glimpses.

Professionalism, controlling panic, is there; but it has become remote and irrelevant. This is my blood, this is my child. He kept breaking into a run.

Lydia is a good swimmer. She knows that the board helps buoyancy and allows one to rest. She knows that if one is pulled too far out it is useless to thrash about.

I am thrashing about myself. And I am no child.

Further out, there are boats. There are also sail-planks. There are always people who disregard safety-warnings.

There is a police life-saver on this beach. There is a police post just the far side, with a Zodiac and a big powerful outboard motor.

This is far enough. Now go back, quartering the beach. She may not be in the sea at all.

Was it the green swimsuit? Or the other, with the big flowers? Why did I not observe, Christ?

Castang is trying to control his breathing.

Then he saw a sort of giant. Huge. Bronzed. Made bigger by the ridiculously tiny yellow satin slip. Bending over. And there is the little knot of morbid onlookers pushing and gawking, which Castang has always seen with cold loathing and now with colder fear. The giant waves his arms and pushes them back. There is a small body. Castang pushes his way towards it through great swells of ice-cold fog. The body is still.

It is stretched across the legs – very nice legs – of a nice young girl, with straight fair soaking-wet hair and very nice brown breasts. The things one notices . . . the little body is 'indecent', having lost the bottom of its bikini in the sea. The ridiculous, white, frog's buttocks are Lydia's. He has sometimes kissed, sometimes smacked them.

And as he bends down to it, it heaves. The girl arches her knees, to help, bringing the narrow little back higher than the head. It vomits seawater, coughs feebly. It manages to spit. The girl holds it firmly. It vomits again, all over her but she doesn't mind. Castang watches, impotent. The giant takes him very gently by the shoulders and says, "Not drunk – not drown," in approximate French. Castang gabbles something in Spanish, realising ten minutes later that he was attempting to speak German.

Then there is a large, square, navy-blue, professional presence in shorts and a jerkin with upon it the triangular insignia of the Republican Company of Security.

"Very good, Miss. That was smart work. She'll do. We'll whip her up to the post though, to make sure. Wrap her so that she doesn't take chill. Anybody an idea where the parents – ?" Castang stands on jelly legs.

"Me."

"You, eh?" Blue eyes and fierce brows stare neutrally at him but Castang knows that he is getting a big, direct, deserved bollocking. "You had better start," making a very stylised salute, "being bloody well ashamed of yourself."

"I have to find my wife," says Castang dully, but he turns to the girl. "Thank you," he says stupidly. Lydia has vomited seawater and breakfast over the pretty breasts.

"It washes off in the sea," she says with a nervous giggle. She looks at him then. "Are you French?"

"Yes."

"Then remember," pointing to the giant. "A German saved your child."

"Austrian," said the giant mechanically grinning.

"I' vergess' nicht," said Castang. 'Nie. May I know your name?"

"No no no no. Nichts, nada, rien, nothing."

"He means 'il n'y a pas de quoi'."

157

"Nothing it is not to me." He has still no idea what language – if any – he is speaking.

"You go look after your daughter," said the girl gently. His shame is showing and not only in stupidity.

He cannot find Vera.

He finds her at the police post. She stands immobile, holding her youngest child in a clenched grip. The nasty little twitch along her nose comes and goes whitely. The rest of her is stone.

The CRS lifeguard has found a doctor, who is sitting holding Lydia on her knee, laughing and joking with her; a young woman with a long Spanish face which looks up hard and professional at Castang.

"No great harm. Her eyes react well, her reflexes seem normal, her pulse is rapid, there's shock there but no brain damage I think, she probably wasn't unconscious more than a few seconds. Colour's coming back. Keep her warm, take her straight home, put her to bed. A hot drink if she wants it, if she sicks it up no harm but call your own doctor to take a look at her and if she shows any sign of abnormal behaviour take her straight to hospital. She'll do, I think. I'll just check her again," feeling her pulse. "Niña – look at me. Straight in the eye. Now follow my finger with your eyes. Left, right – good. You're okay, dolling," patting the child's cheek. "Narrow squeak," at Castang, rather stonily.

"Name and address," said the CRS man, filling out a form. "Learn your lesson. Bit of a chop on an ebb tide, some current, what d'you think we have the flag flying for? You think we haven't enough to do, with those fools out there on the stinking sail-planks? No thanks to me – go give your thanks to that German and his girl friend." He lifted Lydia up. "Can you walk, honey? Swallowed a lot of sand, didn't you? But you're all right. Keep the board for half flood and an easy sea, till you're more expert."

"I've lost it," said Lydia sadly. "It'll have been pinched."

"Anything left on the beach," said Castang outside, heavily, "gets pinched." Vera without speaking lifts her other hand. Firmly clutched are the two bags.

158

11

Painter, and subject, had had their share of difficulties. Monseigneur, in common with most active men, thought of the portrait as a piece of rather tiresome business. It was 'expected of him'; very well, he had submitted to the necessity, but it rapidly became irksome, and he had had to combat impatience and irritability. The dressing-up – a thing he rarely did and avoided where possible – was an irritation in itself. A modern bishop was in his eyes above all a business man, an administrative, executive, telephone and tape-recorder man. He worked a sixty-hour week, and would have found himself doing more, but for the absolute necessity of keeping hours of thought, of prayer, of meditation, of reading, of music (you couldn't do any of these while being painted). But without them you are no more than a vulgar materialist; they are indispensable. Sitting, at first a novelty and even a relaxation, became a mechanical chore. The old man was an amusing conversationalist, but what the dickens was taking him so long?

"The xerox machine I should be painting," grumbled old Marklake. The equation, never an easy one, of painting a spiritual authority, which he had seen as a challenge in the context of a modern world, was giving him trouble.

"These," pointing with a brush at the predecessors hanging in the gallery, "academic jiggery-pokery. Monseigneur withdrawn from the world, contemplating eternity in the shape of a work of pious devotion. Fakery."

Indeed, Monseigneur was ashamed of the job done on his immediate forerunner, an oily work of abject pietism, not even fit for the seminary's diningroom wall, there to edify the spirit while the flesh is mortified by stodgy food.

"Or *that*," with sarcastic emphasis (reverend gentleman known to Marklake as the Bank Manager in the Biretta).

"One or two are good. These we must equal or surpass. That painter has looked to some purpose at good pictures. Vermeer's *Geographer*." Monseigneur had his share of human vanity.

Then there was the dreadful moment when exactly like Vladimir de Pachmann in the middle of Chopin dynamics, a thick Polish accent said, "No no no no, begin again."

"We're losing time. You're losing money."

"Interest you want to calculate?"

Concentration was disturbed by the perpetual hovering of nuns of either sex and Monseigneur's deplorable habit of taking planes at no notice.

It had built up a considerable tension.

"I begin to understand," said Monseigneur.

"Henri Matisse said that to learn, you had better cut your tongue out. It would teach one to look."

But to keep his subject still, and interested, the old man does not obey the precept of this illustrious mentor. He is an Ancient Mariner.

The onset of hot weather, in the closing stages of the picture (Monseigneur has set himself severe norms of selfcontrol, but is tetchy, on account of the soutane) brought it about. The old man, in a check shirt, had rolled his sleeves up and the number showed, tattooed on the tough brown arm. The bishop's eye, an unusually luminous blue (this passage of the painting has been most successful, everyone agrees), rests upon the jagged blue numbers.

"Yes," said the old man tranquilly, "Auschwitz."

"The worst."

"No. Not the worst. There were others, where you were killed through work. I was a strong, a very strong boy. A tough, obstinate Polish boy. They could have killed me, at that game. At our camp, there was a policy of extermination, yes.

If you went through a certain gate, there was no coming back. The only exit was the chimney. But it was possible to avoid the gate."

"How did you do that?"

"In the train, I learned some things about painting. It was not easy, you understand, to survive the train. It took a great deal of effort, to learn how to breathe. One thought for a long time before deciding upon even a very small movement. This is important, in painting too. After the train, the camp was easier.

"Questions were put to one. What are you, what do you do? People answered, I am a carpenter, I am an electrician, and if they wanted such people, one was put aside. I said, 'I am a painter.' Aha, what kind of painter? A decadent, Jewish painter? A maker of cubistic toys? A surrealist? No, I said with arrogance, I draw. I am a draughtsman. I draw like Rembrandt himself. You understand, it was a good answer.

"Here, they said. Here is a piece of brown paper, a pencil. Draw, draw that chair. Let us see. They were pleased. 'Major,' said the SS lieutenant, 'we have an artist. We have use for such, I think. Culture must be maintained.' 'Send him to me,' said the major. This lieutenant you understand was a fool, a slapper of faces, a kicker of arses. The major had contempt for such savages. 'Draw,' he said. 'Draw anything.'

"I had looked, before my arrest, at much Chinese painting. For instance, Chu Ta, a seventeenth-century painter from the very highest period. He was called the Dumb Man, because long before Matisse he had learned to be silent and to look. I had thought much about him, in the train. The Single Line, le Trait Unique. Much thought, much preparation, and then a line. Of a rapidity and fluency unsurpassed. I had not much time. I thought quickly, I drew bamboos. They are very important, and highly symbolic, in Chinese painting: just in one aspect, because they are hollow at the centre they symbolise humility.

"The major was a cultured man. I want this man put aside, he ordered. I do not want him hit or kicked. I want him given the materials he asks for. This place, he said to me, is anus mundi, the world's asshole, and you are going to change that.

Oui, mon Commandant. Chu Ta had moments of insanity. I thought, I will not become insane.

"It was of course necessary to have a protector. Himmler knew this well. We all agree, he said, that it is necessary to get rid of them, and every single man comes to me with exceptions, they've all got their own good decent Jew.

"I did his portrait. Indeed I did many portraits. I painted for him like Titian. And I filled the camp with Chinese classical subjects. Rocks. Birds. Flowers. One learned living as one learned drawing. I wonder, sometimes, what became of those many pieces of paper.

"My major was a ruin. His fear of being sent into Russia had made of him a hollow man, and I was the only person who could give him back joy, hold out hope. He suffered much. He had been machinegunned, in the abdomen, in Norway. He knew he had not long to live. When as often he was ill, or sleeping, or absent, then I had to be very careful. There were many who were fiercely and we can say too murderously resentful: the camp teaches one also the value of words. A word is like a line. One must be careful with it. Think before using it.

"Take this word life. When the hyena lies in wait for the antelope about to give birth, devouring the baby before it has even struggled into existence, we shudder, but who fails to understand the idea of life? The hyena or ourselves? Helpless we ask – what are the purposes of God? This was a question a great many Jews asked themselves. There were those, in the villages of Poland, who held debates as to whether it could be lawful to resist or even struggle against a purpose of God made so manifestly clear to them.

"So in using this word murder, we also meet with theological subtleties. If we disinfect, and in so doing kill some millions of pathogenic bacteria, it is ridiculous to talk about murder. Nobody questions whether we thereby promote or deny the purposes of God. This was one common attitude.

"Equally, there was a peasant, you might say an agricultural viewpoint. Postulate that there are a great many rabbits. They

162

are destructive, of plants, of crops, of young trees. They proliferate. A decision is taken, at the Préfecture, that this is declared a disaster area. Every peasant is hereby ordered to make war upon rabbits. The sanitary authority will provide the equipment, the cans of cyanide, for a rapid, hygienic and really quite merciful destruction of rabbits.

"Furthermore an instruction is issued, signed by the Prefect, that any peasant so stupid, so lazy, so antisocial as to neglect these wise and necessary precautions will be himself treated as criminal and punished according. Hah?

"If, lastly, I catch the hyena at its horrible task, I put a bullet through it, no, and count myself virtuous as well as fortunate? Is it not a vile and ignoble being unworthy of living? Does it not look horrible, smell revolting, have utterly disgusting habits? Excellent work we are doing, with God and the Préfecture to help.

"Possibly, it has often been claimed, only Germans think like this. And of course Poles. Lithuanians. Ukrainians. Russians. Untermenschen all these folk. In England such things would not be possible."

"Until of course," remarked the bishop, "it was noticed that several hundred thousand Untermenschen had got crowded into the city of Dresden, affording an excellent opportunity for a highly hygienic rabbit hunt conducted with flamethrowers."

"Good, you are learning," said Marklake with playful sarcasm, "but did your theological studies include any history? You recall perhaps that in the fourteenth century the Black Death, plainly brought about and planned by Jews, achieved notable results? To take one small example, that the Jews of Basel and of Strasbourg were shut up in their synagogues and houses which were then set alight? Not of course only Jews. Crusades were directed at all non-believers. To be subhuman, it sufficed to be unbaptised. Poor Mr Churchill did not invent crusades, any more than poor Heinrich Himmler. Both had read some history. Either could readily have recalled Colonel Chivington of the United States Cavalry."

"I don't know him."

"It was a small and unimportant feature of the Crusade against Indians, dramatically known as the Sand Creek Massacre. A few hundred Cheyenne. The only interesting feature is that some simple-minded troopers enquired whether to spare the women and children. The gallant commander replied that they were to kill them all, since nits breed lice.

"We might notice, lastly, an amusing reversal of roles in the State of Israel these recent years, in which it is held that only a small segment of Fromme Jüden, pious Jews, will be allowed to escape judgment. Everyone else, including myself, is sub-human. Especially myself. It was very wrong of me to have come out of Auschwitz."

Monseigneur, nailed down in his chair, for once had not thought of moving.

"I must let you go," said the old man, cleaning his brushes.

"Is it finished?"

"I am a perfectionist," looking closely at the canvas. "It is finished but for one or two minor retouches. I am not quite happy with your nose."

"So one more? But then no more second thoughts? I will be free, then? I apologise, but I've given a lot more time, you know, than we had counted upon."

"You will then be free," bowing. "Do not apologise. It is for me. An old, silly man. An uncertain hand. A garrulous tongue. But it will be very short. An hour, at most."

"I do not mean to complain," said Monseigneur hastily. "Besides, I want to hear about Auschwitz."

"To hear about – " open-mouthed.

"I'm asking it as a favour."

"Well! I shall do my best. Half an hour. With magic-lantern slides. The old man will tap with a stick. Next, please."

"I have learned much, in our time together," said Monseigneur, "and I have still much to learn."

"We shall both do what we can," said Marklake scrubbing his palette.

* * *

"Yes . . . the nose just a fraction," rubbing his own, which was high-bridged, Roman. "That eyebrow is a scrap too heavy. And a hand. A little too much knuckle, but I must be careful with the ring." The bishop fiddled with it nervously; a nice dark amethyst, a Victorian seal-ring. "Tsk tsk, stillness! But to keep you from fidgeting I promised, yes, to tell about Auschwitz. It will be very short.

"So on the one side, there was the suppression of germs. Most hygienic and meticulous. All run by Jews, you understand, that was policy. Hairdressers. The collectors of clothes, of shoes, of teeth, of spectacles. Of money, of jewellery. This was the dividend of the factory, to be paid to shareholders. Most important and most scrupulously weighed and counted. A company of accountants and stocktakers.

"This had nothing to do with us. We did not go through the gate but we were concerned, because at any second a whim might send us through the gate, a possibility not to be neglected.

"On our side, a multitude of little tasks. Some pleasant, such as the mowing of grass and the care of flowers; others less so; but sometimes these were rewarded. Perhaps a little soup, a vegetable, even who knows a bit of sausage.

"Also there were hazards. Besides the SS officers there were others roaming about. Hyenas. At Treblinka there was one justly celebrated, though they exist everywhere – his speciality was kindness. He would walk about the whole day, his hands behind his back – like this, a strange bobbing walk. Smiling, and so kind.

"Silently he would come up behind you and tap you on the shoulder. 'My poor friend,' he would say in his gentle voice, 'you look tired. I fear you are ill. You need treatment. You must go to the hospital. They will care for you, there.'

"In the hospital was one doctor, a Jewish doctor. One treatment, an injection. You guess, perhaps, what was in the injection. Do not close your eyes, please. Yes, that was a hyena.

"I was fairly safe. For the most part, I was under the eye of my major, at work. But outside . . . Others there were, brutes.

There was a captain, who had a great wish that I should have broken fingers, perhaps, or an – oh, anything which might incapacitate. Because once you were unfit for your given task, you see, there would be no other task. A finger would point to the gate, and you would be on your way. There was also the separate establishment, for which the good Dr Mengele picked his Chosen-Ones.

"There were also guards, naturally, a further hazard for they varied widely. Some were lazy, others bribable. Some, vicious. It was hard to tell. One day, up a ladder. Next day – down a snake. It kept one alert.

"And one day, such a one hit me, with a spade. Here. On the shoulder. I was strong still, and healthy, for my major saw to it that I ate well: a potato, an egg, even. But I was badly hurt.

"How to conceal that? I could not work: I was down the snake. It is finished, I said. Notice, then, how accidents happen. My captain, who had been longing for such a thing to happen, had chosen the day before to go on pass. His replacement, a creep, thought to himself Oh, the major will notice. He will be angry that his artist has been sent to the hospital, and that can mean for myself the Russians, oh-oh. So he had a smart idea. Marklake, he said, here, I give you a chit. You go to the infirmary, and maybe they can fix you up, but it better be quick, because Monday the captain is back from pass, and nothing more then can I do. So it's up to you.

"This infirmary is not the hospital. This is an SS post next to the guardroom, for small injuries. Like a lot of things in this world it is not what it seems.

"I see the guard. 'What you want, you?' Very humble I show the chit. Lucky it is a good chit, my lieutenant is a highly correct type – a formfiller, a rubberstamper, so it is all right and he just say 'See the nurse.'"

Marklake was not forgetting his work, which was delicate, even minute, and had his full concentration. The bishop noticed that the power of these memories was such that in his speech, though still talking French, he became again the persona adopted at the time. With a guard a shambling, uncle-tomming sort of nigger slave. Grammar broke down to pidgin, and the Polish accent, always thick, became almost incomprehensible.

"Inside is an office, very clean and neat, desk with papers. I knock on the door beyond and there comes a girl. We did not often see women, you understand. A German woman, tall and straight and blonde hair, in her nurse's uniform, and she say also What you want – just neutral, neither nice nor nasty but like any nurse. 'You are hurt? Come in here then, and show me.'" His voice for the nurse was clear, speaking a correct high-German.

"I was ashamed. That was a funny feeling, I can tell you – to feel shame. Shame! – in the camp – where if they told you to, you went on your knees to shovel shit with your hands. In those striped rags I knew I smelt bad. An examination room, smelling of disinfectant and of ether, bench with a clean white sheet, and a clean white girl. Strange feeling.

"I could not move the arm. She went to cut the rags with scissors and then, 'No, I better not, that might get you into trouble.' When she saw the wound she goes, 'Ay ay ay.' Carefully she clean and disinfect. A good nurse, strong hands but gentle. And she look, and say, 'It is not broken; good. It is cut bad, and bruised worse but that is less bad.' I tell you, I was glad to have strong bones then. 'Anti-tetanus injection you have to have.' I was not frightened because I knew I could trust her. She bandage me up good, very firm and solid, but so as not to show, under the jacket, and she put painkiller tablets in a piece of paper and say, 'These you must hide. Only for when the pain gets bad.' So I told her. That I don't care for the pain, but I must move my hand, I must look normal, I must act like nothing happened. 'You must do your best,' she said. 'I will help you. You must come back, tomorrow if you can. I will give you a strong chit, for your officer; who is it?' When I said the major she looked relieved and said he will be all right but look out for the captain, stay out of his way, there I cannot help you. 'But first I give you some medicine.' She came with something in a glass and I swallow quick and you know? – it was cognac. My eyes went open. And she start to laugh. A letter then she wrote for me, that I am okay, fit to work, but must come back for treatment. And her stamp. Sign, Field Army Nursing Sister, Corporal rank, Schmidt."

"Was that her name?"

"No. But her name I don't tell." An oddly vivid little scene, thought the bishop. I can see the neat little office, smell ether.

"Go on."

"I showed it to the lieutenant. He was satisfied; he was covered. He get the major to make a still stronger chit. In case I meet the captain, maybe I am covered and maybe not. If the captain says You are no good, you are for the gate, paper won't help me. Maybe next day or the day after the major say Where is my Jew, the schwein will just laugh and say Why worry, there are plenty more. So all next day, the schwein back from pass, I am dodging about, waiting that he go for lunch. Because the girl tells me to come in the morning. After that, there is another girl on duty, and she perhaps say Get out, I treat no Jews here, go to the camp hospital. And that . . ."

"But was there no doctor?"

Marklake began to laugh.

"Oh yes, there was a doctor. This doctor got blown up in Russia, his nerve is shot, he is all the time drunk, but the general has said Ach, he's a good chap, cover up for him, find him some phony job where he can't do any harm, and here is where they send him. One guard got an appendicitis and the nurses say Mein gott, get an ambulance, get him out of here, we don't want our captain operating on him, likely kill the poor bugger."

"So you went back?"

"Yes. The lieutenant was a decent man, he helped me. He came back pretending he had forgotten something, and said 'Go now. He is in the officers' mess, he is drinking and telling stories about a girl he meet on pass, he is safe for an hour.'"

"Why'd he do you a good turn, d'you think? I'm glad to hear it but – "

"Hard to say. They were all, you know, in some sort of

trouble or disgrace, or why send them to this filthy place? That lieutenant had done something to put him on a shitlist, and the captain would have known what it was."

The old man was back to his normal voice. "The picture is finished. You want to see it?"

"Yes, of course." The painting had been covered between sittings with a cotton cloth to keep dust and insects off. Most of the bishop's helpers had stolen a peek at one time or another, and made comments he had mostly thought in poor taste. Why had he chosen never to look? Vanity? False pride, or false shame? Even a sort of superstition? Monseigneur had not felt himself on very firm ground here. "But I don't want to look just yet. I want to hear the rest of your story."

"I understand," said Marklake. "You wish to look while I am not here. You are embarrassed to tell me you are shocked and don't look like that at all. That I have made plastic surgery on your face. Come on, man – some courage!" Monseigneur got up and stretched himself deliberately, composing his features. He looked lengthily, avoiding comment, schooling himself.

"It is altogether remarkable. I shall wish to thank you properly, when I find the appropriate words. I am a little overwhelmed. Could we approach this subject this evening? – I wish to propose something, a small formal mark of my appreciation, of the honour done me. I should like you to come to dinner – and of course bring Madame."

"It's a deal," said Marklake courteously. He began his formal, ritual cleaning of palette and brushes.

"I leave it on the easel till properly dry," unnecessarily. "Paint handled this way, six months it will be before it is totally right. For the frame, I look in Paris – you can leave that to me." This failure of nerve, thought the bishop, is touching, human.

"But won't you finish the tale? Or do you prefer not to?"

"I prefer not to. I will, though."

"I had been wondering, whether perhaps you have a purpose, in telling me?"

"Yes . . . I think this is true."

"Like a drink?" Human himself, Monseigneur had thought of calling his closest colleagues to 'come have a look' on completion – but the moment is wrong.

"Yes. A drink I will take now. Give me please some cognac. Never I drink it without thinking." The two touched glasses.

"Splendid picture," said the bishop.

"It is not too bad. A good addition to your gallery. Twentieth-century Seigneur, but with a sense of history." He took small sips of the cognac, letting it expand in the broad cavities of his throat and nose.

"Yes," he said, for the third time, as though to himself. "This was September. Of nineteen fortyfour. The mood, among the German officers, was febrile. The failure to hold France, the Fortress Europe, was damaging. But there was much loud talk of the secret weapons, of the great coup the Führer was preparing. They talked in front of me, you understand, freely. Since I did not exist!

"My memory is inexact. A little later, I think, there was much optimism. In the West, the armies were blocked on the Rhine. A great battle in Holland destroyed and captured great numbers of paratroops – was this then? I can recall much exulting – jokes about a bad English general? Poor fellow, he has to have ten to one in men, twenty to one in material, before he feels brave. The bangbang American general, with the cowboy pistols – he should lend this Englishman a pistol, and send a journalist, a noisy bigmouth macho, to teach him to shoot it. I forget their names. It is all so long ago."

"I was a little boy," softly. "Right here."

"But it was in September that I went to the infirmary. She smiled at me. 'Let us be quick,' she said. 'This is a good time. They are all at the mess, drinking to some big victory.' I did not care about the big victory. I was alive. For a little longer. I was still strong, you understand, a strong boy. Getting weaker, but until that winter, we still had food. And she had saved my life. 'Lock the door,' she said. 'But suppose someone – ' 'No. I lock it when I take stock of dangerous drugs, supplies that

170

might be stolen. It is an official instruction.' She threw away the bandage. 'Good, it is healing. The inflammation is much lessened. We must keep it clean.' Some powder they had, to put in a wound. Sulfanomide? I am no longer sure. Some small strapping then she put on. I was alive. I was grateful. I was not alone. A sister I had, Schwester they are not called for nothing. I wished to be gallant, I kissed her.

"She laughed. 'I am glad that you are alive.' You know what she did then? She took off her clothes."

"I'm not quite sure," said the bishop a little stiffly, "that I understand."

"I don't expect you to," said Marklake coolly, helping himself to more cognac. "You are a man with a vow of chastity. These unchaste behaviours and fornications you are bound to frown upon, nicht?"

"I don't quite mean that. I don't understand the psychology of such a woman. That she should have a feminine instinct of mercy and human kindliness, I accept and praise God for, but this – she was after all an SS woman. To give her body to a Jew . . ."

"Psychology is all Quatsch," comfortably, relaxed from the drink. "Especially women's. If you were a painter you would know that. Any woman is four or five women."

"Possibly. I still find it hard to – "

"I offer you just two things, out of many more. She had much secret rage, and humiliation, to find herself in this most ignoble place. She had not seen that as her path. Many, you must understand, joined the SS with high ideals: by no means all were bad. Women do not find it as easy as men to deceive themselves.

"Also this victory. Was it hers? She had looked, I think, for other kinds of victory. I do not know. Perhaps she looked too for a victory over herself. And over Auschwitz. Not a place where many babies were born. Also a victory I think of life over death."

"She had a baby in Auschwitz?" stupefied.

"Piano, piano," smiling. "Count."

"May of 'fortyfive," doing sums in head.

"She could not have known this skilful timing," with an irony not lessened after so many years.

"But you mean – you had a love affair?"

"No indeed. How could that be possible? I saw her again once only, after many months. Let me think. Up to the winter – there was a wave of optimism. Talk of a great SS offensive in the East. Reaction from the conspiracy of the officers to kill Hitler; at last they were freed, purged, of traitors and faint-hearts. I can recall the major – drinking a lot – saying that this was how it had been in nineteen eighteen. But they would not make the same mistake twice. Now indeed they had to fight upon two fronts, as after 'seventeen they had not, but then they had not the SS either. Now they would know how to fight Jews and Bolsheviks. Many of those with easy office jobs were returned to fighting units. My sadist captain went. My poor stiff lieutenant went. At the end even the old major went.

"I remember him completely drunk. 'Filthy Jew Roosevelt – no no, you are my good Jew, Mark.' So he called me always. 'Saint Mark was also a Jew. Was he not a painter? Is there not a tradition he painted the Virgin? These are superstitions but who knows – I look after you, Mark. I see to it you do not go through the gate . . .' And you see me here," recklessly taking a third drink. "I survived all this."

"But her. She – what did she . . .?"

"At the end there was panic. Sauve qui peut. They will be here any day, you can hear the guns. Discipline vanished. She came to speak to me. I saw her – what, five minutes? She was big then, showing it. Nobody had bothered her. There had been jokes no doubt, that she had done her duty to the Fatherland; to have a baby was no disgrace. It was assumed no doubt that she had slept with officers. Who knows? Maybe she had. It was not for me to ask. When she showed me her belly and said 'This is yours', I did not and I do not doubt her. She said, 'We are all going to die. This I am going to save. By whatever means. Will you trust me? I am going. Now.'"

"Poor girl." Monseigneur felt ashamed of this banality even

172

as he uttered it, but it was out before he could stop it. "I wish I could have seen her."

"So you can." The old man stumped across the room to where he had left his jacket; an old man's jacket with many bulging pockets, stuffed with junk, and from the shoulder-holster pulled a worn sealskin wallet, the kind with as many pockets as the jacket, in which old men accumulate the balancesheets of their existence. "At no better than third hand. And poor at that."

From its bowels he produced a plastic sleeve such as is used to protect photographs. The photograph was worn, and fading. Of a picture.

"The picture was not, naturally, made at the time. A memory only. The picture itself is gone. Destroyed." He did not say how, and the bishop did not ask. "So that is all there is. And quite soon, that will be gone too."

The young woman represented wore the same blue overall as Vermeer's girl who reads the letter, but she had no letter, and there the resemblance ended. She was drawn in large planes of simple colour, like a Modigliani; a handsome girl free-standing, with her feet in sensible black shoes and large kindly hands resting on her stomach: her head a little on one side; a questioning, one would almost say a humorous expression, of serenity, of acceptance.

"And that, thus, is also my Robert. Whom I cannot paint, since I have never seen."

"But how do you know then about – ?"

"No, I never saw her again, nor heard from her. But she saw to it, as she promised, that the child . . . and to a man, a kindly man whom she met and learned to trust, she confided one or two essential details." Monseigneur, himself remembering a detail or so confided to him, is feeling too his mind begin to – as it is conventionally called – reel.

"This man in his turn told Robert some things. Such as taking over responsibility from British military authorities for the sort of embarrassments they got stuck with now and again. Like a baby, in this case a male child with a label tied to its ankle saying 'Illegitimate German Wassermann negative'. As well as a kindly man he was both able and adroit. He had also good friends, as I guess, among senior officers of the occupying forces. The English are good at cutting red tape."

"But how d'you know even this much?"

"Oh, Robert has upon occasion written to me. Indeed I still hear from him. Obliquely. From time to time." Marklake is punishing the whisky bottle but that's the least of Monseigneur's worries. "In fact," the old man went on placidly, "I now come to the whole point of my telling you this tale, which to your ear must be sordid listening.

"You see, I know very little of Robert. As much as he has allowed me to know. That he is a complicated and divided personality. That he has talent. That very likely he is a criminal. Just a short time ago – and this story I am not telling, it is tortuous and full of ambiguity – Robert has somehow arranged that I come into possession of a large sum of money.

"For me this has been legal. I mean my possession of it is legal; this the bank tells and assures me. How, where, when, such a sum comes into Robert's hands I cannot tell, I better not ask. I could start something I cannot stop. Now why does Robert give me this? I do not know, I do not want to know, once more it is not good to ask.

"What can I do with this money? I have not earned it. I do not wish it. I should put it in a box maybe, in a locker of the Gare Saint-Lazare? Give it to some poor Jews? I cannot give it to the dead. Monuments they got already.

"One day then I listen to you. It is at the beginning of this picture. You are talking with Commissaire Castang, and there is an honest man who is worrying about some things which to him seem pretty funny, and I listen and I am not laughing either. Like about why does this fellow who has run away with a woman from this town, why does he sign my name? He is maybe drunk, yes, but how does he know my name? You are explaining to Castang about money, some is given, some is stolen, some goes straight and some goes crooked.

"I have painted you. I know more about you now than,

perhaps, you realise. I give you this money. You don't need to know where it comes from. Like for me, a legal title is all you need and this I and a very good Swiss bank we can make for you. You do as you like with it. I am thinking your sisters, the nurses, they got bombed and two got killed and their house was destroyed; some quite good repairs you can make there. I have reasons to be grateful to nurses who look after the poor for no reason but that they listen to their heart and that is as far as I go in matters of theology.

"So we make a little meeting with your Finanzdirector, what d'you call him, that fellow who has been coming in here every day to look over my shoulder at the picture and make intelligent comments I can do without while he is pouring himself a few big drinks. Like me."

Monseigneur is himself feeling the urgent pressing need for a large whisky. And he'd better be quick, before there is none left.

12

"My mind slipped several gears and made some very ugly noises before getting into drive," said the bishop. "But in the end I found it quite a simple story."

"They all are," said Castang. "It's only in these damn detective stories they're complicating matters with missing wills and lost heirs and the putative father who turns out on the last page not to be the real father after all but was meant to twist the reader with a final cunning reversal, oh how clever. But real life is very simple, except of course for the minds of the people involved and this is much too difficult for simple folk like you and me."

"Yes, I have been dealt a smart example of how little I know or understand about human life and human suffering. But tell me, I'm not troubling you with moral tales about my conscience: in the purely police sense can I accept this money, I mean without going to jail?"

"You can," said Castang, who has a letter from Robert in his pocket. But he's not proposing to show it to Monseigneur: it's been a long time since he went to confession.

Vera, maybe. But then she's a woman, apart from being his wife. And Monsieur Sabatier wouldn't want to know about it anyhow. He has said so. Commissaire Morosini of RG; but Castang has learned discretion.

"As I grow older," said Monseigneur, "I find myself less burdened by moral scruples." His fingers stretched and released an imaginary rubber band. "More elastic?"

"What we call elastic," croaked Castang, "the right wing denounces as culpable laxity."

A laugh.

"That's very true. We have a good deal in common. We are both in the service – functionaries, uniformed – of a state. Civitas Dei, or la République Française, it often comes to much the same thing."

"We had both a good deal to unlearn, perhaps, from early training. The rules that seemed so clear and simple at the outset, and which experience teaches to be dark, and full of pitfalls. Like a vow of celibacy. Not altogether a bad thing. A young inspector of police; he's out a lot at night, he risks his skin, he works long hours, he hasn't really got the time and energy for a wife. Which is why a lot of police marriages end in divorce. But as he gets older . . ."

"A good example. It's as you know the subject of much present debate in the Church. I'm not about to go into that. Some handle it better than others. It's never given me any very great problems. It can give marvellous results. Look at Annunziata. Can you imagine her married?" smiling.

"No," laughing.

"There you are. Of course, this fundamental innocence – separateness – makes her a poor judge of a good few basic human conditions. Poor Annunziata; she came to me, you know, in some distress of mind, because she'd had a long letter from the woman who went off with MacLeod. Mrs Sergent. She couldn't make head or tail of that because nothing in her training or experience fitted her to understand it."

"Did she now?" said Castang with assumed indifference. Everybody of a sudden writing letters! Monseigneur thought for a moment, said, "Perhaps there isn't any real rule of confidentiality that need apply here," thought another moment. "Perhaps you are best equipped to grasp this aspect of the matter . . . nothing I can do about it," he muttered, opening a drawer of his desk and passing Castang a thickish envelope.

"I'll be interested," blandly putting it in his pocket. If people did not write letters, my own existence would have been simplified. He did not share this thought with Monseigneur. I have a whole damned file of letters, and all they did was lead Morosini straight to my doorstep.

When one goes on holiday, there are two schools of thought. The first is that mail should not be forwarded. It's all electricity bills anyhow, and who wants that on holiday? And the second revolves around what the bishop might conceivably call a moral scruple. Vera fusses but he doesn't.

This had come to the office. And because it was marked 'Personal' Madame Metz had sent it on.

Thick paper of good quality. The engraved heading 'Erskine MacLeod' and 'Burwash, June' in a fine oldfashioned handwriting.

Dear Mr Castang,

As I learn, your sense of professional duties undertaken has not prevented you from exercising them with understanding, and tempering them with generosity. This accords well with such opinions as our slight acquaintance enabled me to form. I wish to express my gratitude.

The more heartfelt, since the enclosed is largely self-explanatory. I have decided, after some thought, to forward it to you uncensored and in the form in which I received it. It will shed light upon things said, and more that was left unsaid. It is right, I believe, that you should know the truth of both. This knowledge may fortify you in the belief that what you did was right.

If you wish, said Henri Matisse, to learn how to draw a tree, you must grow up with it. I would agree. But while I watched this tree growing, my own capacities for growth did not keep pace.

The sadness consequent upon this culpable blindness, for so I name it, the total opposition to primitive superstitions concerning 'heredity' – all too facile a means of escaping responsibility – is alleviated by the 'unprofessional' sensitivity you have brought to bear upon your subject.

I have answered Robert, as he requires to the Poste Restante in Biarritz, with such remnants of common sense and judgment as are left me. I mention this, since there is apparently a risk that he may not stay to claim it. In that case I should be yet further in your debt if you could use official powers to secure it.

Cordially yours

Yes. Unfortunately 'for all concerned', Mr Morosini's official powers had been the rapider. Still, and oddly enough, Castang had also got that letter. It had been lying about . . . And Mr Morosini had not been bothered about Castang's picking it up and putting it in his pocket. (Like the little girl in the song, A-tisket, a-tasket.) He had read it already and it had no further interest for him. So now it had joined Castang's file; an unofficial file, and one must devoutly hope, would never again see the light of day. Perhaps, finally, one might show it all to the bishop. Might make his moral screws that little bit looser. Or alternatively reinforce his idea that a vow of celibacy is no bad thing. Life's less complicated that way.

But to keep things in their due order: – the 'enclosure' . . .

Biarritz, June

Dear Father,

Probably you shouldn't answer this.

I should rephrase that, I think: I should not expect an answer. But you will make your own decisions, and I had better say that if you reply, then 'poste restante' here, but I have no certainty of getting it, because the police take an interest in my movements. I can tell the truth about this, for once: – I bear no guilt. But I cannot say I played no part. Technically, I should find it difficult to prove clean hands. I have friends on whom I can rely. The Pyrenees are crossable, as they were in your day. But this looks like goodbye.

Doubtless a police detective would notice that this was typed on an old portable Royal with the *e* out of alignment. The typing was neat and even professional, triple spaced with a wide margin. Perhaps, thought Castang, a good detective might reach the conclusion that this was the work of a journalist used to typing in hotel bedrooms, but the paper was a puzzle. Maybe it was a clue? Standard-size writing paper of standard quality, but the heading was printed:

Commissariat à l'Energie Atomique
Centre d'études nucléaires de Saclay
Service de physique nucléaire à haute énergie
B.P. No. 2 – 91 190 Gif-sur-Yvette
Tél.: 941–81–77

The good detective, panting like a bloodhound, might avoid drawing sinister conclusions about Espionage. He might say simply that a journalist, finding himself in a government office, pinched some government writingpaper, because you never know when it might come in handy. Or perhaps first he'd have to know Robert.

I am not going to dwell upon the past. No room left for selfpity; less for rancour. I am guilty of a foolish and hazardous action. This may have more serious consequences than the many such others, across the years.

Why did I always defeat you while defeating myself? And how I wonder now at your never-failing patience. Perhaps it could have been done: there is nothing genetically impossible about taking the child of a Polish Jew and an Aryan Berliner Mädchen, and bringing it up as English. The more since I inherited my mother's cast of features. A public-school-accent does the rest: has indeed operated stranger transformations. Your object was noble and your effort gallant. Perhaps, each tiny

180

mistake compounds, increases the initial error, the 'false deal'. English prep-schools take children from their parents too young. My view of the whole system is that held by Orwell, thirty years before. But it is all water under the bridge.

Hypothesis: if a half-Jewish man were to father a child upon a half-Jewish woman of obscure south-Slav origin (he won't; she's too old), what would that make the child? A good English citizen perhaps, with a passport properly registered by a British Consul in Argentina! Do you smile, at a typically back-handed introduction? Do, please! I found her running a Brussels boarding-house, under circs I won't trouble you with. A widow making ends meet. She has an astonishing capacity for love. Some similarity of background had an immediate effect upon me: a self-discovery? My own capacity for love had been neglected. I love you. But a woman? Never until now. So that I am determined to make good one real affair of love, as opposed to a few miserable love-affairs which were never better than blind, brutal and vulgarly egoist.

We have had some weeks here, of extreme happiness. I prolonged them, unwisely but understandably, to the point where we are now at risk.

About the near future, thus, the less said the better. It is possible that a few weeks further on, I might write more, since you would wish that, and so would I. A letter with descriptions – even with photos? 'Look, this is our farm in New Zealand . . . that is my wife, on the patio.' We had better, both of us, see it as a thin chance.

But whatever may happen, do not lose the belief that I am evermore your loving – and grateful

Robert

No detective work had been needed. Castang would have been delighted to get a picture-postcard of Perpignan railway-station, saying Having a wonderful time, regards to all the boys. But he had a letter of his own, and even without the heading (one could see the Atomic Energy Commissariat as a fairly typical Robert-joke), even without the same typewriter, the two had been written on the same morning, and they belonged together.

PERSONAL TO COMMISSAIRE CASTANG

I understand that it was my drunken fancy of signing my real father's name which put you on my track. Silly, if freudian, since otherwise I imagine your curiosity would not have been aroused.

As you have learned, caprice and impulse have too often ruled a regretted, a silly existence. I do not know where this will end. As it began, quite likely, on the turn of a coin.

Your generosity was unearned, unexpected: I am the more grateful. I am acting, as soon as I can swing it, upon your recommendations. I must see to it that the evasion must compromise nobody.

A prayer thus – two prayers, though they're one and the same. Please let Ada go unhindered. She knows nothing of evil, and owes nothing to anyone.

And please do not pester the old man. I know little of him, but his innocence is intact. This might be the reason why he is a good painter (and you, I believe, have understood that). Please see, also, that after surviving the death camps he has the right to remain free of police interference. I bitterly regret the irresponsible use of his name: blame me, not him.

About Ada – I see this as pretty uncomplicated. She has an incredible capacity for love, both giving and receiving. In her life she has not had sufficient outlet for either. She tells me that you have a lovely wife and magnificent children. Please think of how happy and how fortunate this makes you.

I will take my best pains to ensure that I cause you no

further trouble. For the trouble I give and have given you, my simple and humble apologies, deepfelt.

> Truly yours
> Robert MacLeod Marklake

Well, yes, Robert. Unlucky as ever – you were, genuinely, unlucky and it's not all juvenile selfpity – you come too late. All of us, always, come too late.

Castang put them back in the – there wasn't any file so he had taken a large business envelope and put them in that; keeping it in the drawers of his desk where he stowed personal belongings.

He better not keep it there, either. An office – any office – is always full of spies. The drawers had locks; not very good locks. Could one even feel sure of Madame Metz? No more than fairly sure: an accomplished snooper. He was not being paranoid in feeling even less sure of his senior inspectors. Paddy Campbell, old and hardened in sin and craft, was near his pension. A good cop? Yes – if such a thing exists. A highly competent cop. One does not get that far without knowing a good many secrets. A lot of one's own, and some acquired by ways not at all legal. The preserving of these, the keeping of them secret, means in some minds a suspicion of friends, colleagues and superiors; not to mention the Inspectorate. What better way is there to preserve one's own secrets than to know other people's?

Castang would not feel sure either (maybe still less sure) of the other senior inspector, Fabre; who was younger, more ambitious, and even more secretive, presenting a cold, still face to the world, and nobody ever knew what went on behind it.

Castang is not paranoid, and holds the view that the best way to protect oneself is to have nothing which needs protecting. If he has been in trouble in the past, as he quite often has, it has been through reckless overexposure. He has not the temperament for excessive prudence, nor discretion. But it's a fact: nobody reaches even middle level in a police hierarchy without having things to protect. There are envious people. They don't have to want your job. They don't even have to want to see someone else in your job. They're after power; often only a petty selfimportance and the malice which goes with mediocrity.

This is a case in point. He is not especially uneasy about Commissaire Morosini, who is in a different service (one devoted to collecting information of every sort concerning practically anyone), who has the same grade as his own – and is a scrupulous man, with a conscience. He is also secure, and Castang poses no threat to him. But there are colleagues of his own who might feel rather gleeful about evidence that the Commissaire has aided and comforted a fugitive from justice. You could build that up into quite a pretty little intrigue.

And of course – by definition – Divisional Sabatier has an ear planted in this office. And Castang knows who it is. He must get rid of these papers: they are better burned. They have no value . . .

Thinking twice, he took a sheet of plain paper, pushed away the typewriter, uncapped a fountain pen (pettishly rejecting several ballpoints and felt-tips which live in a jamjar) and sighed heavily.

'France, July the – ' (his calendar is from the Irish State Tourist Office, full of improbable views of Connemara in which it is never raining, which promotes a sense of unreality, perhaps an impudent evasion of reality, quite suitable to himself).

Dear Mr MacLeod,

I appreciated your gesture, which has been useful and valued. The letter is your property, and I am returning it with thanks. I add another, to myself, which I prefer that you should keep if you wish.

Officially, the matter is at an end. Unofficially, a little time to let the dust settle. If you are in touch, the dust is better unstirred. It has been for myself a sobering, I should hope a humbling experience.

Another document has come into my hands. I think it

right that you should see this, and if you should so wish keep it with the others.

Castang stopped. The letter was of no further value to Annunziata: she had given it freely to her superior, and Monseigneur in turn had learned all he could, or wished, from it before handing it on, which he had done freely. Yes, it could – and it should – go on to old MacLeod. Who could see from it that his hopes in his adopted son were not as futile as he had feared.

But he would read it again before slipping it into the envelope with the rest. Finish off first, quickly.

When you regain contact, I should be grateful if you would forward my kindly sentiments and assurance of friendship. Please tell the lady that everything she wished concerning the disposal of her property has been seen to.
Yours in all sincerity
Henri Castang

And he would post that himself, in the main postoffice, on his way home to lunch. Misuse of official stationery, Commissaire.

And before closing the envelope he reread Ada's letter.

Cheap scribbling-pad paper bought no doubt at the local newsagent together with a scratchy sixpenny ballpoint; poor tools for an important message. But strong bold handwriting. Loose and quick; he was no expert, and a graphologist might have interesting things to say of it. Intelligence certainly, firmness of character. And generosity. And that would do to be going on with. The education of any ordinary French child twenty years ago, meaning more attention to spelling than you'd get nowadays, as well as articulate.

Midi, June

Dear Annunziata,

Surprise? We've known each other a longish time but never really well. But to start with the essential I was

185

terribly shocked and horrified to hear about the bomb, bitterly unhappy at girls killed and wounded. I've said prayers. I'm thankful for lots of things and specially that you are all right. Selfish? But I've nobody to pour out to. Perhaps you won't understand my doing so to you – but too bad for me. I met a police officer who says he knows you (Commissaire, name of Castang) and this has started me off. We worked together a bit before you went off last time to S. Am, but I was never much use to you. I had my little hotel which my man left me and a living to earn and never found proper time & never told you how much I respected you (envy's a bad word). I hope that the time is coming when I'll be of more use. Zia dear (old joke) I don't think that you would be condemming me, I'm sleeping with a man which will make you frown, not so much wrong as the waste, you used to say, but it doesn't always work out, one can have certainties for years and then one day it dawns that one has been all wrong & just humbly have to start again from zero & try to do better. You can't answer this even if you wanted to because I'll be gone by next week (long complicated story). I just can't see we've done anything *wrong*. You'll probably say I've started wrong, sex is a trap and all the rest and this involves one in worse, and sorry but however hard I try to listen I can't take that, I'm giving everything the way I never have – certainly not to my poor husband dear though he was to me, and this giving is to me everything. I can't have a baby of course & alas but I have a man who relies utterly on me, who has had an unhappy misspent life & who is a good man but lonely & tormented. Sounds bad like he was a drink-of-water (one of your phrases) with no will or strength of character and this isn't true at all, he has an immense potential to good. So *please* don't think harshly, he had *nothing* to do with that horrible attack on you, he's utterly opposed to all violence, I couldn't bear it if you thought that.

I stopped because I got all silly & hysterical & you

wouldn't put up with that (imbecile women). I only wanted to say that he did do something wrong but wishing & trying for right. Really evil people looked for vengeance on him, and on you too! because they thought you helped him – that's all confused but he says you can untangle it for yourself. I asked him whether he minded my writing to you & he said please do because I owe her more than apologies. Now look Zia you always said that knowing is forgiveness, so now though I'm breaking confidence & giving away a lifetime secret I know you'll respect that. You just *have* to understand, this man was brought up as English and even highly posh, university & everything but was adopted as a baby by a man as kind and good as yourself who was there because a war correspondent. A prison camp in 1945 imagine that & he's half Jewish & the baby was begun in a deathcamp! Can you see what an awful thing, but the fact is love existed even there. I'm half Jewish myself: I never told anyone but I had it as a child from my father, he lost relatives in those terrible nazi camps so this will help you forgive me. Imagine now a child getting to know that (he never knew his mother died herself with malnutrition & bad winter in 1947 it was very cold & long, on top of neglected TB). Well he just can't endure all that fascism means, the women of Argentina the Mothers of the May Square and in Chile and Brazil and Paraguay but you yourself *know all this*. You are disciplined and trained but he never learned anything useful, years of drinking and acting the fool, but when I think of how sterile and stupid my own life was for years – so Zia all I ask is that you understand. Don't just say oh Sex, stupid & selfindulgent, because there are things you & I both never learned & remain ignorant about so do please keep your mind open & think of me without shutting the door. We're going to S. Am because that's where we're needed. love love love

    Ada, formerly Mme Sergent forgive

No comment, thought Castang licking the envelope, and if it isn't understood then as Ada says Tant Pis, for you, her, me, and the lamppost.

There's black-and-white salad at home; raw mushrooms, goody. The habit, thought Castang, of that detestable crowd the Dominican Order – great Condemners (a word Ada can't spell) of the Infidel. Powerful orators; theologians of great erudition, proving to you quite irrefutably that women were the cause and root of every evil. Heart-warming stuff.

13

The tumbledown shack with the suspect roof was exactly the sort of house, frequent in the French countryside and especially anywhere near the sea, that nobody wants to live in: whose only reason for existence is to be let to tourists at exorbitant rents. It was seven or eight kilometres outside the little town, on an obscure, winding country road.

Castang got hold of a doctor, with difficulty; explained, with rather more, how to get there; waited a long time, imagining a variety of horrors.

He appeared at last, a rather acid young man with a new and noisy Renault which he revved unnecessarily while turning in the lane, and voiced a complaint at how difficult the house was to find.

"Yes. Well. In here." But patient and gentle with the child.

"Uh. *Who* said she was all right?"

"Spanish woman on the beach."

"A doctor?" disbelievingly.

"I didn't dispute her claim," said Castang.

"Yes, well, the child is perfectly all right. Over five kilometres I have to add mileage for a house call."

Vera sat in the bleak livingroom with stains on the ceiling: rain did come through the roof.

"I want to go home."

"Come. That's perhaps not fair on the children, they're having a wonderful time and we've ten good days yet."

"Vile house," said Vera bitterly. Indeed it was typical of the local cleverjack who finds an awkward bit of terrain going cheap, throws a jerrybuilt bungalow on it getting cutrates from his connections in the local trade, sells it quick to a starry-eyed Parisien 'for investment', and is never seen again. The rooms were badly designed, leading awkwardly into one another under ceilings which were too low. The kitchen featured blackbeetles. The bathroom had a peculiar stink, attributable one hoped to damp. Vera sat upon the lavatory with the gravest misgivings. Most of us have known houses like this. There was a nice view of the sea, meaning the wind and rain of the Golfe de Gascogne. The terrace was shaded by a bent pine. Some very fine weeds grew through the cracks in the concrete. A long narrow strip of garden began overgrown and ended in scrub. Except when boiling-hot this house would always be chilly. Faded garden furniture stood about showing beerstains from previous revelry: the barbecue was a sticky graveyard of burned sausage. Holiday: Vera reading historical fiction on the beach learns that Indians have a Holi Day. They strapped on a great wooden penis and flung red dye about: she doesn't think she would have enjoyed this much.

Lydia stirred and muttered in her sleep.

"Chevillé, pas collé." Castang's lip twists recognising the allusion. Wishing to move a rickety-looking whatnot to a more auspicious position, Vera had fussed at his brutal methods, fearful she said of the thing's falling to pieces.

"Dowelled, not glued, you Czech asshole," had said an irritable Castang, and the children, tickled, used the phrase on one another. He felt better. Lydia, sitting up, said,

"Need to do pipi," and when she came back, "Want to go to the beach."

"No question," said Vera, austere.

"Good, we all feel a lot more like ourselves. I have a suggestion," he said, "which is to go down to the village, buy some entertaining food, come back here and make a big fire to cook it. Why don't you phone Judith and ask if they will come over and help eat it?" Lydia dances; oh yes please: I want to go down to the village.

"You're a tiresome young woman and you gave us a fright. You stay here and collect firewood."

190

"They'll come," said Vera returning. "Were just looking forward to a boring evening."

Castang, more relieved than he wished to show, bought a lot of extravagant goodies. Having spent more than he intended – a male commonplace – he was standing with his trolley in the supermarket, gazing into space and sternly repressing the equally commonplace urge to steal something, known to the French as winning-a-little-back, and the main reason why supermarkets are so dear, when he felt a gentle tap upon his shoulder and started guiltily. Lucky for him he hadn't any contraband because just behind his shoulder was the dark, round face, perpetually smiling, of Commissaire Morosini from Renseignements Généraux. He felt he'd had enough frights for one day.

"Hallo, Castang. Planning a party? 'm I invited?" Whimsical.

"You gave me a fright." Pointing to the trolley, "I was just wishing I had a shopping bag with a false bottom and you come jumping me like a security man, please follow me quietly to the manager's office. Think though, hundred francs for a bottle of pastis, that's ten thousand anciens. Pauvre France." Talking too much. But gain time, asshole. He was aware that Commissaire Morosini was also thinking he talked too much. "On holiday too?"

"Not quite as much as I could wish," joining the queue for the checkout.

Castang did not know Morosini well but recognised a method akin to his own. The man's hands were empty. He wasn't going to make a pretence of coming in here to pick up a packet of razorblades. There were two conclusions. He had come in here specifically to let himself be seen, meaning to convey a warning. He had come in here because it is a tactful, discreet place for doing so. He could have had a plainclothes gorilla lounging outside. Standing perhaps – it is a technique he has himself used – idle on the pavement, one negligent foot on the bumper of Castang's car, absentmindedly rocking the suspension. He had chosen not to bully.

He assembles – quickly because the checkout girl is already

191

pushing his parcels down the slide while the fingers of her other hand twinkle expensively upon her keyboard – what he knows about this man. He is young; thirtytwo or three. That is indeed young for an officer of the same rank as his own but Morosini had come out of school top of his class, gone into 'RG' after a spell at the PJ service in Versailles. Fast, but a reputation for straight. Has opinions, publicly and strongly held, of extreme conservatism, way over on the right wing, but has never been known to persecute Arabs. Given name is Dominique. Is said to be a good colleague, considerate and fair-minded. This is all Castang knows. He goes Wow at the total on the printout, pushes his credit card at the girl's impassive hand, tumbles all the rubbish into a cardboard box and makes his mind up. Do not try to be cunning with someone a lot more cunning than you are.

"Want to ride with me in the car?" unlocking the back to heave the box in.

"If you invite me," politely.

"I'm only going home. Up the hill a way."

"I know where it is."

"I thought of a quiet evening," starting the motor. "On the terrace if as I hope there's a pretty sunset."

"Nothing's nicer than that," with unexpected warmth. Castang tried to remember whether he was married, decided he didn't know.

"One doesn't get much family life," steering out of the maze of one-way streets, "and we had a nasty shock this morning. Little girl surfing in water too rough for her and I blame myself for not paying proper attention. She had a narrow squeak. Big German boy caught her. I've never been so grateful to Germans," changing gear.

"It's a banal thing to say, but one can't often dismiss trouble from the mind. Has a way of appearing when you least expect it."

"One tries to create a distraction – a sort of antidote. She's all right now but I promised something nice for supper and

192

invited an old friend. Ex chief of mine now retired around here, but I don't suppose you ever knew old Richard, did you?"

"No, but I've heard of him. He left a good reputation I believe, as a straight cop, and skilful."

"Deserved," turning into the country road. "He taught me a lot, I owe him a lot: it's a friendship I value."

"Not political, as I heard it, but wasn't he pretty adroit, as a young man, in getting clear of all the dirty work after the liberation?"

"Some of it was very dirty," agreed Castang. "Not just political backbiting but real knifing. There's always a certain amount of this. Comes from people too fond of power, and unscrupulous about getting it."

"Why beat about the bush? That's a simple diagnosis but I'd go along with it."

"Here we are," driving through the rusty gate. "Come and have a drink and meet my wife."

"I don't drink, but I'll be happy to, for just a minute."

The children were running to and fro building the fire. Lydia's voice came through the window saying "Czech asshole" to her sister. Vera appeared, smudged and dirty, was introduced. Mr Morosini was courteous, said something nice about the children.

"Have you yourself?" she asked.

"One little boy. He's seven."

"I hope you'll excuse me," Vera knows when to be tactful, "so I can change into a clean frock."

"Don't let me get in your way, Madame."

"Henri, you haven't given our guest a drink."

"Would it be a trouble to ask for a glass of milk? Water will do."

"None at all. There's plenty of milk. Do sit down, even though the chairs in this house . . ." Morosini watched her slight limp going away, turned to Castang and asked, "Polio?" softly.

"A bad fall, traumatic paraplegia. One never quite gets shot of it."

"I understand. I wish I knew you better. Here's to that," drinking milk. Castang, who'd be drinking enough later, was having the same. "I have this artificial sort of existence," Morosini went on, "like those tiresome spy books. You know? – lots of clever talk. A great deal of knowing information negligently let fall, about the sort of passes the Cabinet Office uses, the private habits of the Israeli Secret Service, to show how familiar the chap is with the corridors of power." Castang, who sometimes reads these in bed, nodded grinning. "Fearfully knowing too about the right brands of cigars and champagne, or where to buy the best clothes. Very thing-minded . . . They're boring these books. I mean that there is never anything in them about real human beings. The people in them refuse obstinately to come to life. Back to Graham Greene," unexpectedly disclosing likings.

"We don't make literary criticism," boomed Castang in a fairish imitation of a famous phrase of General de Gaulle's. Morosini smiled.

"And we don't make literature. We try if we're any good to think about what human beings do. They love, for instance. On account of this they sometimes do very silly things, which are hard to understand, but become easier if one accepts quite simple facts."

"I'm only a PJ man, but I agree warmly."

"I thought as much. Clever books, clever people – stop thinking of being clever, take emotions into account . . . I'd like to meet Richard some time. Be interesting to hear about those bad years."

"He doesn't talk about it much. But stay on: he'll be here in an hour."

"No no, I've no wish to spoil your evening. Indeed I must be going now, with my thanks for your hospitality and my respects to your wife."

"I'll drive you back."

"No need," said Morosini smiling. He sauntered down the badly laid crazy pavement. The roof of a car gliding along showed just above the hedge.

Castang smiled too. Morosini stopped at the gate.

"Castang, I'd feel unhappy that a job I get given should interfere with your enjoying a holiday." These subtle uses of the subjunctive tense; that's very RG.

"We have to do the jobs we're saddled with," said Castang waving a cheery byebye.

"What was all that about?" asked Vera.

"Tipping me the black spot . . . no no, not that dreadful," seeing her consternation, grinning. "Generalised formula for keeping my nose clean, not engaging in politics, and so forth."

"But how . . .?"

"I don't know," sobered. "He must have got a line on Robert somehow; the silly ass has been making phonecalls or – how should I know how the RG gets news? Not so much the fact that's aback-taking as the speed. But just when one's expecting a stately progress through bureaucratic channels is sometimes the moment when – tough on Robert."

"Oh Henri – that poor woman on the beach this morning."

"Quite, but you know the notice on the railway-lines – 'One Train may conceal Another' – and that's a legitimate warning."

"But the least you can do is convey – "

"I already did. I told him my train had lurched to a standstill and that RG might be stuck in a shuntingyard somewhere but not to count on it."

"Still – "

"No. Morosini sees me down here, this is a small place, I'm legitimately on holiday, he may be no believer in coincidence but there's not much he can prove. If he knew exactly where they were he'd have gone straight in and there's an end of it. Chatting me up is to close a conceivable bolthole: I make no secret of having left-wing sympathies. But if I put a finger in his pie he'll chop my hand off. Those children are putting much too much wood – Don't make it so big," he bellowed through the window. And shot off to rake the bonfire down into embers.

Vera, left brushing her hair and wondering which frock to put on, was in two minds about more than this.

Adrien Richard was fond of her, treating her with a paternal affection she found touching in this childless man. But she had never stopped feeling rather frightened of him. It was anyhow silly to suppose for an instant he wouldn't say the same as Henri.

She told herself sternly that this was official business. Or at least, semi. She also told herself that she did not know Robert MacLeod. She had not set eyes, she could not care less; q.e.d.

Judith Richard, a strange and solitary woman, had as a child crossed the Pyrenees – going north – just a step ahead of General Franco's . . . that woman on the beach this morning . . . she herself did not find it easy to make friends. She too had crossed a frontier, as a silly young girl. Yes, and only Henri's sympathy had stopped the French police taking hold of her, turning her round and sending her straight back . . .

She was sitting here like a fool doing nothing. Richard and Judith could arrive any moment.

That woman on the beach – Ada – Vera had looked at her, listened to her, instead of keeping a proper eye on Lydia's capering about. Lydia had nearly drowned, and there had been a moment when Vera had felt like blaming the woman instead of herself.

Wasn't there some way? – the black spot . . . A phrase she had herself taught Henri. It came from *Treasure Island*. Even if he, even if it fell into Morosini's hands he could make nothing of it surely; the words yes, but not the sense, because a minor classic of Eng. Lit. was not reading matter for the French police. Whereas . . . there wasn't surely even today a single English schoolboy who could fail to understand this phrase . . .? Two monosyllables . . .

Vera zipped her frock in a hurry, ran to the telephone. Henri was busy building half-burned logs into a bed. She tore a leaf off the phone-message pad (ballpoint would leave a trace on the next sheet; vague memory of detective stories) and printed with her left hand.

YOU'VE BEEN TIPPED THE BLACK SPOT. HOUR OR TWO AT BEST.

She folded the little square of paper and put it in her pocket. No pocket – she put it in her bra, like a schoolgirl.

"Ho," boomed Richard's voice, jovial. Tatty trousers, an

old bush shirt, the retired English colonel to the life only no moustache, kissing her.

"I did try one but I shaved it off – a parody. My dear child, how tanned you are. This is Lydia? – heavens, how they shoot up. Henri dear boy, you're black as a nigger. Judith's made a cake, I warn you it's probably lead-heavy. I warn you too I've been fasting all day, if it's only sausage I'll go straight home. Duck, by god. A chinese duck. Ju, we're in luck."

"Duck!" as though she'd never seen one before. One of the nicest things about Judith was her simplicity.

"Take ages still because the children put too much – I've got honey, and ginger, and soya, I don't quite know – let's have lots to drink first."

"Leave this to me," said Richard, grandiose. "I've become an excellent cook. Need to, since Ju gets worse and worse. Some mustard, Henri, and lemon juice to mix this with. The skin must go dark," in commanding tones, "and of course crisp." It was exactly like the old days when he was teaching Fausta how to make scrambled eggs to eat at his desk at lunchtime. "Hitch it up a bit higher, dear boy, or it won't be done enough on the inside. Two ducks," with joyful gluttony. The dear-boy act must come from playing golf with colonels. "More ginger!"

"Yes, well, Lydia nearly drowned her bloody self so there's something to celebrate."

"Can't drink pink champagne with duck."

"No, that's for the girls."

"And behold!" producing super-Cahors from Judith's basket. "Properly bloody." The children were unwrapping cardboard boxes.

"Raided the salad counter," said Castang modestly.

"Crab," like a child undoing Christmas presents. "Cold ratatouille, goody. And behold!" An alufoil parcel from the basket.

"Whoopee, mullets." Let the children enjoy themselves, thought Vera drawing Judith into a corner. The two lonely women had always been friends, and hadn't seen one another 'properly'.

The men got a bit drunk and the duck nearly fell in the fire. They remained however cop.

"I don't suppose," said Castang, sweaty, "there's any chance of getting a word-of-warning to that ass Robert? A swarm of RG bees has descended upon Biarritz."

"No way. Assuming that wasps and other nasty creatures will be nervously a-buzz. Just recall, I've had one house burned under me: no wish for a second." There is no further argument. Castang has himself an unusually vivid souvenir of the time Richard's house burned down: it was there that his upper left arm was shot to pieces by a large-calibre pistol. These magnums make a hole the size of a football. Only the minutest deflection had stopped it being his chest, and then there'd have been nothing left between his head and the belly he was busy filling.

"I rather thought not. Does Saint Lawrence here need one more turn?"

"We'll take the wings off and let his ass grill a little longer."

"Sounds like the story of my life," said Castang.

Commissaire Morosini stopped with one hand on the garden gate. Before making up his mind whether to ring or cough, to attract the attention of what was presumably the lady of the house, he did a bit of observation. She had not noticed him, which made for a favourable position. The street mounted a round hump or hillock a little outside and above Biarritz, in a curve so that the desirable villa residences did not overlook one another. The house was not large, as such places go, but the garden was; admirably situated with sun all round and backed with a screen of trees. He had heard that she was an enthusiastic gardener, though right now she was only smoking a cigarette and studying a malignant-looking datura bush; a bony weather-beaten woman in a shirt and trousers, with a mop of frizzy grey

198

hair and an air of taking little interest in the world at large; meaning himself.

The house was a pleasant adaptation of local architecture to suburban villa style: walls clothed in wood, the roof-eaves projecting far out to shelter the balconies, in the Basque style. Four magnificent camellia trees: the roses were wonderful too. Morosini, who likes gardening, never finds any time, felt a pinch of envy.

The French dislike being invaded, a fact that horrifies neighbourly Americans and discourages the dropper-in. Garden gates do not open on a simple latch. It seemed unnecessary to ring so he coughed politely. Judith looked, and drifted across. She saw a stocky, bullet-headed young man with a round fleshy face, closecropped hair, a thin clever mouth tucked inside heavy, close-shaven jaws, peepy eyes, big flat ears. She knew who he was from Vera's description. It was early in the morning, but he looked like someone who got up early; solid, tenacious, and dangerous. She took her time and looked vague, which comes naturally to her. Judith likes being out early in the morning.

"Madame Richard, would it be? Commissaire Morosini of the Police."

"I know." He is disconcerted but not for long.

"Castang told you?' She nodded. "Then you'll forgive the intrusion this early. I was hoping for a word with Monsieur Richard."

Judith nodded again. "Hoping he'll tell you where to find Robert MacLeod." Again!

"Do you know where he is?" Perhaps it is her being Spanish, this directness: she has the accent.

"No," cleareyed. "But it's not a secret, is it, that you'd like to?"

"Perhaps Monsieur Richard will know."

"I doubt it. You can always ask. He's out at present. He shouldn't be long. Perhaps you'd like to come in and wait," undoing the gate latch.

This was true. Richard also likes to get up in the morning,

but not to potter in a dressing-gown: to go down to the village and do the marketing before there are a lot of people about.

"I'm admiring your garden."

"People do. It takes a lot of work. Thought. Study. Love. Do you know anything about love?" Thus touched like a fencer, for the third time, Morosini realises that he needs his wits about him.

"Not as much as I should like." He hasn't much over for observing – a nice livingroom, a lot of books, a lot of flowers, a lot of litter, and quite a lot of dust. Richard is not as meticulous as Castang about objects. Judith is even less enthusiastic about housekeeping than Vera. She has a woman in once a week, and cleans things when she thinks of it.

"Sit down, do. You'd like a cup of coffee? I'll get you one."

"That would be very kind." An English sort of cretonney sofa. The *Guardian Weekly* – Richard's antidote to *Telegraph*-reading golfers, and he likes to practise English.

"The thing about commissaires of police," giving him a cup of black coffee with no sugar in it, which as it happens he likes, "is that they will insist on reasoning. They don't trust emotions. But one never gets anywhere with reason." It is as well that his wits are collected: this woman's sudden lunges . . . In fact he is both amused and interested: he has a theological turn of mind.

"It is true that we rely overmuch, perhaps, upon reason. People are not very rational. But it's the thread of Ariadne."

"No wonder it breaks all the time." She took a cigarette, blew a plume of smoke, sat down. "People are forever telling me I smoke too much." She had seen his disapproving eye! He must sharpen up. "Atheist? Agnostic?" in a milk-or-sugar? tone.

"I believe in God," said Morosini beginning to enjoy himself. "I am a Christian." She nodded as much as to say there were a lot of them about.

"God's a man, mm? Father Son and Holy Ghost."

"Prefer a woman, you mean?" If she were just a feminist . . .

"Don't see why it shouldn't be both. Lots of plants are. Wouldn't be any odder than a Virgin Birth. What about hell?" Mr Morosini thought about hell, which he did quite often.

"I'd say yes, I've seen too much of it to think the contrary. Doesn't have to be anyone in it though I've known a few who'd qualify – but I'm not there to judge. Only to collect information."

"It's quite normal that Satan should be easier to believe in than God. Have you ever been in the Jacobin church, in Toulouse?"

"I'd have to think. Is that the one with the double nave? Tomb of Saint Thomas Aquinas?" Two nods. "Then I think so, but only superficially."

"Rarely have I had such a sense of concentrated evil as there."

It was just beginning to be stimulating when he heard the car; characteristic garage-gate manoeuvres.

"I shall hope to know you better, Monsieur Morosini," said Judith politely, drifting out through the french window to the patio. He heard her calling in front of the house. "Darling, may I borrow your beautiful car? There's a man I want to see about caterpillars." He could not hear Richard's mumbled answer but the motor started again. He felt rather a fool; she'd left him high and dry. He stood up. But perhaps she had after all mentioned his presence. A tall thin man came in from the kitchen-direction, loose and comfortable, no way disconcerted at finding a stranger on his hearthrug. A bit of stoop from years of paperwork but an alert springy walk, an outdoor tan, thin silver hair, long expressive hands; casual oblique manner. Quite unsurprised, but after forty years in the PJ . . .

"Ah, Mr Morosini. The spycatcher." The word sounded insulting but not the tone, which was neutral. "M'wife been entertaining you, has she?"

"We've been talking theology."

"Yes, she generally does. You've had a cup of coffee, like another? Then you'll forgive me if I have one. Happy here or would you prefer to sit outside? You're after this chap Mac-Leod." She hadn't had time to tell him all this. Mr Morosini realised that this man was formidable too. But in a way he understood. "Make yourself comfortable," said Richard, throwing papers on the floor to give himself space to sit and cross his knees in an English way. "Let's get it clear. Castang's an ex-pupil of mine, and a personal friend: I found him a holiday place and was delighted to see him. He was interested in this fella. Got a line on him, tangentially: the subject came up because it sounded interesting, as a matter of character or behaviour. But you understand – I'm retired. In what way can I serve you?"

"Were you all that detached, perhaps?" When Richard did not answer, drinking coffee and looking around for a rather horrible-looking cigar, he was forced to unveil batteries. "You're an interesting man, Monsieur Richard. I've always wanted to meet you and I'm glad to have a pretext. You had an unusual career – a sort of history of the French police back to the Liberation. It makes you a figure with a particular kind of profile – there's hardly anybody left in public life like that. Monsieur Chaban-Delmas in Bordeaux, and who else, now?" Richard went on looking bland and indifferent.

"I'm not writing my memoirs, you know. Unprintable, yes, and boring too. The secret of retirement is to retire. This, as I need hardly tell you, is a nest of political activity. The two northern Basque provinces which happen to be part of La République, causing embarrassment to all concerned, but I came here simply to give my wife good gardening conditions and because there are three golfcourses giving me a healthy existence for a man my age.

"Understand me, Monsieur Morosini. I had a very nice house, with a garden twice this size to which my wife gave ten years of her life. One fine day through political and police manoeuvres, it was burned over my head. That day, I pulled the curtain down.

"Castang knows something about that. A crooked cop shot his arm kaput, so he has a little souvenir to carry about with him. For myself, make no mistake, I have no wish to find it happening a second time. Basques, be it the Iparretak or however they spell it, who would like to see an independent province with no allegiance to the Spanish crown or the

President of the Republic; the Gal who present themselves as a loyalist franquist movement preserving Spain – they none of them interest me a sou's worth, cher monsieur.

"Nor Robert MacLeod. I know rather less than you. My wife, as it turns out, likes the illogical, irrational sides of things. She was interested in this tale. Can't say," blowing his nose, "that I was."

Plenty of people have slithered about on Richard, scrabbling for a foothold. Mr Morosini drives in pitons with his little hammer, but finds the ice thick.

"So you have received no confidences from your friend Castang?"

"My dear colleague – and suppose I had? Should I have the good fortune to be taken into your confidence, you'd expect me not to blurt it out, wouldn't you? You said last night, as I understand, that you'd like to meet me. Here I am. You said you were interested in how I kept my feet in the years after the war. There's a simple answer to that – no blabbing."

"Monsieur Richard, I do have to tell you that I've some evidence pointing at a contact between your former colleague and a fugitive from justice."

"You're suggesting a dereliction of duty? Some collusion?"

"That would be serious, wouldn't it? You couldn't countenance such a thing."

"Man, I've known every kind of crooked or collaborating cop, some of them living today in an odour of sanctity, just like myself. Doesn't worry me for a second and never has. So don't talk to me please about the safety of the state."

"I wonder," said Mr Morosini gently, "whether perhaps I'm giving this problem the wrong emphasis. I find your attitude cynical, but with your long experience of politics that's understandable. As a guideline for human conduct, perhaps we should be taking a moral standpoint. I had the pleasure of a short conversation with your wife. I don't mind telling you that I'm a traditional moralist and make clearsighted distinctions between good and evil – you find me ridiculous?"

"Not in the least."

"I'm a practising Catholic and not ashamed of it."

"I have the greatest possible respect for you."

"This country's survival as an entity hangs on a thread, and the thread is belief. Political talk isn't going to change that. I like Castang. He's a good cop and I respect him as a colleague. But you know, that kind of left-wing liberalism which encourages anarchy through the destruction of moral principles is causing fearful damage."

"Is that what Castang's been doing?"

"Let's not be frivolous, Richard, nor sentimental. I have intercepted mail which gives me some idea what Robert MacLeod has been getting up to, and which is strong evidence that Castang had closed his eyes out of sympathy. I don't want him to get into trouble, because his motives are good, but a dangerous flirtation with materialist marxism . . ."

"Why are you telling me?"

"Your influence with him may be decisive."

"I influence no one."

"I'm not an extremist. I don't share the theses ascribing every misery to Arab immigration and Jewish finance, and suchlike catchpenny stuff, and I don't by any means approve of all the counter-insurgency tactics, but what I do see is the necessity for a crusade, and I hope that you're both man and patriot enough to back me."

It was said quietly, with dignity. Richard wonders, even now, whether his own silence conveys sympathy. Even shame? He can remember being a patriot. True, in the nineteen forties he had been very young. We can remember too the confidence; the security; the courage; the sense of honour . . . He remembers the companionship of simple folk, of Breton fishermen and Languedoc vineworkers. How they despised, while fearing, the intellectuals, the Parisiens, the dialectical-materialism boys. He remembers the young Belgian Benedictine monk who had left his monastery, humbly asking permission 'under obedience', and was told to follow the dictates of his conscience. Whose motto was 'Allègrement' – joyously; laughing: and who had led them into dangers they'd never have faced alone, after

204

giving them absolution, a blessing, and saying Mass for them wherever he could find a table. A Mass, then, according to the Ritual of Pius V, as it is now called. There wasn't then, any other. Never had been, never would be. 'You are put under the protection,' said Athanase in his Belgian accent, 'of the Star of the Sea. The Navarrese fight under the Sacred Heart but The Lady will see us right.' Every one of us with a Stella Maris medal round our neck. 'It won't keep off a bullet but the Lady bears the pain.'

He keeps his silence, but not without a struggle.

"Nothing to add, I'm afraid."

"So be it." Courteous. "I shall hope that when I lay hands upon Robert MacLeod nothing will come to light that might give you cause for regret." Richard sees him out, with a moment of wishing he had a medal to put round the man's neck. Comes back and relights his forgotten cigar.

14

Judith had driven the car (painstakingly, she is not a practised driver and people hoot at her from behind when she stops to give priority at intersections) down into the town and up the long sloping avenue to the area Castang calls 'Santa Monica'. There is no 'Venice' up here but Judith too is aware of the slide-area feeling. People had built these rich, confident houses, but how many of their children or grandchildren still lived there? A lot stand broodingly empty, with ghosts behind their barred windows sheeted and gibbering. Judith drives soberly. She is looking for a house called 'Folle Brise'. Vera, if she had been there, would have been translating – such is her habit – the phrase into other languages. 'Careless Breeze'? 'Wild Wind'? Since she likes poetry of a classic sort that she can understand, she might have come across 'Frolic Wind' – Zephyr with Aurora playing: Milton, is it?

There is no sign of Zephyr, nor Aurora; it was a still, grey day, hot and with the promise of thunder. But to tell the truth Judith was not looking for them, but for any sign which might indicate plainclothes policemen hanging about. She is not sure she would recognise them: she tells herself she is becoming an old woman. Her most vivid experiences of suchlike people date from the Civil War; even before Ray Chandler put Laurel Canyon Drive on the map . . .

Frolic Wind is in any case ludicrously ill-assorted: a heavy mansion of a suffused dark red colour. Good, it is pure California-Spanish in style, and certainly dates from very-early-Lillian-Gish: it has an immovable solidity. The doors and windows are strongly barred against housebreakers, squatters and hooligans. The stucco, the ironwork, the wood, are thick and of excellent quality; good careful building to the highest specification. Unobtrusively they have been kept in good shape and given the necessary paintwork. Judith does not notice any of this. What her eye is given to is the garden. Sand, she thinks. Pine, mostly pretty scrubby. Some raggedy palm, marram grass and tamarisk and – but from this far up the headland there is a pretty view of the sea and the lighthouse and both bays. Not a garden where one could grow anything really interesting.

This house had been a pretty good buy, picked up for a song in remarkable condition. There should have been a nineteen-thirty Bentley or Bugatti, a Hispano-Suiza, or even perhaps a Packard phaeton on the weedy gravel: they had liked their cars to be as flashy as their houses. It had appealed to something atavistic in the present owner, who had been attracted by the big billiardroom as a place to entertain one's friends and gamble to heart's content. A schoolfriend of Robert's; it is surprising how many rich Englishmen like to indulge this taste, popping over to Deauville for the race-meeting and the yearling sales. Biarritz, whose raffish Edwardian smack only exists in the imagination, appeals because handy for cards and claret. The big wrought-iron conservatory, behind the house and facing the sea, had somehow escaped having its glass broken by horrid boys: another inducement, for nowhere does a man look better in a dinnerjacket or a girl in a lowcut frock.

It is only of course for six weeks in the year, a houseparty between the yachting season and the vintage in Bordeaux. For the rest of the time the big problem is a caretaker. Robert's proposal to camp there for a few months had been accepted as casually as it was offered: until September – sure sure, old boy, keep the Frogs up to the mark is all I ask. And it was round the back at the servants' entrance that Judith got an answer to a ring, after trying the front in vain. Robert had been observing her for some minutes from a top bathroom window, wondering who this odd biddy could be before deciding that it could do no harm to satisfy curiosity.

"I was asked to deliver this," handing over the black spot.

207

Vera's bit of phone-pad folded small, like the sort of note schoolboys slip one another in class. Robert thanked her gravely.

"No answer, except a thank-you to the sender – if the occasion arises – and message received." Judith would rather like to have laid eyes on the mysterious Ada, but plainly she's not getting asked in and hasn't the cheek to try: says "You're welcome" humbly and whisks back down to the gate. Robert had run upstairs but could see nothing except that she had a car parked some way along the road and went straight to it without hanging about.

He prowled about a little, seeing that the house was in good shape and the fastenings sound; and glancing out now and then, for sign of any other hangers-about. Everything fine, he thought, and Luigi can see to things: Billy is an ass but has been generous and I've no wish to leave him dry or drop him in the shit. For himself he has no worries. This is a bit premature but was to be expected. They have been very comfortable here and he would like to have stayed on awhile, but the retreat is organised. He has Basque friends, both here and on the Spanish side, all expert border-crossers and policía-dodgers: he is in good standing with them and they value too an English journalist: they don't know that his credentials nowadays are unsound. A phonecall will do it, for if the house is still unmarked then neither is the phone. He wonders if he can risk the poste-restante to see if there's any mail. There's just Ada . . . and no worries there either.

The basement, rabbitwarren of passages and butlers' pantries, has been converted to a good comfortable staff flat and here they've been living. Robert looked about affectionately – how good she is at making anywhere a home. His typewriter stood on the table – like any journalist abroad he is used to being selfcontained: he can be ready in twenty minutes. And she hasn't much . . . He found her in the bathroom, characteristically leaving it spotless-neat behind her, kissed her neck and said, "The bell's rung." She turned and kissed him back, opening wide those enormous eyes. A plain woman, slim and light but visibly fortyish; nothing to look at but for those extraordinary eyes. You'd never notice her in the street.

"Already? Today?" She hugged him then. "I'm glad." Yes. She has been uncomplaining about his messing around here, this tedious and sentimental farewell to France which he has loved. But she has 'felt useless' as well as feeling the risk. Happy to be on her way to something she can do, and do well. Solemnly learning Spanish on the beach out of newspapers and a pocket dictionary and practising with him. There have been lovely still evenings listening to music – and dancing together sometimes on the smooth black-and-white marble of the conservatory. She loves to dance. "Can I have an hour?"

"Of course. The car will take that long at least. Just be ready when it comes. We want to slip out like going – say for a picnic." She was nervous, but had fear brought at once under control.

While Ada did her packing and his (hardly more than two shopping bags – 'only for the plane really, whatever we want will be cheaper the far side as well as easier') Robert knocked off a couple of notes on the typewriter – friendly word to Billy and leave it behind; compromise nobody and clear him of complicity.

And then zip, there was Bertrand in the Fiat which looks like any other but has a Lancia motor under its tatty hat. And Robert took the risk he knew to be a silly one, and Bertrand complained about it, but he did just want to see whether there were any letters.

The motor screamed. Bertrand gets away, easily, and with plenty in hand. This for three excellent reasons. He knows the traffic patterns better: Mr Morosini's driver was not a local man but had been brought down here with him. The Renault while gifted with a turbo engine had not as much power as the Lancia, which had been fitted by a mechanic as skilled as any the policía had. And Bertrand was ready, which the police driver wasn't.

Robert had got his letters, and was pleased he did; they were important to him. But the poste-restante, as one might have and had suspected, was tagged; a young man sidled up unobtrusive and said 'Mr MacLow' (to rhyme with cow, typically French), and before he could add the make-no-scandal-please everReady Robert gave him such an unmerciful knee in the balls. And there was only the one besides the driver.

Bertrand went on nagging like an old woman all the way up the hill.

"That was really stupid, Robert. Now I'll have to put you straight on the boat and you might be there hours and that's your tough luck; if it's very uncomfortable too bloody bad and if they search it you're a gone goose and nothing I can do. All right, I head up into the hills and they'll think we're going for a border crossing. But it's still a pest. I don't think they even saw the car but I can't take the risk of leaving it like this, it'll have to be resprayed and tarted about; won't do just to change the plates. You've compromised me, you know it?" Robert can't say much except Oh belt up, because it is useless to explain that he always does take unnecessary risks and always has and isn't about to stop now. Ada is shaking but rather enjoying herself.

"So now I'm running straight into Saint-Jean and going to dump you straight at the hut. Pierrot will put you on board. We've about a halfhour before they have the whole harbour area sealed off and your one hope is that it won't occur to them you could be there already. If it's hot that's too stinking bad, you'll just have to piss in the goddamn jamtin, you and the lady both. All this drama in the streets, tyres leaving rubber on the turns, stupid young man running after you – even if his ass is dragging on the deck, he's still waving a gun and screaming: we don't want that here, it's bad for our public relations and upsets the people, and even if there's plenty happy to see some RG boy kicked in the zizi, there's also a considerable schweinerei thinking of the notice that says Ten Thousand Francs reward, the motherfucking traitors – well I bloody hope you sweat."

There are ways of passing time, in the dark and a smell of fish. You regress into childhood, for example. Contented, Robert found himself eight years old, reliving a summer holiday. Burwash was used in those days as a country bolthole, a place of weekend escapes and short, magical passages outside time. Not much more than a cottage then but from the start a livingroom full of books and an attic where the boy read even after being sent to bed while the summer twilight dwindled into a candle. Erskine's books . . . an eclectic lot, and full of joys, going back to the turn of the century. Here one had read E. Nesbit, preferring *House of Arden* and *Harding's Luck* to the facetious coyness of the Bastable Family – and here he had read *The Scarlet Pimpernel*. He could feel the rubbed, faded scarlet cloth and a soft, coarseweave paper. Broad margins, a blunt, rather attractive typeface. Saving the aristos from the guillotine, nothing preposterous then! A yacht called the *Day Dream*. Was one a bit in love with Marguerite Blakeney? Did she too have to dress up as a fishwife? She didn't have to piss in a jamtin though. Heaving with silent giggles he felt Ada's hand reach out for his own.

It was a while later that a mouse whispered, "I hope we don't have to get on a plane. Everyone will notice the stink of fish." Later still being frightened by a light footstep, furtive and sinister, until recalling that the crisp, not to say heavy step of officialdom would be more sinister. The step recalled himself aprowl this morning (a world away) in the bedrooms of 'Folle Brise', linking thought-bubbles to a week ago reading an old English paperback in bed; a country house, the light footsteps at night of a burglar; taken by all to be those of a French duke, well-known seducer, so that such men as were still awake (Ada's gentle breathing told him she was asleep, confidence flooding him with happiness) muttered 'Only me, old boy, try next door', while the wives 'lay in a happy trance of desire murmuring such terms of encouragement as they knew in French': a piece of prose to make anyone grind envious teeth; a bit above Nancy Mitford's class and more probably Evelyn Waugh, characteristic mix of economy and insolence. Another silent giggle; in vain did Gaston Palewski (Robert remembered interviewing him in Rome) tell Mitford that 'real French dukes are not like that'. Palewski himself could never keep out of bed with any woman. The turn of Robert's hand to reach out to Ada's small confident paw.

The change in rhythm; a new buoyancy and a lurching pattern like dancing in heavy boots, which told him that the tide was turning, and soon after the growl of voices whose patois he could not follow; confident feet whose movements were those of chores done every day, in practised sync. with one another. A moment when the blood ran cold at the sharp bossy voice of unmistakable officialdom alongside and one metre from his ear. The relief of the sudden stink of diesel oil and the monstrous loose clatter of the motor next door outraging the eardrums, Ada's rigid fear gripping him as tightly as though she were in labour, and at last at last the heavy slap of watersoaked rope warps on the deck, the clatter idling down to a persistent soft thud, mingling with the thick chuckle and ripple of moving water, startlingly close to his skull; a drift of tobacco which cleared the sinus just as the combination of fish and diesel fumes induced nausea. A fishingboat running down the harbour of Saint Jean de Luz at twilight on the first of the ebb. But no freedom yet.

Commissaire Morosini was very distinctly vexed. (It will be tomorrow morning before patiently backtracking all the way detail by detail he will find the cross-reference to 'Folle Brise': twentyfour hours before he too will pick up the Nancy Mitford paperback, not 'left lying about' because Ada leaves nothing lying about, but at the head of Robert's bed, and will think *Love in a Cold Climate* a funny title, peculiar not -haha, containing some ironic resonance.) Mr Morosini did not show vexation in a raised voice or hasty movement; it wasn't his way. Nasty to his people though, some of whom had been acting like a crowd of constipated assholes. Nasty also to Castang.

"Very well, Castang. I have not had, and do not have, grounds for more than a strong desire to hear this fellow MacLeod explain in my presence how he comes to be friendly with the local independence groups. We'll go on then to the links and causalities that led to an explosives-outrage back where you and I started from. My desire is stronger than ever now that I learn he slipped my fingers an hour ago at the postoffice, and I have some strong pointers to his having made a run for it. Odd coincidence. Just as we had him gentled down and feeling comfortable in this honeymoon he's been having with that woman who interested you, he suddenly takes fright, in company with a friend who has a souped-up Fiat car, and whom my local colleagues have been anxious to interview for quite a few weeks. They are busy with the frontier between here and Roncesvalles, and they assure me that they've got everything bottled. I'm not at all convinced of that, since the degree of neighbourhood collusion is very high indeed, but I'm in the position of being parachuted here, and my colleagues on the spot aren't interested in my version of affairs, nor do they have any interest in nuns in Flanders. I intend to pursue one or two notions of my own."

"If you imagine that I carry disloyalty as far as tipping off Robert MacLeod when I know that you're wanting him, then say so and be done with it."

"I don't think so. I'd have trouble believing it. I'd have even trouble imagining it. I had a talk with your former colleague and chief, Monsieur Richard, who answers for you."

"I had a talk with him too," confident in a clear conscience, "and we agreed that Mr MacLeod would have to come clean as your witness, taking any lumps along the way. I've no interest beyond the sentimental curiosity I mentioned to you of knowing what bee bit that woman. As you know, Sabatier decided to switch the juice off – the PJ has no interest in pursuing the matter."

"I'd like you to tell me formally. Did you give any sign or warning to this MacLeod?"

"I have done nothing whatever," said Castang. It was the truth.

"I accept that. I'll put it flatly: pretty funny coincidence. I don't much believe in such; you don't object, I hope, to my co-opting you temporarily in the interests of justice."

"Since I'm on holiday I do object, strongly, but I put it aside in a collegial spirit. Since as I take it you're stuck."

"I'm stuck all round. I'm short of people here and I'm getting the big fart from the brethren. They're full of their Iparretak or whatever that private army's called. And they conduct their own vendettas; I'm the hair in their soup. If I don't pick up this pair in the coming hours I've a very thin chance of doing so at all. All right, you're on the team for the next turn of the clock, willing or unwilling, that's a matter of indifference to me. Sure, blackmail. Not a word you use of your colleagues." Smile if you can call it that: sour, and one-sided.

The police mind at work, thought Castang. Morosini had a small doubt about my involvement even if there was nothing he could prove. So when he catches up with Robert, which he is confident of doing, he wants me alongside so that the fellow can see my face, all welcoming smiles, gun under my jacket and the little notebook in my pocket. Robert might say something instructive, then.

Since he had done nothing to tip MacLeod off, who had? Not Richard, certainly. Morosini himself, no doubt. The sort of thing they teach at police school now. When you have pinned down a suspect – particularly if armed or holding hostages – if possible avoid surrounding the house with weaponry before kicking the door down, which is a wasteful and laborious business, and bad public relations. Hold off and see what you can find to 'destabilise' him. The classic little note saying 'Fly at once, all is known.' It is also typical RG thinking. Even if not much interested in the man himself, find out what you can about his friends.

As the morning went on Castang began to feel better. It wasn't going to be quite as easy as all that to walk up to MacLeod wreathed in merry beams, slap him on the back and say jovially 'You got shopped, laddy' and wait for his eye to swivel round to Castang . . . Either Robert was smarter – and luckier – than anyone thought, or he had some good, and efficient, friends.

Castang has been amused by the Swedish 'Martin Beck' books; recognising and knowing well the cop who is forever blowing his nose and the one who is forever in the lavatory. And the two lazy ones always sloping off for a cup of coffee. Witnessing the great telling off of the two unfortunates who had missed Robert at the postoffice he remembered their names – Kristiansen and Kvant. They get bawled out by a very tough inspector whose name he can't recall but who doesn't resemble Morosini. He fashions his bollocking in a quiet style – not unlike Richard's in similar circs.

"Do you realise that through your stupidity a golden opportunity has been let slip? That the description of the driver may correspond with a man needed for questioning, suspected for complicity in several bombing incidents?"

"Like what?" asked Castang when the headwashing was finished with and K & K were scooted off with the injunction to watch the shipping in Saint Jean harbour.

"The local people think it's a man called Bertrand Lama, well known but small fry; a courier. They believe he may lead them to something bigger if they could flag him for a minor infraction – pretext for holding him awhile and heating the pot. He's said to be quite an artist at frontier crossings . . . As you know, Castang," with the lemonjuice smile, "it's nice to have something to give the locals, when expecting them to take trouble on one's own behalf."

It is not certain, but it is at least possible that the bollocking of Kristiansen and Kvant may have been the episode which delayed surveillance-of-shipping.

"The neighbours want this fellow Lama. By overlooking charges against him they might turn him around," went on Morosini. Into an informer, Castang needs no telling. "They have no interest in Mac of course. He's headed into the hills, and they hope to booby-trap him up there. Nothing to do but wait: I – no, we – get the man and woman on a plate.

"However, an item on the computer has attracted my attention. We'll go and have some lunch," looking at his watch. "In Saint Jean. That'll make a better mobile headquarters than this dump. For reasons I'll explain to you," ushering Castang into the passenger seat of his car.

Saint Jean de Luz is the next little town southward along the coastline from Biarritz, a quarter of an hour away. Smaller, a different character. Lying on an estuary it has a fishing harbour with real boats, canneries and small industry. The boats fish the Golfe de Gascogne, in competition with the bigger ports along the northern coast of Spain, which leads to some acrimonious disputes about territorial waters.

Morosini said nothing in the car beyond, "You got a gun, Castang?"

"No. Never carry one unless I'm forced to."

"Just as well perhaps."

"You don't imagine MacLeod to be armed?" with sarcastic emphasis.

"No, I do not. His friend habitually is."

He knew his way about, leading the way to a restaurant in the old quarter of Saint Jean, under the shadow of a fortified Renaissance palazzo, formerly some governor's residence, now demoted, in Republican style, to a ridiculous amalgam of museum and town hall. Morosini explained all this over the grub. If watch has to be kept, Commissaires like to do so in comfort. A good lunch does the job in proper style. Sitting in the plain van, smoking too much and picking their noses while on the lookout for illegal activities, if need be for several hours – that is a job for Kristiansen and Kvant. And proper punishment for them to stew there with a horrible ham sandwich while their superiors are feasting.

"Now where's the name of this goddamn boat. Officially," dragging out a piece of torn-off computer printout, "number sevensixteen."

Sevensixteen, thinks Castang vaguely (just a little blurred by maïmu and plonk) that's a big number for a tiny place like this.

There can't be that many boats in Saint Jean, surely? He didn't say so, though.

"But nobody surely-to-god tries using a fishingboat to cross a frontier, do they?" is what he says. "Too obvious, no? Too slow, too easily isolated."

"That's oversimplifying, if you don't mind my saying so. These fishermen are a law to themselves, unruly crowd; there've been some ugly episodes with Spanish boats who don't give a damn about territorial waters and claim ancestral rights and liberties, don't take at all kindly to rules about quotas. Government had to slap a gunboat in down here to calm them down." Castang has a vague recollection of reading about it.

"But the Basques have their own solidarity. Laws and regulations, French, Spanish or Brussels, could go climb up their thumb. Terrorists, lord knows who, hitching a lift across. Every local force, gendarmerie or guardia civíl, came to an unwritten agreement to avoid perpetual hassles. They don't do it often because the risk's too great – massive fine and possible confiscation. Always one or two willing to try a bluff."

"Then why not raid the boat while it's still in harbour?"

"You off your nut? That's a strong union, sticks together no matter what. Send a couple of gendarmes there in the little Renault van – tipped into the harbour is where they'd find themselves pronto; van and all. Also it's indiscreet. I don't want to stir up a lot of dust; onlookers, press maybe, lot of stroppy fishermen arguing the toss. If I have a pinch, rather make it out in international water."

Castang, visited by recollections of his own, thinks that Mr Morosini is a landsman: but keeps his mouth shut.

"Time for a tour and see those clowns aren't sleeping. I've four men along there. I'll put your bill on the expense account, Castang," rubbing it in, "since you're here on business."

Reports were that among the moored boats, all was quiet.

"Won't go out till the tide turns," quite nautical. "Nothing definite out of Bayonne," after unsatisfactory conversations with his carphone. "We'll take a look up there in the hills. I don't like using these radio frequencies; however often they're changed they're never secure."

"You see?" two hours later. "Pinned down. Nobody could make a move till after dark and wouldn't dare then."

"Lay up for a day in a safe house – they must have a couple out here. Knowing you couldn't keep it running round the clock – an ear on the shortwave frequencies."

"No no," said Morosini, "these people wouldn't take that trouble for a fellow who isn't even one of their own. Must have paid over heavy money as it stands. Got 'm bottled, and out to sea they'll try and go. That's commencement of execution: under the flagrante ruling they're floored, run them in front of the tribunal tomorrow morning and nobody dare say boo."

And Castang had to admit, some helpful equipment laid on. Not of course a fishery-protection vessel; that belongs to the Navy. But a muscular twentytwo-metre civil-defence launch from the Gendarmerie Maritime out of Bayonne. This is a lifeboat really, used mostly for rescue work. Tourists *will* go out too far on rubber rafts, sail-planks, nonsense of every sort. The almost impossible enforcement of yachting regulations, a complicated tangle of inshore and offshore speed and power limits on outboard motors, children under sixteen in charge of waterscooters . . .

"In July–August," said the sergeant, "we could have fourteen cops where we've one, there'll still be mayhem, and as for the Mediterranean . . ." words failing him.

"Comes a moment when the whole of fucking-France thinks it's defending the America's Cup. Back before I was born, used to be one simple rule, saying steam gave way to sail 'n' port tack gave way to starboard. Now I've ten thousand yobboes like this was the Etoile at rush hour. Fall off a scooter, scream for a helicopter to come save them."

They slipped out past the little pier head, a discreet distance behind the wake of fishingboats. The water was calm, glassy even, with a little sucking swell. The late-afternoon air was hazy: distances were deceptive.

"Tja," said the sergeant, "be foggy further out. No strain," to forestall disquiet among the landsmen, "every navigational aid y'can think of," casual wave at the banked instruments.

15

Castang wasn't happy at all. No need to underline or put three exclamation marks or 'wistfully, he said', belching when the thing hit a bump. I want to be at home. I want to be abed mit Frau. If this goes on much longer, quite likely I'll throw up. People always do throw up in the Golfe de Gascogne, otherwise Baja de Viscaya, what's the difference, and why should I be an exception?

Nor have I any confidence in all these bleeding echosounders or whatever they're called now. (Castang's small-boat-naviga-tion has mostly consisted of D'you see the lighthouse? Not that one, asshole; the other one. Now ten degrees left d'you see the white stone? No! Primitive peoples coasted and how right they were.)

"Not a good sailor, Castang?" Morosini, being breezy. You wait!

He's done this before. Off the coast of Dorset. With the Royal Navy so-please-you. That was not a fiasco, just rather pathetic. This is, and I'm the more sure of it with every second that passes.

And when the fiasco appeared, after an interminable (and bumpy) prologue, it was beautifully sudden.

"We in international water?" snapped Morosini suddenly.

"Christ, yes." The sergeant's official grade is called a maréchal des logis, which sounds pretty landlocked. Italian carabinieri have the similar rank of maresciallo: what do the Spanish have? Being skipper next-to-God, he's a bit resentful of a Commissaire in the pissing RG. He's on my side, thought Castang.

"Well, close up on him then." They aren't in any cockpit. They're on the bridge, with a great big wraparound all-weather windscreen or sprayscreen or what's it called? The marshal levelled his impressive binoculars.

"Did you say a *three* letter group?" Not believing it.

"Seven sixteen."

"No such number." And yo ho ho, the computer has Fucked Up. And they're out of range of the police shortwave ashore. They've only their own maritime ship-to-shore wavelength, which isn't going to take at all gladly to a cocked-up computer query. It might be seven-six. Or seventyone. Or sixty-bloody-seven.

"Close up on him just the same."

"I'm not going to risk a bump, you know. This cockleshell might look solid, and it ain't." What the English, bless them, call the Tupperware Fleet. "I can lay alongside, no less than ten metres." We've two bloodybig Marine Volvos, but we watch our ass just the same.

"What's the man think he's doing?" bawls a hoarse jeering voice. "Danger to legal navigation." The marshal had throttled back the motors to keep pace with the thumping waddle of the fishingboat. A touch of port helm veered them a little closer. Castang eyed the evil water between the two boats and did not like what he saw.

"Make your number, port of origin," cried the marshal, close enough to need no loudhailer. The hairy villain opposite thought this funny.

"Oh. José. Lève-toi. Get out of bed, captain. Navy wants you." Leaning with two elbows on the ragged bulkhead he produced a bottle, drank from its neck, looked at it disbelievingly, shook it, and threw it overboard. A smaller, hairier figure appeared, this one with a knitted stocking cap. Scarlet, like the one Captain Cousteau is fond of. Well, had once been scarlet. Eyes the same colour.

"You piss off," said this one. "We got our license, we got our quota, go fall in it." The boat tripped on a swell, lurched: he steadied himself with both hands on the bulkhead.

"Jesus-gott," said Castang. The left hand lacked the two little fingers. The right hand lacked the forefinger.

221

Commissaire Morosini had decided it was time to show authority.

"Check your way," he bellowed.

"They won't, you know," muttered the marshal. "Nets down."

"You are suspected of harbouring fugitives." The two savages looked at each other, thumping the bulkhead in delight.

"You," said the big one, "are suspected of harbouring pederasts."

"I propose to board you."

"You do that." Stockingcap dived with surprising agility into the cabin (nobody seemed to be steering), reappeared clutching a shotgun. Rusty gaspipe thing no doubt, and no doubt too, full up with buckshot.

"You prepared to use force?" asked the marshal mildly, glancing forward at his two sailors, standing stolid behind the canopy. Castang knew them to be armed with riot guns as well as assault rifles. The marshal had a pistol in a polished holster. He and Morosini both had large revolvers. And that old sod opposite has fingers enough left to pull both triggers.

"Why the hell not?"

"We'd have to put the dinghy over. Those two clowns are both totally pissed and capable of anything. And it's the wrong boat. We've made a balls-up."

"Fuck it," said Morosini. "Disengage." With an obedient touch of reverse helm, the launch veered off to starboard. Cackles went up from the disgusting wreck left behind.

"Very likely," said the marshal, "those savages haven't a license, haven't a quota, and their nets aren't even the legal dimensions. But is one going to risk men and material finding out? As for your fugitives – given a big enough bribe, boat's in San Sebastian by this time."

Morosini controlled himself. He was even good company on the way home. The only further reference to Robert was "That MacLeod of yours must bear a charmed life."

True, the Renseignements, the Police Judiciaire and the maritime Gendarmerie had all been put to ignominious rout.

But it was not surprising. Robert had friends, as journalists generally do, in this awkward corner between France and Spain, where the Basque country lies on both sides of the frontier, in centuries-old disregard of diplomatic arrangements made by Cardinal Mazarin. It is a natural terrain for guerilla warfare.

"I grant," said Castang, "that a lot of little coincidences went his way."

"Rather too many," said Morosini, without sounding over-embittered about it.

And all that Vera said was, "Why do you smell so of fish?"

Nobody ever did find out whether Ada took a shower in the airport washroom, or even whether odd, discarded, fish-stained garments were later found in the dustbin. As any airport employee will tell you, the things passengers get up to in the washrooms you'd never believe anyhow, so don't think a little thing like that would ever attract notice.

Castang, studying the atlas – long after he got home – thought that a dozen airlines will shift you from Bilbao to Casablanca. Royal Air Maroc have a handy flight from there to Dakar. And that of course is the handiest staging post on the whole West Africa coast for the long hop across the South Atlantic. Robert is on familiar ground anywhere in Argentina. He will find a job there easily enough. Not exactly the penniless immigrant of folklore, castrating calves in Cordoba.

Nor would Ada-the-innocent find herself at a loss. A solid bedrock of common sense and ability: an excellent hotel manager. Any country club in Tigre province would think itself lucky to have her. Six weeks to learn that horrible Porteno Spanish and people would be saying that never had they been so well looked after, never had they felt so comfortable; they'd be eating out of her hand.

Commissaire Morosini? There's nothing one can do about a chap the Polizei is wishful-to-interview, once he's in someone else's jurisdiction. The most he'd do would be post a name and description, in case the fellow gets homesick and runs back to France. Not very likely where that pair is concerned. It has a priority a lot lower than the large band of fraudulent bankrupts all highly confident they'll never be extradited from Switzerland.

Castang can forget the whole thing. No more nuns got blown up, so that Divisional Commissaire Sabatier in Lille sleeps, as the French say, upon his two ears.

The bishop? He works away there in his library at laundering money. So does the Mafia. He is a soldier. There is a moment when he broods about the exact meaning of the word 'soldier'. So that he looks up the word in the dictionary called 'The Little Robert' and finds the etymology is from *solidus*, a small Latin coin. We are mercenaries. To be sure: we always were. He feels unaccountably reassured.

From time to time, his eye is caught by the picture hanging in the gallery: a great improvement on the predecessors, most of whom were painted by the gentleman immortalised by Anthony Powell: Horace Isbister RA.

Marklake, in Paris, grumbles at Gabrielle about the flowers going stale before he has finished painting them. She had bought in the market a bunch of the flowers known as 'gaillards'. They are damned difficult.

Now if he had consulted 'Le Petit Robert' he would have understood why. An old celtic word, *galia*, meaning force. In old French 'robust, of good health'. By extension 'jovial or gay'. In modern French a sexy connotation: earthy, racy, near the knuckle. A dirty joke but a good one, calling for a rough belly-laugh. It is not easy to get all this into just a flower-painting.

They are rural, rustic flowers. Their coarse, bright petals form a red-and-yellow wheel of fortune. They have a strong crude smell. They sit in a coarse, round-bellied, earthenware jug. There are some cherries, also some walnuts, lying about. Gabrielle looks at all this with something of a sniff on her face.

"Cherries and walnuts you are getting in the same season now?"

"You stupid woman!" says Marklake. "In paint you do."

* * *

224

Nelson Walter has been learning his responsibilities. His first field captaincy; that is not the same as being one of the fifteen field players.

Nor is it the summit. Perhaps he will reach this summit. He wants it and he wonders whether he fears it: certainly he has a distrust of it because then he would have to be the right-thing all the way through. Every tiny vein and capillary of his bloodstream impregnated with the Blackness, and he isn't convinced that this is the case; and neither are the high priests whose decision this will be.

The summit is when you lead the AllBlack team on to the field at Christchurch, South Island. This is not like Wellington; still less like his native city of Auckland. And that is the city on the neck of land which runs up to the Northland peninsula. Almost completely surrounded by sea and by islands. And there are people down in Christchurch who think it a sissy place. And who say too that Nelson Walter is a fine player, yes, but not right for a captain. Or not anyhow in Christchurch. Pressed, they would become vague in stating their reasons. Dreamy? – whatever that means. Thinks too much – he knows what that means. Sort of over-sensitive . . . aye-aye; Christchurch. The very name tells you what it's like.

Of course New Zealand is different to anywhere else. It is way out at the end of the world and nobody would ever have heard of it unless we Saw to It. And the heart of Seeing to it is in the tough spiny uplands of the South Island. Ask them in Auckland and they'll tell you that's Antarctica down there. There are jealousies yes, and pettinesses. But when it comes to being Black then we are bound by the one common purpose. Which is to show the world at large that it's smaller than New Zealand is. A formidable proposition, but we are a formidable people. We do it by being more bloodyminded than anyone else, most especially on the rugby field.

This is all causing Nelson some worry.

You couldn't get it expressed any simpler than in his present thoughts: the question may have become more complex in recent years but the basics are very simple indeed. The fore-bears came out from England and especially Scotland – a place of poverty and of deprivation. And decided that in their new country nobody, but ever, would again dictate to them. With them they brought religion, rugby, and agricultural skills on poor soil.

Religion, of an evangelical sort attested by the neogothic spires of Christchurch, may have decayed somewhat. Rugby hasn't: there's an argument for saying it has become religion.

AllBlack rugby is simple too: it just says Win. It has two other basic rules. Nobody pushes you off the ball; the whole team supports the ball-carrier. Given that we are big, fast, hardy, and Black, we do win. Anywhere. But especially in Christchurch. To lose there has been very, very rare; and if it happens the whole population goes into black, and the captain will never quite live it down.

Some of the Stone Faces think Nelson isn't quite good enough for the task. Physically he is right. Technically he is even very good. Heart yes, and bowels, but we aren't quite sure that the two are welded together as they ought to be. Perhaps it is the fault – like most other things in this world – of Europe, where Nelson spent a basic formative year at a tender age. Their attitude towards Europe is crude in the eyes of his generation. Europe is the origin of all that is deplorable, a place without ethics, and without bowels. It is admitted that we play a lot of rugby with these people: ergo it's no bad thing to see the boys seasoned there awhile. More reluctantly it is admitted that some intercourse is desirable with universities and the like (Don't really see why: perfectly good colleges right here in Hamilton!). This witchword Research . . . All this talk of modernising. Tja, or Tchaaa, we have a good big boy, some spring in his heels, all these damn computers won't teach him to jump any higher in the line-out. There are some who hold that Nelly Walter is the best number eight we've had since Murray Mexted, and maybe so, I don't see that Europe has given him a damn thing. If anything, the contrary. Women, probably. The stonefaces can go on a longish time about drink, but are a never-failing source when it comes to females.

A compromise was reached. We are sending a team on an Argentine tour. They aren't really First Division there – too Latin, huh? – all right for football . . . But tough and they've talent: Pumas are never a pushover. This is a chance for Nelson to prove himself, leading the sort of team we usually send: mostly young-uns, with a few veterans to give experience, seasoning, and add bowels (stonefaces are also inexhaustible on every aspect of bowels).

Today Nelson has captained an AllBlack team in a test-match. We won, yes. It was also a narrower squeak than we like. We were led at half-time. Those Pumas are clever as well as hard. The Chief Stone Face sitting by the touchline is forbidden by the rules to intervene, but it said all he ever says or wants to. Roll your sleeves up. All six and a half feet of sheepfarming pillar.

Young Walter rallied his team. Scored himself, made two more. Home by seventeen points to twelve, and he knows it may be thought not good enough. There is a second Test coming, and he will get a second chance. His mind has gone over and over the technicalities. He doesn't want to think of it any more. He is happy, at doing his job right. He feels regret, that it was not better done. A little sadness, that he does not want that job in Christchurch more than anything in the world. He shouldn't be having these mixed feelings. He shouldn't be having *any* feelings.

Face said nothing beyond "Clearer cut next time, all right?"

After an international match there is always a banquet. The host country lays on a mighty spread. How these boys do eat. And drink. There are speeches; every broad-bottomed plati-tude ever heard. Nelson felt profoundly unhappy until his turn had passed. He felt better then, because afterwards comes the singing. Anglo-Saxon legend is that these songs are of limitless obscenity. True insofar as rugby is a medical students' game, and a Hospitals Cup Final is stronger meat than an Ire-land–Wales. It will not be the same in France – or New

Zealand. Many of these boys are barely a generation away from hill farms where to see another human being makes an eventful day. When that bow-legged cannibal stands up, ludicrous in a hired dinnerjacket, he is again a Basque shepherd. It is just the same in Argentina. You will not hear about Eskimo Nell, but you will hear of Highland Mary. Here too – as in Russia – you may hear the songs of the peons, of those who have known serfdom and lifelong suffering.

By this time everyone is pretty drunk. Shirt buttons undone – big unaccustomed cigars. Little knots of two or three convivials begin to become sentimental about the shepherdess, *mi pastoretta perdida*, but Nelson is sitting by himself, drunk enough to feel the extreme lucidity, and the sadness: he is listening to the song of the little black horse.

Really they ought to be forbidden, the journalists; a greasy backslapping crowd, who have got in among the free drinks without doing anything to earn them.

But this one he has known in Europe, as well as in Auckland. Brussels correspondent for the *Herald* at a time when a familiar accent was a rarity, and a homesick Nelson had stood in need of comradeship. His appearance now was jarring, even hideous.

"Well, Nelson, you stood up for Auckland today." Yes . . .

But he's loyal, young Walter, to dreadful old pals known in the army. Polite boy, too.

"Sit down then," however rumpled, fattish, sweaty, and despite his having sat down uninvited. The table is full of half-empty bottles. This soft Argentine wine 'se laisse boire' – a phrase we both learned. What the hell is his name? Barry, yes, Barry. "What you been up to then, in this neck of the woods?" Talking like him too – one slips straight back in!

"Just the same," the neck of the bottle clinking on the glass, spilling, mopping with a napkin which has seen duty. "Like you, standing up for Auckland. Brussels or B.A., what's the odds. But I've been up-country, Tucuman way. In the north," helpful.

"What for?"

"Oh, politics . . ." Laying a finger alongside his nose. "You

228

know. The army, up there. Gets short-tempered at the liberal viewpoint, indignant at what they call revolutionary propaganda fed to the campesinos. That's a pretty backward part of the world, right? Like in northeastern Brazil. The colonels don't want to see any more Sandinistas in the driving seat, once was too many, right? I turned a piece in for the paper, you know the tune, Resolute in Defence of the Free World. But the thing I meant to tell you, I met a couple of types up there who said – or she said – they knew you."

"Uh?" We're getting a bit muzzy, here.

"I know the man a bit, as it happens. Brit type I've knocked up against betimes, in bars and such."

"Shouldn't have thought the army would be dead keen on Brit journalists; or am I wrong?"

"Not perhaps a lot," laughing over-heartily. "Passing, as they say in South Africa. A bit finger-on-lip, at seeing me.

"But this woman, lemme tell you, she's Belgian, or French. And hearing who I was, she brightened up, asked whether I knew you.

"To which I make the facetious answer; you being a Great Man, sure I do, and furthermore, you being on the tour here this winter, I'll be seeing you.

"Right, she says, laughing, give him a special message, say Ada sends her love, her special love. What you been getting up to then, hey?"

Nelson has taken some hard jolts today.

"Hey! Nelly? Boy, what you need is a drink."

"Barry, do me a favour? Like personal?"

"For the great man? Sure. Just ask." But he pulled a face, when he heard.

"That's not going to be too easy, Nelly. Like I said, people are sticky up there. You don't ring up the local ayuntamiento to ask if the local water's safe to drink."

"Too much to ask?"

"Not that. But it might take time, you know. And Bobby MacLeod – I wouldn't want to burn him, you understand?

Enquiries might shed an indiscreet light. He got into some trouble with the French, I heard, I don't want to add to it."

"It's the woman who interests me. We'll be going home soon. But you could send a telex, or whatever you do, back to the office in Auckland. Tell them it's for me."

"Sure, Nelly."

From then on the story reached Castang by indirect driblets. Not evidential.

Barry Waterfield was a good journalist, and he kept his promise. It had been a promise made while drunk, and this ought to absolve one from keeping it. Then he heard a rumour, and thought he ought to verify it. It cost him the best part of a bottle of Chivas finding out, and he was still a bit drunk composing his message, while wondering whether this was professional conscience or personal, and whether there was any difference.

YOU WON'T WANT TO PRINT THIS. PERSONAL TO NELSON WALTER. REPEAT, THIS ISN'T ON AFP NOR REUTER. TRUST-WORTHY EYEWITNESS REPORT STATES TWO EUROPEAN ADULTS OFFICIALLY UNKNOWN/UNIDENTIFIED, ARRESTED BY PRIVATE MILITIA, CHARGES DENIGRATION STATE POLICIES. QUOTE TRIED UNQUOTE TURKISH CRIMINAL CODE, CONDEMNED EXEMPLARY PUNISHMENT EDIFICATION LOCAL POPULACE, EXECUTED SAME AFTERNOON VILLAGE PLAZA. WITNESS IMPECCABLE NATURALLY REFUSES ATTRIBUTION SOURCE BUT SORRY NELSON NO DOUBT WHATEVER.

The editor read this. Of course there was no printing that: unattributable and unsupported. And would only make the readership in Hawke Bay turn that much smarter to the sports page.

Where they would read that after deliberation, the Selection Committee had decided not to name Nelson Walter to the captaincy for the forthcoming series of Tests against the touring British Isles team. It would be Wayne, instead.

Quite right, the populace was disturbed by this item of news. Some ill-feeling was expressed. Wayne was a good fullback, felt to be a little old, maybe getting a little slow: there was the usual muttering about the South Island Mafia. Questioned, Nelson Walter declined to comment.

Weather forecast is scattered showers.

And another three months later, Mr Waterfield got home, to his relief and wishing for a nice quiet assignment as Contest Editor or whatever, and saying Nelson owed him a bottle of Chivas.

He found Nelson quite willing to pay it. Mr Walter had been puzzled, over 'a quiet beer in a quiet bar' with the editor, at one or two details of the original message.

"What's this shit about the Turkish Code?"

"Sort of shorthand. When they hold people on phony political charges, and even fake up a trial. Happens to journalists too, in Afghanistan or wherever. That article really exists, and they use it. You know what it says? 'Dissemination of propaganda tending to weaken national sentiments shall be punishable by between five and ten years' deprivation of liberty.'"

Nelson, openmouthed, was shaking his head.

"You mean getting five years for – for telling a traffic cop he's an asshole."

"For saying your national newspaper printed bullshit," dry, "you'd certainly get ten."

"I just don't believe it."

"Time's not so far back, Nelson, you could have gone to jail for joining a union. Could have got lynched, come to that. Drenched in petrol and set alight, like your friends there. Or hung or castrated or beaten to death with a whip. Saying that a worker ought to possess basic rights is Communism, and that's unpatriotic. We've no time now for the lecture in political science. Just be grateful your name isn't Sacco or Vanzetti."

"All that woman ever did was love people."

"That's what we call guilt by association."

* * *

231

Mr Delaunay, an inspector on the French Railways, got a letter, and 'some time after' (Castang never did quite sort out his muddle at remembering that winter here is summertime in New Zealand) showed it, in that same pub where eighteen months earlier . . . with Nelson; with that funny old Jewish painter . . .

Dear Franck,

Here's greetings from Auckland way down there, and it's been a long time but I think of you often. I don't forget friends, and our sessions in the old Caravan, and I better say it, Franck, I've got stinking news, our Ada is dead. This is horrible but I owe it to you. She went to South America with that fellow, he was a journalist. It wasn't pretty, they have gangsters who call themselves Counter-Insurgency in all these countries, said they were exciting the villagers into discontent. I got this or rather a reporter in B.A. got it for me from an eyewitness, German chap on some water-purifying scheme. They lined up the village after a 'trial' and made their usual speech, that shit about the justice of the People.

Now hold tight Franck, this is bad, they marched those two out and roped them and tripped them up in the dirt, the German said they could all see it coming because this socalled soldier came walking no hurry carrying a can of gasoline. He found courage to speak up and say Barbarity, and they laughed and said Shut up, you did it to Jews and we do it to Communists and it's exactly the same. I won't say any more, Franck, because it isn't good to think about, but knowing you you'd want me to tell you. I guess we none of us know until it comes to our turn.

Well I think of you often. I'm in fair shape though they didn't make me captain. I should worry, there's a lot more I lack.

So have a beer now with your old friend

Nelly

Castang handed the letter back. As he had given the others back – there wasn't any 'file'. A lot of messages come to the police and stop dead there. One wouldn't hand the news on to Marklake: to old Erskine MacLeod . . .

For this winter (summer in New Zealand) an AllBlack touring team came to Europe, captained by Nelson Walter, and after giving the French a rugby lesson in Realist Thinking, in Toulouse, there'd been a day off, and Nelson had taken a plane to Stuttgart: a bare two hours away, a German city where they don't play much rugby, save for fun, but where they make, among much else, water-purifying equipment, and where a lot of people speak Spanish as well as English. A business man, who had made a technical field trip to South America the previous summer (winter in the southern hemisphere), was surprised to see this giant enter his office.

"I don't want to talk about this, Mr Walter. It was not an experience I wish brought back to my memory." Careful, pedantic English.

"Yes. I've come a long way to hear this."

"If I might ask – why?"

"That woman and I; loved each other."

"I see. I mean, I see that I must make the effort. I'll tell you this much, Mr Walter, you're right: that woman was good at love." During the explanations he had asked his secretary for a cup of coffee. One cup – Nelson found this German coffee too strong. He fiddled with it: it was still too hot to drink. He picked up a pencil to gain countenance and held it between his hands. He concentrated his mind.

"When they struck the match, that woman rolled herself. I do not mean she rolled about. I mean that she forced herself, in that pain, to join herself to the man. She was trying, Mr Walter, to hold him in her arms." The pencil snapped.

* * *

233

Castang, giving the letter back to Delaunay, found nothing to say. A line from a song came into his head, by a well-known Argentine artist. Nelson had heard it sung, the night of the banquet.

"*Ay! Vidalita.*"

Delaunay knew the line and completed it.

"*Mi ausento de aquí.*" Since he takes trains to Spain he has spent careful hours – it is part of his job – with a little Spanish Grammar book. He is familiar with the reflexive verb *ausentarse*. He can give the literal meaning of the line.

"I am going away from here."

There would be no point in telling Marklake. Or old Erskine MacLeod – but there must be somebody he could tell, apart from Vera.

Another six weeks, and the path of the Commissaire of Police Judiciaire crossed that of the bishop. So he told him . . .

The bishop said nothing for a long time, sitting stilly.

"If a proof were ever needed, Castang . . . you go looking for proofs, don't you? You need them. Here would be one more among so many. In, also, our human circumstances, love is always stronger than not-love."

M
Freeling, Nicolas
Not as far as Velma